The Brimstone Offensive

BOOKS BY THE AUTHOR

GENEVA INTRUSION

PRIMARY PROTOCOL

ISLANDS OF PEACE

THE BRIMSTONE OFFENSIVE

BEHIND YESTERDAY
"Love, intrigue, and espionage in a time of war."

AT RANDOM
"Thoughts from a marginal mind."

The Brimstone Offensive

RICHARD D. TAYLOR

Pacific Grove Press

The Brimstone Offensive
Copyright © 2022 Richard D. Taylor

"This is a work of fiction. Names, characters, businesses, places, events, and incidents either are the products of the author's imagination or used in a fictitious manner. Any resemblance to actual persons, living or dead, or actual events is purely coincidental."

All rights reserved. No part of this publication may be reproduced, distributed, or transmitted in any form or by any means, including photocopying, recording, or other copying via electronic or mechanical methods, without the prior written permission of the publisher, except in the case of brief quotations embodied in critical reviews and certain other noncommercial uses permitted by copyright law. For permission requests, write to the publisher, as shown below.

Cover Copyright © 2022 by Richard D. Taylor
Interior Illustrations Copyright © 2022 by Richard D. Taylor
Pacific Grove Press
Printed in the United States of America

For more information on this and other books, visit my website by clicking the button below.

[Link to visit my website www.richardDtaylor.com]

RichardDtaylor@gmail.com

I would love to hear from you.

Version V112

To my supporting family.
Writing is a lonely craft.
It cannot be done without them.

Table of Contents

IMPORTANT CHARACTERS AND TERMS	9
PROLOG	12
CHAPTER 1	15
CHAPTER 2	19
CHAPTER 3	23
CHAPTER 4	25
CHAPTER 5	32
CHAPTER 6	38
CHAPTER 7	41
CHAPTER 8	45
CHAPTER 9	52
CHAPTER 10	54
CHAPTER 11	58
CHAPTER 12	61
CHAPTER 13	63
CHAPTER 14	66
CHAPTER 15	71
CHAPTER 16	75
CHAPTER 17	82
CHAPTER 18	88
CHAPTER 19	91
CHAPTER 20	93
CHAPTER 21	95
CHAPTER 22	100
CHAPTER 23	102
CHAPTER 24	109
CHAPTER 25	112
CHAPTER 26	117
CHAPTER 27	120
CHAPTER 28	122
CHAPTER 29	126
CHAPTER 30	129
CHAPTER 31	131

CHAPTER 32	138
CHAPTER 33	140
CHAPTER 34	147
CHAPTER 35	156
CHAPTER 36	161
CHAPTER 37	166
CHAPTER 38	168
CHAPTER 39	171
CHAPTER 40	173
CHAPTER 41	177
CHAPTER 42	180
CHAPTER 43	184
CHAPTER 44	188
CHAPTER 45	193
CHAPTER 46	195
CHAPTER 47	197
CHAPTER 48	200
CHAPTER 49	203
CHAPTER 50	207
CHAPTER 51	211
CHAPTER 52	218
CHAPTER 53	223
CHAPTER 54	230
CHAPTER 55	233
CHAPTER 56	236
CHAPTER 57	241
CHAPTER 58	244
CHAPTER 59	247
CHAPTER 60	250
CHAPTER 61	254
CHAPTER 62	259
CHAPTER 63	263
CHAPTER 64	267
CHAPTER 65	270
CHAPTER 66	273
CHAPTER 67	275

CHAPTER 68	279
CHAPTER 69	286
CHAPTER 70	292
CHAPTER 71	297
CHAPTER 72	299
CHAPTER 73	303
CHAPTER 74	307
Chapter 75	309
CHAPTER 76	311
CHAPTER 77	318
CHAPTER 78	320
CHAPTER 79	323
A COMPLETE LIST OF IMPORTANT CHARACTERS AND TERMS	327

A COMPLETE LIST OF
<u>IMPORTANT CHARACTERS AND TERMS</u>
IS AT THE END OF THE BOOK

A Partial List of Characters

Adi Nymagu—President of Tanzania
Avery Stanton— CEO Adler Industries Chairman
Brad Danner— Co-worker of Kate. Cartel communications, Security group, a friend of
Dr. Stephen Austin Devroe— Director of National Intelligence   (DNI)
Elena Maleeva— Manager of Geneva9 surveillance system (Mom) and security group.
Havel Vanek—Enforcer for Teradyne
Jordan Duma—Agent providing security for Nymagu and his   friend.
Kate Adler (Katerina)—Protagonist, Executive Director of Cartel, Owner of Adler Industries.
Konner Houston—Special assistant to U.S. president and Kate's love interest
Loren Sorrel— Assistant manager of Geneva 9 asset field operations, Directing the G9 asset in the real world.
Martin Perez—President of the United States (POTUS)
Milosh Luka Petrovic—CEO of TerraDyne
Nuri Koffman—Prime Minister of Israel.
Penn Hauer—Director Cartel Field operations, security group
Security Group – Brad, Penn, Elena, Loren, and Kate.

Then the Lord rained upon Sodom and upon Gomorrah brimstone and fire from the Lord out of heaven;
Genesis 19:24

People never know what they can do until they have to do it.
Richard D. Taylor

PROLOG

Wonsan Naval Base
North Korea

A canopy covered the dry freighter, shielding the entire ship from satellite observation. Dust rose to the lights as tons of iron ore poured off the loading belts onto the cavernous holds below. The dust caught beneath the canopy, made breathing difficult for everyone and the biting cold made constant movement necessary.

It was thirteen hundred hours, and the early morning frigid air from the Pacific caused Captain Anton Kikorov's arm to ache where he broke it over ten years ago. "How can that be?" He thought.

"I'm going outside for a smoke," he told the political officer and walked out onto the bridge port wing.

The officer was with the State Security Department (SSD). The special department reported directly to North Korea's great leader Kim Il Sung, resulting in an arrogance tolerated for only the briefest periods. It was not unusual for a political officer to be on hand to load a smuggling ship, but a visit from the SSD was unprecedented.

Chul, Kikorov's first officer, pulled down the wool knit cap over his ears. "Do we know our destination yet?"

"No, it's another anomaly in the normal routine."

Chul said, "I've finished my inspections. We'll be lucky to get anywhere in this hulk. I mean, the term rust bucket was meant specifically for this ship. It has to be its last voyage." Kikorov knew precisely what lay beneath his feet. He had walked the vessel stem to stern. He said, "The desalination is not working. Did you bring extra water?"

"Yes," Chul replied.

Cigarette dangling, Kikorov rubbed the pain. He was part of a select group of captains piloting ships that transport all manner of illegal cargo, working around various international sanctions. He was used to the secrecy, having watched numerous times, the usual cache of guns, ammunition, or rocket launchers loaded onto his ships. Munitions and natural resources were critical deliveries needed to generate the hard cash to keep North Korea's elite in power. It was the worst kept secret in a secretive society.

However, this shipment's security exceeded that of any previous voyage. For one, he had no idea what, other than iron ore, was being transported or why it needed a contingent of three armed guards plus the intense scrutiny of an SSD officer. In addition, the supposed crew were soldiers, not sailors, which meant the journey would undoubtedly hold its surprises. During the loading of this mysterious shipment, they herded the dockworkers into a large building for two hours. At the same time, they ordered him to his cabin with a guard outside.

Eventually, called to the main deck, he saw the dock crane, had completed its mission and was moving away. "Whatever it is, it must be heavy," he thought. Standing before an outside storage locker at the base of the superstructure, the SSD officer gave him the combination of the newly installed heavy door.

The SSD officer said, "When you arrive at the rendezvous point, give the lock combination to the SSD officer that boards your ship. Follow his instructions and ask no questions. Under no circumstances are you to open this door yourself."

It was a most unusual set of instructions.

The SSD officer called out, "Captain, a dock worker wants you on the radio. Pay attention to your job. I promise you there will be no room for error on this voyage, or it will be your last."

Kikorov threw the cigarette onto the deck with a disgust the officer didn't detect. "Of course," Kikorov responded, "I'm sure it's the loadmaster reporting the weight of the cargo."

"Did you pack warm clothes," he said to Chul, "because the boiler steam for the radiators doesn't seem to be getting to the cabins."

CHAPTER 1

Marseilles, France

In every direction, monolithic walls of shipping containers slept, and loading cranes reached into the dark sky. The area was traditionally the driest region in France, but heavy rain fell, and rushing water searched for drains.

Four men sat in a van in front of an office at the massive Marseilles-Fox Port 2 terminal. The largest container port in France. Havel Vanek, head of special operations at TerraDyne Industries, was inside. Vanek's job was to do whatever Milosh Petrovic, founder, and owner, directed. That included everything from leaning on someone to get their cooperation to blowing up part of a competitor's business.

Vanek looked through the rain-spotted window then down to the picture on his phone to visually confirm the address. "What do you see up there?" he asked the driver.

"Nothing from up here, all clear." the driver said, looking out the front and side windows of the van.

His team had gone over the details of the operation many times. But Vanek's knack for survival depended on never assuming anything. His obsession with details kept him alive to tell the stories of his previous assignments.

He nodded and said to his team, "OK, let's do this."

He pulled the balaclava down, and the others followed.

One man opened the rolling side door of the vehicle. The three of them left the driver behind and rushed to the front door of an office. All of them were grateful for the protection of the overhang.

Vanek looked up and pointed. "Get that," he said.

One of the men ripped at a surveillance camera covering the front door.

Vanek tried the key, and it didn't work. He said, "Why am I not surprised that our inside man gave us the wrong key. I want his name." Disgusted, he pointed to another man and moved back.

"Take care of this lock. I don't want to be standing out here without an excuse."

The man pulled out a spray can of compressed air used to dust off electronics. With thick insulated gloves, he began spraying the metal lock on the heavy wooden door as frost began to form outside the can. As he emptied the can, the metal got icy cold and became more and more brittle. He hit the lock with a hammer and watched the shattered pieces fall out from the door to the ground.

"Alright, move over," Vanek said as he walked past, making his way to the alarm panel. He thought of the wrong key, "This better work."

He entered the number code given to him by the same employee—someone whose family had been threatened and forced to cooperate. Vanek saw the green light and let out a sigh of relief.

Vanek reached up and sprayed black paint on the lens of a security camera just inside the door. "Take the place apart, boys," he said. They proceeded to reduce the ordinarily sedate office into something resembling the aftermath of a typhoon. They overturned desks, chairs, and emptied drawers onto the floor.

"Pull that bookshelf down, and someone destroy the glass partitions," Vanek said. Compared to some operations he had directed, this was a frivolous activity, but it would send the required message. The computers were on, and Vanek sat at one, trying to use the password from the inside man to no avail. He cursed and slammed his hand onto the keyboard. Vanek looked at the safe but knew it was never a target. He walked down a hallway to the manager's office, trying that computer with similar results. After looking at some papers in a basket, he reached down and over-turned the desk, ignoring its noise.

Vanek pulled a printed message from a pocket and left it on the manager's office floor. Vanek turned to look directly into the one security camera they'd left in place. The prolonged look made it a defiant gesture and challenge to anyone monitoring the footage.

Vanek had lived a tumultuous childhood in and out of foster homes and a life of crime. During that time, he fought with anyone and everyone.

For Vanek, violence protected him from the dark internal forces and his anger about the failed efforts to help him

After a series of standardized tests, one of his schools told his foster guardians of his inability to perceive others' emotions and physical pain. His extraordinary life and mental state qualified him for this position. Petrovic had harnessed Vanek's "defense" mechanism. It resulted in Vanek finally feeling he had found a place where he belonged.

A voice spoke in his earpiece. It was the driver outside. "Boss, we have two harbor security vehicles approaching. Something or someone tipped them off."

"Are they driving by?"

"Hold on. No, they have stopped a hundred feet away and are blocking the road. One is getting out."

"Are they blocking the only way out of here?

"No, but it's the best way. I've another option."

Vanek thought for a moment. "Disable the vehicles with the M130. Make sure they can't follow us. While you're doing that, we'll run for the van."

"Got it." The driver reached between the seats and pulled up an M130 assault rifle. He stepped out and sprayed the front tires and radiators of the two cars from behind the door.

Vanek and his men bolted from the front, running to the van.

"Get us out of here," Vanek said, looking at his watch. "I've got a plane to catch. I need to be in Tanzania tomorrow."

The driver circled, taking the van up and over a sidewalk, destroyed the sign for the office next door. The driver pressed hard on the accelerator, and everyone felt the van surge forward as they pulled away and into the damp night. Behind them, above the open door of the destroyed office, the sign read, "Morton Roth Shipping and Maritime Services Company. A division of Adler Industries."

CHAPTER 2

Zanzibar Resort
Tanzania

Standing in the sand, Kate felt the edge of a small wave roll over her feet. Her hand was up, shielding her eyes as she looked at the emerging reds and oranges projected above the ocean's horizon. The sun reflected its light to the clouds above, signaling the day's end. "It's going to be another beautiful sunset," she thought. She moved to the private patio of the finest bungalow on the beach the Zanzibar Resort offered. She dried herself off after a quick swim, feeling she was in a good place in her life. "We need more time like this," she said.

"I agree," Konner Houston said, approaching and placing another drink on the table between their lounge chairs.

"Are you trying to get me drunk?" She asked the handsome and very fit man standing in front of her.

"The answer is yes, and to further my plan; you will find this drink a little stronger than the last one."

"Mr. Houston, you're devious at best. You should know by now you don't need to get me drunk."

"I do know by now, so I'm making sure there won't be any complications."

Kate laughed. "And what would a complication look like?"

Konner clinked her glass on the table and said, "I'm taking the fifth. By the way, the Tanzanian president had every opportunity to talk to you yesterday at the signing ceremony. Why does he want to see you personally tonight? Does he have a thing for you or something? You have that effect on men, you know."

"Did you ever think it might be as simple as I own the company mentioned in several major contracts we signed? You do know that's the reason we're here."

"Look,' he said. "I'm glad, as it means we could be together. However, couldn't Avery, being CEO of your company, take care of everything. Actually, do you want my opinion?"

"What opinion?"

"About the president," he said with fake impatience.

"I'm not sure." She said as she wrapped a towel around her toned body.

With disappointment, Konner looked at the towel and said, I think President Nymagu has a crush. I know I do." He said, putting his hand over his heart.

Kate shook her head, ignoring the feigned gesture. "I don't know why he wanted to meet me in person, but it's certainly not your unlikely fantasies. Anyway, we'll find out over dinner with detective Duma."

Konner looked at Kate as she watched a family playing in the surf. Her blond hair was wet and dark as it lay on her shoulders. She was beautiful, rich, and as intelligent as anyone he had ever met. They were very compatible, but their lives were very different. He recounted the last year and how it had gone down a path; he would not have guessed. Had he fallen in love? He thought so; he wanted to, but he wasn't sure it could work given their lives and schedules. He gently rubbed her back with his hand and noticed the time on his watch.

"Uh oh," he said.

"What's up?"

"It's "seven-thirty," Konner said with a playful smile. "That means there's still time to play before dinner with Duma and the drive-by meeting with the president. Why are we having dinner with Mr. Duma again and not a full night right here?"

"We're meeting the president of a country, and Duma is in charge of his security. I guess he's just doing his job." Besides, over the last several days, we've grown to like the guy."

"I still think it's just another man who wants to meet you."

She said, "Konner Houston, you're jealous."

He took a sip of his drink. "Perhaps." He said with a sheepish grin. There's still time for us, but only if you wear something simple and forget the makeup routine."

Pulling away the big beach towel wrapped around her, she asked with a wide grin, "How much time do you need, big boy?"

Konner laughed into his drink, spilling it over the top in the middle of a sip. Holding the glass up and away because it was dripping, he said, "According to you, not long at all."

"That's not what I meant."

"Even if you did, it's the journey, not necessarily the destination."

With that, they were both laughing. Kate made her way to his lounge chair. "Move over," she said, laying down next to him. "Isn't this place wonderful?"

"I'm not sure it's the place as much as the company."

She looked up at him. "Oh, that's nice, aren't you sweet."

Konner said, "As far as the place, it's the best place I've ever stayed. Those of us on a government salary only see places like this on the internet. I am, however, happy to be the guest of an extremely attractive billionaire who rides in on a private jet and simply has the bill sent to her office."

She punched him in the arm at the comment. "Keep complaining, funny man, and I'll throw you off the plane next time we're over Russia. Speaking of which, how did you get the time off?"

"In my line of business, there's no such thing as vacation or personal leave."

Konner remembered the conversation well when he asked Dr. Stephen Devroe, his boss, for a few days off to be with Kate.

"What?" Devroe said. "Do you think you work for Google or something? No free meals either because President Martin has an assignment."

The disappointment was evident on Konner's face.

Devroe asked, "Is it important?"

"Yes, in fact, it is."

"Who will you be seeing?"

"With all due respect, sir, it's none of your business. That's the definition of personal time."

"Look, Konner, you have a super-secret security clearance, and I've got the right to know. However, if you're going to be with Ms. Adler, we could squeeze some time in but don't get used to it."

Konner shook his head, returning to the present, and asked Kate. "Did you call Devroe or something regarding our being together? Because I'm not going to be happy about that. I can take care of my own problems; I can fight my own battles."

"Of course not," Kate said. "Why would I do that? He might think he owes the Cartel or me for things in the past; I don't know." She leaned forward and kissed him. "However, you got the time; I'm happy you're here. With our schedules, it's hard to spend time together."

"I know this relationship takes working at, but I'm willing to try if you are."

"Of course. I'm really happy right now, Konner." She put her head on his chest.

Konner looked at his watch again, then looked at Kate, and then with a mischievous grin on his face, pointed to the extra potent drink he just brought over and said, "Prove it."

"You're one tough guy."

He jumped up and started chasing her into the suite.

CHAPTER 3

Tanzania
Zanzibar Resort

The fading sun lit up the worn panel van, whose sides promoted a bakery in Swahili. It pulled over at a secluded part of a small road that ran high on a hill. It gave the van a viewpoint high above the hotel's presidential suite of the luxurious Zanzibar resort. Thick tropical under foliage was interrupted by tall trees looking down on the complex. The van contained extensive communication and video gear. Jarmil Novak, manager of this operation, watched a monitor fed from the camera atop the vehicle. It provided surveillance footage of the suite in the resort's main building below.

"Are you ready?" He asked the two men sitting patiently inside.

"Yes, just waiting for the go-ahead."

"Well, we're there. It's time for you to take your positions. I want you out early as I'm unsure when this comes down. We wait until we get the signal from the informant inside. Sorry boys, but that's the job."

"Not a problem," one of them said. "We're snipers and used to waiting forever. You will be serving snacks later, right?"

Jarmil laughed, "Get your ass out there." He opened the doors. "Com check as soon as you're in position."

"Roger that."

The two men dressed in dark clothing stepped out, and each was carrying a sizeable long bag strapped to their shoulders. They made their way through the vegetation surrounding the resort. The two men proceeded to their pre-scouted positions and set up their equipment, settling in for a long monotonous wait that was part of their profession.

Once they were in position, Novak, inside the van, said, "Position one, com check."

"One here," a man said.

"One, I'm not getting video from your scope. What's the problem?"

"There, I just turned it on."

"Jesus, pay attention. Didn't I tell you this was a highly visible job? Get your act together as Vanek is on his way, and you don't want him to find out you're the one who screwed up."

"OK, OK," he said, "It's on."

Novak continued, "Position two com check."

"Two here," he said. "Video is on."

"Good, I now have two clear video signals. Settle in until dark and stay undetected."

CHAPTER 4

Tanzania
Zanzibar Resort

Having chased Kate into the suite, Konner stood with his arms around her at the foot of the bed. "Let's get this thing started," he said.

"Well, sir, you're certainly direct." She said in a flirting manner.

Just as Konner picked her up in his arms to put her down on the bed, they both heard the buzzing and ringing of Kate's phone.

"Don't look at it," Konner said. "Whatever it is, it can wait."

"It's Avery's ring-tone," she said. "He's spent this entire trip purposely staying out of our way to give us time together. It must be important."

Konner put her down with a guttural sound and waved his arm towards the phone.

She picked it up, saying. "Avery, what is it, and are you coming to dinner?"

"No, I've got a few things I'm looking into and something you should know. Do you have a second?"

"Yes, I do," she said, looking at a dour Konner sitting a few feet away. He motioned if she wanted him to step outside, and she nodded no.

Konner looked over at Kate, phone to her ear, and studied her face. It was a window into what was happening to her at any given moment. Right now, she looked worried. That was another problem in their relationship. Each of them dealt with issues that were never small. There wasn't anything like a cat caught in a tree. It was somebody trying to kill seventy thousand people in a stadium using poison gas or a terrorist trying to start WWIII by blowing up the NATO headquarters building. It was the nature of their jobs. At least he had only one job. Kate was head of the Cartel and recognized internationally as the head of a children's charity and had more than a few of the world's leaders on speed dial. He didn't understand how she could take it all on.

He studied her hand movements as she talked. She moved them smoothly through the air. How did he, a kid from Topeka, Kansas, end up in a relationship with an incredible woman who would put up with his bazaar schedule? Whatever quirk occurred in the universe, he was utterly thankful for the anomaly. He wanted to fall in love with her but feared she'd wake up one morning and admit this relationship collided with reality.

They said they would try and see how the relationship would develop. It had been a year, and as far as he was concerned, it was going just fine considering the obstacles. Initially, with a history of avoiding anything but brief encounters, Kate was the one who declared anything serious off-limits. They had both survived a kidnapping by a group of terrorists before being rescued by the Cartel's tier one team. That certainly had a way of bringing people together, and after that, things changed.

Kate put the phone down, then turned and said, "why aren't you undressed?"

"I was busy watching you. It's one of my favorite sports."

"*Sport*? I'm a sport?"

"Don't get excited there, cute stuff." He got up and walked over, pulling her into his arms. OK, *one* of my favorite things to do is that better?"

"Nice try, a first strike is a first strike. You can't take it away. But I would accept you making up for it."

"You're on; get that bathing suit off."

She started to undress when Konner's phone interrupted the moment. He looked over at it with contempt as the ring tone told him it was not his tax guy with a question.

"That's Devroe's ring, isn't it?" Kate said.

"Yup," he said with a dejected slump of the shoulders.

"Better take it; they might be demanding you jump another tall building in a single bound."

He laughed. "It's being faster than a speeding bullet I'm worried about."

She looked at the phone on the dresser insisting on being answered. "Are you going to answer it?" She pushed him away and pointed at the device. "If you don't, you could be court marshaled or something."

"I'm not in the military."

"What are you then?"

"Something in between, I guess."

"Either way." She said, reaching over and handing him the phone.

Konner said, "Konner, here, sir, what do you have?" He smiled at Kate.

Kate stepped away and watched this man who had entered her life when she wasn't looking. As he talked to the man closest to the President of the United States, she was somewhat in awe. Konner completed important, dangerous assignments worldwide for the president, treated her like a queen, and was handsome to boot. His travel schedule and hers created a noticeable strain on the relationship. She wanted this to work, but a steady headwind reminded them of their completely different lives. That's why she was so happy they had this short time alone.

She could hear one side of the conversation, and it didn't sound good. Konner kept asking questions, and she knew something had gone wrong. She was patiently sitting in one of the soft chairs, watching him talk. Finally, adding a bit of humor, she picked up the small clock on the nightstand and pointed at it with a silly smile and big comical gestures. He waved his hand and nodded. He understood.

Still, it was minutes later when he finally put down the phone.

"How much can you tell me." She asked.

"Iran," he said. "It could get serious."

"That's all?"

"Fraid so. How about you?"

"It's just things Avery takes care of but keeps me informed."

"You mentioned Marseilles."

"Last night, French time, we had a break-in at our local office, mostly vandalism and the like."

"Doesn't your company have a bunch of offices?"

"Yes, we're in most of the world's major ports. There're over forty, I think."

"Why would Avery bother you with that level of information?"

"As to the break-in, he normally wouldn't have bothered, but Avery said they made an unsuccessful attempt to break into the management system. But more concerning is they left a note saying it wouldn't be the last. Add to that, one of them made a point of staring down the security camera. Avery thinks he was trying to make the point; it wasn't your average burglary. In addition, harbor security discovered them, and the thieves quickly destroyed two of their security vehicles with an assault rifle. No one was hurt."

Konner said, "That certainly changes things as far as an average breaking and entering."

"He has the Cartel staff looking into the cyber side, and the office manager is working with local police, so I'm not worried. Does your phone call mean you can't come back to my place before going to the states?"

"I don't know yet. By the way, how can you call that sprawling estate a house? There has to be a bigger word than that like, say, a monument."

"It's my home, you brute. That's what I call it, and it's the first real one I've had in my life. Everything else was on the way to somewhere."

"Calling it your home is certainly important, but I think Rick Steves will be establishing a tour there anytime now."

Kate laughed. "Hey, big boy."

"Yes?" he said, moving closer.

The phone went off again with Avery's ring. They looked at each other.

Kate said, "I've got to take this. This must be important. Can I answer it?"

Konner's twice falling shoulders were his reply as he walked over to the minibar to grab a beer.

"I won't be long," she said.

"Avery, what's up?"

"I'm sorry to barge in again."

"Avery, I pay you to barge in. I'm sorry that didn't come out right."

Avery said, "The New York office received an express delivery from a law firm in Manhattan."

Kate wondered why he was providing that kind of information. It was something he'd usually never bother to tell her.

"I'm confused. There has to be a reason you're telling me this."

"It's an offer to buy Morton Roth."

"What?" Kate said. "Why?"

"I think who, is the real concern?"

"TerraDyne?" Kate asked.

"No, at least it's not the name on the paperwork. We checked. It's registered in Panama, where they specialize in companies within corporations within partnerships. It's going to be hard to trace. We have Mom on it."

"Avery, we aren't selling."

"I know, but we should try to find out as much as possible to know what or who we're dealing with."

"It's TerraDyne."

"No doubt, but that's still a hunch. I happen to agree with your hunch, but if we're to get to the bottom of this, we need to know who this is because I feel it's not a friendly takeover. I'll have more later but wanted you to know."

"Is the offer just for Morton Roth or Adler Industries? Do they want part or all of the company?"

"Just all of Morton Roth, at least for now. The offer is substantial. Actually, more than it should be."

"Look, do what you need to, but we aren't selling."

Kate hung up and thought for a moment. A takeover put a whole different light on everything. She felt she was being pulled further into the business side of her life.

Konner said, "Everything all right? Whenever you start to stare out into space, I think something's wrong."

"Yes, something is wrong," she said. She pointed at the clock again and said. Superman or not, we seem to have run out of time.

"Damn it," Konner said in a jesting manner. "If it wasn't for *your* phone calls." He tailed off the end of the sentence.

"*My* phone calls? I don't think so. Either way, I agree with your sentiments. However, we committed to dinner with Agent Duma, and he asked us to be on time. Besides, it wasn't my short phone call that was the problem. It was Devroe going on and on about something that you can't talk about."

"Dinner with Jourdan Duma," Konner said with a horrible French accent. "Now, there's an interesting man."

"Do I have to remind you that I'm on a business clock? That I was here to sign huge contracts on behalf of Morton Roth worth around one hundred thirty million over the next six years? It's the reason we're staying here and enjoying ourselves. Besides, since we met him two days ago, he's been very thoughtful, so what's the problem?"

"I've got to agree there, but it's not what I had in mind like him or not."

Kate put a finger to his lips. "Patience, my dear. The best is always worth waiting for."

"Well," he said with fake sincerity. "We'll always have Paris."

"What's that supposed to mean?"

"Oh, how soon they forget." He said. "That night when I was your knight in shining armor and saved your life. It's humor. You're supposed to laugh."

"Funny man, You should stick to being a spy."

CHAPTER 5

Serbia to Tanzania

Milosh Luka Petrovic was uncomfortable sitting in his office at the rear of his Boeing business jet. The room had become cold, and he could feel his heart's rapid beating. His psychologist was sitting just outside the door, but it was doubtful Petrovic would tell him about the latest symptoms. He had just finished reading the summary page of the latest report from Anakin Holland, Chief Financial Officer and trusted deputy. He hit a button on the phone and said.

"Get Holland in here."

A short time later, a thin, bespeckled man stood in the doorway. Detailed to a fault, but otherwise an immensely capable CFO, he was at the center of Petrovic's empire. Nothing moved, was purchased, or sold without his signature.

Holland said, "You wanted to see me, Sir?"

Petrovic held up a set of papers. "What's this?"

"Well, it's the report you asked for on TerraDyne's remaining gypsum and gold operations in Tanzania."

"Why did you remove the copper and nickel contracts with the government. I wanted them included."

"Mr. Petrovic, the report reflects the revised revenue estimates resulting from the loss of those contracts to Morton

Roth. That's what I thought you wanted to see in the review. We're still in excellent shape in that market even with the reduction. Also, our quarterlies are going to look very strong. You're running a very profitable operation across several continents."

Petrovic ignored his comments. "Didn't I say I wanted them included?"

"Yes, Mr. Petrovic, but if I added them, the report is of no use; it doesn't reflect reality."

"In this company, I alone determine what reality will be. Go back and do this again and leave in the contracts."

"Yes, but even your version of reality has to be based on facts. The new contracts now belong to Morton Roth. We lost them. I don't understand."

"You don't need to understand. Where are the quarterlies from our operations in Brazil and Australia?"

"They're ready, but your request singled out Tanzania, so that's all I provided."

"OK, bring them in after the Doctor. Also, you saw Seaward Marine has agreed to be acquired by us. You weren't in that meeting yesterday as you were coming back from Hanover."

"They agreed?" Holland smiled. "Yes, I saw that. I'm having the paperwork drawn up as we speak. I don't think they agreed as much as finally acquiescing after the series of accidents that their company experienced. Mr. Vanek is a talented member of the organization. They were a stubborn takeover, but I guess they decided something is better than nothing."

Petrovic gave a satisfied look, "Most companies we go after usually have to come to that decision."

Holland said, "Having Vanek convincing the Liberian government to revoke the registration of their ships seemed to be the tipping point."

"Yes," Petrovic said, leaning back in his chair, pleased with himself. "Remember Holland, the loudest voice in the room is always money. The Liberians understand this more than most. As soon as we have ownership, have the tankers re-registered in Panama like the rest of our fleet."

Holland said, "That will add another fifteen ships to our total, but it's still not enough to fulfill the North Korean commitment."

"I know. I plan to get the additional ships we need by acquiring Morton Roth. Then I need to change the mind of the new Tanzanian president and get the contracts we lost back into the company.

Holland realized Petrovic had his own idea of what he wanted in the revised financial statement. "How are you going to do that?" Holland asked.

"Leave that to me for right now. Go back and add in the contracts we lost and do a proforma plan including Seaward."

Holland closed the door, and Petrovic reached for his desk's center drawer. He pulled out a pill container and took a pill with the bottled water on his desk. For a moment, his face reflected the bitter taste. He hated them but had no choice. Again, he thought of going to his bedroom at the plane's rear and catching just a few minutes. Something he seemed to need more often recently. The cell phone display said it was Vanek.

Havel Vanek, TerraDyne's solution when it required a heavy hand, said, "You wanted me to call boss. What's up?"

"I'm checking on the status of the next operation. Are we all set up for the next phase? Any problems yet?"

"No, everything is in place, and I'm on my way there. Don't worry; I'm overseeing this one personally. Did Morton Roth accept the offer you made to buy the company?"

"No, I expect that later today. That isn't your concern. Do your part following my plan, and we'll have control of Morton Roth soon. It's a proven formula, and they won't know what hit them. Are you all set for the Brookhaven office? Do you have the press release ready?"

"Yes, I've got one of my best guys on it."

"You're not doing it?"

"I'm good, but I can still only be in one place at a time. Your schedule calls for operations quickly, one right after another."

"Just don't screw up. The Morton Roth takeover has become personal."

"Have I ever let you down?"

"Istanbul, Turkey."

"What? Someone tipped off authorities. I found out who contacted them and dealt with it."

"You asked, and I responded. As I said, this is personal."

"Is it because she's a woman and won the contracts?"

"Careful, Vanek. Just do your job before I decide it's *you* that I need to deal with."

There was a soft knock on the door. Petrovic said, "Vanek, I've got to go. Keep me informed."

Petrovic said, "Come in, Doctor. Have a seat."

It was Doctor Jozef Matic's first time on the Boeing business jet. Matic looked around at the office furniture and said, "We usually meet where you can be more comfortable laying back in my lounge chair, which is certainly closer to the ground."

"I've got urgent business with my subsidiary in Tanzania. I didn't have the time to make our weekly session at your office, and I appreciate your accommodating my schedule. Besides, I'm still the same person whether lying on your lounge chair or sitting here."

"Just not as relaxed." The doctor said, sitting down and taking out his notepad. He flipped over several pages and said, "We left off talking about your mother."

"No," Petrovic responded in a raised voice. "We *finished* talking about my mother."

"No, Mr. Petrovic, "*You* finished talking about your mother, not me. Are we done with these games? We need to address this issue thoroughly. Our discussions have revealed a wave of anger at your mother for leaving when you were young and your father thinking you're a failure. These two situations have had an outsized influence in your life."

"What mother doesn't have an outsized influence?"

"Not in this case, Mr. Petrovic. Yours is a near obsession. Your anger at your mother has driven your life to date. Until you recognize this and clear it up, it will continue to dominate your actions. You're the center of your universe. You have set up your life to control everything around you."

"I don't see the problem there. I run a business doctor, and I need to know where the moving parts are. I need to control the moving parts. I do control the moving parts."

"And that's the problem." The doctor said. "Finding your mother has fallen into the category of beyond your control. Not being able to dictate an outcome is unacceptable to you, but it's there nonetheless. Your anger at your mother has manifested into your anger against all women. It's affected your ability to sustain any meaningful relationship. You have to let this go. Even if you eventually find her, she won't have the answers to help you."

Petrovic wondered why he let this moron talk to him this way.

Matic said, "When a parent chooses to leave a family, especially a family with children, it's under extraordinary circumstances. You've tried to find your mother and so far have failed. This failure manifests itself as a lack of control and inability to dictate the outcome. It's the conflict eating at the center of you and the source of your panic and anxiety attacks. Over the years, they've also been the cause of your deteriorating health. It would be best if you addressed this. You have channeled all your energy into your business because it reacts to your orders."

"Mr. Petrovic, if you remember, when we started these sessions, you said you were having problems concentrating and overcoming anxiety. That you felt your health was being affected. I said I could help, but you had to agree to the solution if we found one. We found one, but you insist on denying the problem exists."

Petrovic said, "According to my doctors, my health issues aren't caused by anxiety. I keep telling you that."

"Milosh, their conclusion is from treating the symptom and not the cause."

"You seem to forget, Doctor; few people on the planet have been as successful as I have been in business. I don't need my parents' approval."

"On your success, I do not argue, but your dead wrong about not needing your parents' approval. You need to understand that your mother leaving you and your father's criticisms of you as a child have no meaning today."

"My dear doctor, you weren't there when I was a child."

"I don't need to be. I'm not the one with anger issues. We're not trying to cure me. It's you we're worried about."

Petrovic let out a heavy sigh.

"Milosh, you will not get better until we address the problem. You need to talk about it and let it go to be free of their grip on your life."

Petrovic looked out the window and over the tops of the clouds. He thought to himself. "Is this working?" The continued shortness of breath convinced him to stay with it a little longer.

CHAPTER 6

Tanzania
Zanzibar Resort

Agent Jourdan Duma, an independent contractor, provided security to high-ranking political and business figures worldwide. Formerly with DGSE, the French equivalent of the CIA, he started his own security business. With the help of several close friends in high places, it had become very successful. The men of his security detail were gathered in the room, going over the details of their latest assignment. They were currently engaged in providing security for Adi Nymagu, the new president of Tanzania, during his stay at the hotel. They had protected him at a formal signing ceremony earlier in the day.

The president signed a series of new shipping and distribution contracts transporting its natural resources to its export customers. TerraDyne, the previous company, filed lawsuits contesting the loss of a substantial amount of business. The actions by the president benefited the people but disturbed forces within the country. The president felt he needed additional security and contacted his close friend. The assignment was more than just another job for Agent Duma as, for twenty years, he was very close to the Nymagu family.

"OK, listen up," Duma said. "All of you know my opinion of TerraDyne, the empire built by a Mr. Petrovic. He doesn't do business like the rest of the world. We made it through the signing without any incident but don't think for a minute we can relax. Mr. Petrovic is anything but predictable, and his methods of furthering his business interests are unlike anyone else. He's more like a corporation with guns. At least his track record paints that picture. This assignment isn't the first time I have dealt with him. During my days with the DGSE, he was constantly coming up connected to nefarious people of the world from gun runners to drug lords."

"Yes, boss," Patterson said. "We get you don't like him."

Duma turned to Mansell Brin, his second in command, and said, "That was nice work by all of you today. We have to get him through a dinner meeting, the suite's political socializing, and back to the palace tomorrow morning. I want to go over the assignments and schedule again."

Brin said, "The president will arrive with his palace security detail at eight, and then, at the president's request, we take over. Three armed men are patrolling the grounds, and we'll have three men in the portico for the arrival." He turned to Duma and said, "Then you will accompany him to the restaurant area on the ground floor."

Duma said, "There, the president wants to meet with a dinner group that will include me. The dinner starts at seven, and we should be sitting with after-dinner coffee when he appears."

Brin continued, "We'll cordon off the dining area where you sit. Geffery will take care of the kitchen and service hall with two men; Perren and Del will accompany the president in the service lift up the suite and will stay outside the door for security and checking guests."

"Does everyone understand?" Duma said, "Once he's in the suite, no one will enter without my authorization. The president has invited about twenty guests, all cleared by his people. Two men will be with me discretely inside the room with the president. I don't want you standing there like bouncers with menacing faces, no drinking, but talking to guests is permitted. You can say you're security but no personal information."

Duma addressed one of his men. "Patterson, this is not an opportunity to score this evening, am I clear?"

"Yes, boss," the agent replied. "I'll try harder this time." The comment generated muffled laughter.

"OK, gentlemen, stay out of sight until he arrives. Brin, call me when he pulls up to the hotel."

"Yes, sir."

CHAPTER 7

Tanzania
Zanzibar Resort

Vanek heard the ring and the pickup. Jamil, Vanek's manager for this operation, picked up. "It's Vanek; I'm five minutes from touchdown. Is everything under control?"

"Yes," Jamil said. "No problems. See you in a bit."

The chopper pilot had come over a series of hills and hovered over the designated landing zone in his flight plan.

The pilot brought the chopper to a hover and looked down. The lights underneath the craft and the fading light from the sky helped him assess the area and what he saw was troubling. He moved the craft back to get another angle and finally said, "We can't land here. Didn't anyone pace out the LZ because there isn't enough room to land. Look at those trees. The margin of error is almost none. He grabbed the center control arm and raised it, and the chopper started to lift.

"What are you doing?" Vanek, said.

"I'm going back. This is too dangerous."

The passenger's hand pushed down on the control arm. "I'm telling you to land anyway, margin or not. I need to be on the ground and now."

"Are you crazy? If we clip one of those trees with a rotor blade, we could roll and not land on the skids. Then it's anyone's guess what might happen."

"Bring her down anyway."

"Sorry, I don't want to die today or be responsible for damage to the craft; TerraDyne will kill me." The pilot then felt a stabbing pain in his left ear. The force pushed his head into the window to his right.

He said, "Jesus, what are you doing."

The passenger pressed his gun harder against the pilot's head as the man struggled to maintain control of the craft.

Vanek said, "Land the plane, or you will certainly die up here and possibly die down there."

"That's crazy. How are you going to get down if you kill me."

"I'll take my chances. I'm waiting."

The pilot rotated the helicopter on its axis to get a better view of the clearing. Slowly, he lowered the craft as debris rose from the ground. Checking both sides for clearance, he was feeling better about his chances. He couldn't see the tail rotor at the back, and just two feet off the ground, it struck a small branch. Because the rotor provided counter thrust to the main blades, the chopper was no longer stable and started to spin. This threw the craft to the right causing the main rotor blades to graze a tree. The contact created a crushing noise and violent vibrations as they hit the ground hard. The pilot immediately shut down the engines and scanned the glowing control panel with red emergency alerts, but none indicated a fire in the engine area.

The pilot shouted, "Are you bloody trying to get us killed."

Vanek reached over and unbuckled the seatbelt, and started opening the door.

"Now, because of you, I can't fly this damaged piece of junk anywhere."

Standing on the ground and looking into the cockpit, Vanek said. "Shut up; you've had your say. Call the TerraDyne office and ask for a tow truck. Give them my name. Tell them it's my fault." He slammed the door and pulled out his phone for directions.

Vanek walked through the thick roadblock nature had placed before him. He looked at this phone again to check his position and found himself just yards from his destination with the growth obscuring both the road and car. Coming out onto the road, he signaled the waiting driver tasked with taking him to the van

"Do you know where it is?" he asked the driver.

"Yes," was the brief reply.

A short time later, the car pulled up alongside the van. Vanek got out and looked towards the resort. He could barely make out the lights through the growth. Jamil Novak was his best man and had previously set up the effort. He seldom needed Vanek to be on-site for operations. This time was different for two reasons. First, the boss was pissed at someone, and second, the amount of money involved. He opened the door of the van and asked for an update.

"Any sign of the target?"

Jamil said, "No, not yet. Our informant told us he's expected around eight, which is still two hours away. But we don't know for sure."

"Are the men in position?"

"Yes, they're in position but not checking through their sights. We're doing active monitoring through our rooftop camera. I need the men deployed and waiting, given we're not certain of the time. They can be there for hours. They train for that."

"Are they our people?" Vanek asked.

"Yes. We brought the men in from Germany for this operation. Video and audio checks are complete. It's now a waiting game."

"You better get this right."

Jamil said, "We have done everything we can."

"Well, sometimes that's not enough."

Vanek's phone rang. It was Petrovic. "Yes, sir," he said. "Can you give me a second to get private?"

Vanek walked out of the vehicle and to the car that brought him in. He told the driver to take a walk and climbed into the passenger seat.

"Okay," Vanek said.

Petrovic said, "Is everything in place?"

"Yes, I just got here, but I've had time to go over everything. Novak did a good job. We'll soon find out if those snipers we keep paying and seldom use are worth it."

"Vanek," Petrovic said, "this needs to happen. This man is in the way of my plans, and that's unacceptable."

"I know, generally, getting in your way is not good for anyone's health."

Petrovic said, "What about Marseilles?"

"I was there last night. We're all set; it was successful."

Petrovic said, "Our people are monitoring police reports of a shooting."

"Not to worry. We had authorities arrive, but we escaped with no unnecessary causalities that would initiate an investigation."

Vanek said, "I've got the next one set up in Bremerhaven, Germany. Each step gets progressively worse for Morton Roth. I left the note at the site. They know it's coming but don't know where."

"We're on approach. I'll be at the Zanzibar shortly."

"Don't worry, even with the slightest opening; we'll get it done tonight."

CHAPTER 8

Tanzania
Zanzibar Resort

The Zanzibar hotel's dining room was very formal. Konner had on a double-breasted suit, and Kate was radiant in a full-length black gown with bare shoulders. Following Kate into the room, he looked at her and wondered how he could be so fortunate. He addressed the maître d saying, "The table for Jourdan Duma."

Without looking at this book, the maître d said, "Yes, of course, Mr. Duma hasn't arrived. Would you still prefer to be seated?"

"Yes, thank you," Konner said.

With clipped, efficient words, he said, "Please follow me." Menus in hand, he led the couple over to a table. It was in a corner away from the windows that overlooked the pool area's lighting and activity.

Konner asked, "Is there a reason we aren't on that side of the room?"

With the slightest nod of his head, the man said, "The location is at the express instructions of Mr. Duma."

"This is just lovely," Kate said as the man pulled out her chair.

Konner looked around the room. "This is nice. So Avery decided not to attend?"

"Remember, I said how he had insisted on giving us some privacy? Besides, he's dealing with the problem on the phone call."

"Too bad," Konner said. "It's not like he keeps us from enjoying the time here. I like the man." Then Konner surprised Kate by taking her hand. With a very mischievous smile, he said, "The fact he oversees your welfare is something I sincerely appreciate."

"To use one of your lines, did you just change the subject?"

"Of course not," he said with a wide grin.

The waiter approached. "My name is Antone, and welcome to the Zanzibar Restaurant. I'm the senior waiter at the hotel and will be serving you tonight. I trust you had an enjoyable day." He said as he pulled napkins from the table and placed them. "Can I start you with something to drink as we wait for Mr. Duma?"

Konner looked at Kate, who nodded. "Yes, we'll have a bottle of Veuve Clicquot, thank you."

"Of course, I'll be right back with the champagne and answer any questions you might have on the menu."

Konner told Kate, "Any thoughts on why they stuffed us into this corner away from all the other guests. I can insist on another table."

The maître d made his way back to the table, followed by Mr. Duma. Both Kate and Konner stood up as he approached.

Duma motioned towards the seats and said, "Please, let's sit. How wonderful to see both of you again." He looked at Kate with his arms open wide, saying, "And look at this radiant woman, aren't you a sight lighting up the night." He reached for Kate's hand and, bringing it up, took a deep breath of her perfume and said, "Magnificent as always."

Kate said, "Jourdan, you're so French and so attentive."

"And Mr. Konner," he reached out. "How are you this evening. I would like to thank you both for being here tonight. The President so wanted to meet you personally."

"You mean he wanted to meet Kate," Konner said smiling.

"Well," he said, getting the inference, "we men must always take second place, do we not? I trust you had a restful day. It's the finest resort property in all of Tanzania."

"Yes, Jourdan, it's a lovely place, and the views are spectacular. Has the president been keeping you busy? We didn't see you at all today after our breakfast."

"Sometimes, as we enjoy life, we must fit in a little work." He said with a charming smile. "The president is quite demanding when we're on call."

Kate said. "We look forward to meeting him."

"How's your security business coming along?" Konner asked, having toyed with starting a security firm at some point. "I would think protecting presidents and high profile figures would make a successful effort."

"I must say going into business for myself was the best thing I ever did. It's certainly more work than my position at DGSE but infinitely more rewarding. In the military, I was in command of a demolition team. It's a skill wasted in civilian life."

He raised a finger and said, "However, don't be fooled. There's a lot of fun in blowing things up." He gave out a sincere laugh as though he was enjoying old memories.

"In this case," he continued, "President Nymagu is a very close friend, so this assignment is more personal. We go back many years, and our families are close. Our children go to the same private schools. His state security team is responsible for getting him to the hotel. However, his wife insisted I keep him safe here and at the signing earlier. It's a responsibility I take very seriously."

Duma's attention wavered as Kate and Konner saw his face turn towards an approaching man. "It seems we're about to get a visit from Mr. Petrovic, the CEO of TerraDyne, the company losing the contracts."

Brin moved swiftly across the room.

Kate said, "I recognize him from my briefings, but I didn't see him today."

Jourdan nodded and waved at Brin to let him through.

Petrovic said, "I'm so sorry. May I interrupt for a brief second?"

Jourdan stood and said, "Mr. Petrovic may I introduce Ms.Kate Adler and Mr. Konner Houston? This is Mr. Milosh Petrovic."

"Yes, I know of Ms. Adler," Petrovic said. "I follow your wonderful work on behalf of children through your foundation. It's quite a success story. You must find it very rewarding. I, of course, know why you're here, but I hope you're also having a relaxing time as it seems you arrived a few days early."

"Yes, it's been most enjoyable. Were you here for the signing?"

"No, I just arrived. I'm here for other business, but this is my hotel of choice. The president's event is a personal triumph, so I wouldn't think of taking the limelight from his event. It's important for the country. His efforts to eliminate corruption from the system are courageous and inspiring."

Kate pressed. "But your company is a major player in this country. I would think you would want to make an appearance, at least. The company is losing several contracts to Morton Roth, so in a way, it involves you."

The comment took Konner by surprise as Kate usually didn't confront people, but he sensed something was going on. She was egging him on, and it was unlike her.

"Yes, I guess you're right about losing the contracts. But TerraDyne is still the biggest mining, processing, and distribution company in Tanzania, one of the biggest in the world. We do business in over other 30 countries. Granted, some of the countries are small, but there's enough for everyone."

Kate said, "I would think it's much easier to influence smaller third-world governments to accept your business practices."

Petrovic felt the anger rise within and looked decidedly uncomfortable as he stammered for a response. "This little bitch he thought. I'll crush you."

He avoided eye contact with Kate and spoke to Konner, "I believe I've interrupted your evening enough. It was very nice to meet you both and continue to enjoy this country as it has so much to offer."

With that, he walked back across the room and out the entrance.

Kate went at this man out of nowhere, and it struck Konner as curious.

Kate said, "He's everything the press says about him. He drips of insincerity and arrogance."

Konner said, "Do you know something I don't? You went at him pretty hard."

"I don't know." She said. "I sort of surprised myself, but I know the man is evil."

"Still, he built a massive empire. Perhaps you have to be an ass sometimes."

"My father built an empire, and he wasn't an ass."

Kate brought her hands up as if trying to stop the moment. "I'm sorry about that; I'm not sure what got into me. I just brought the mood of the table down."

Duma said, "Your feelings are not misguided as the man has many enemies. Many have suffered the consequences of his business practices. That's why he never goes anywhere without his security team." Duma leaned forward as if telling something confidential. Then he broke out a large grin. "In fact, the man has a specially built Mercedes. He sits inside the equivalent of a bulletproof bathtub that surrounds him. All the same, let's talk of other things."

Kate said, "Jourdan, why did the president want to see me personally. Lang Gerlach is managing director of Morton Roth and reports to Avery Stanton, CEO of Adler Industries. I'm not complaining, mind you, as this is a great place to do business." She looked at Konner, acknowledging that it was also an opportunity to spend time together.

Duma said, "The president wants to do business with your company due to your reputation."

"The company's reputation?"

"No, specifically you. The president wants to change the tenor of his administration from the corruption of the previous president. He wants to create one recognized in the world as just and for the people. You're part of that plan."

In jest, Konner said, "All this time, I thought it was because Kate was a beautiful, successful woman, but it turns out it's her international diplomatic credentials."

Everyone laughed. Duma said, "I understand the president is a known ladies' man, but I feel he's sincere in his request to meet Kate personally."

"We shall see," Konner smiled, looking at Kate.

Sheepishly he added, "If I'm truly honest, I'm also a fan of Ms. Adler and used my position as a friend of the president to insert myself when offering to look after your stay. Then, of course, I found both of you wonderful company."

Kate said, "We have certainly enjoyed our time here. I have to admit the time away was wonderful as it doesn't happen often. I would like to hear your take on the abrupt change in the president's commitment to TerraDyne?"

"The agreements that you signed were negotiated with the utmost secrecy. As you know, mining, specifically cobalt, gold, and diamonds, are a pillar of the economy. Duma looked around the room before saying, "To make this change carries with it risks from many factions. Shortly, he'll also sign legislation nationalizing the production of cobalt. TerraDyne, the existing company, stands to lose even more of their very lucrative business in this country."

Konner said, "It's been my experience that it takes a special person to pull all this off."

"Indeed, six months ago, Adi Nymagu did what others couldn't. He defeated Ahmadou, the incumbent president who had remained in power with the background help of TerraDyne. Ahmadou is now under investigation for corruption. They've charged him with accepting payoffs from TerraDyne. The company has reaped huge profits at the expense of the country's treasury. Petrovic's company stands to lose millions with the mining and distribution contract and tens of millions in infrastructure due to nationalization."

"All of which sounds like he deserved it," Kate said.

"Yes, but TerraDyne is a vast company and will not go down easy. Throughout their time here, people have crossed the company and been deported, ended up in the hospital, or completely disappeared. So your instincts about Mr. Petrovic are correct. Thus the increased level of security.

CHAPTER 9

Tanzania
Zanzibar Resort

Sitting in a tree for hours was not what everyone would call a great time. Both snipers listened to confirm the final step before the rest of their instructions could play out.

One of the two snipers hated the long hours and sometimes wondered why he chose the profession. Patience was not part of his toolset, especially when the targeting had to be done after a long wait and while supporting himself in a tree. In another part of the resort, three more men crept up on Duma's security guards as they patrolled the property. Their job was to disable them when the shooting started.

Number two sniper adjusted his leg keeping his balance pressed against a large branch. "It won't be long now." He thought.

As the sun had fully set, number two thought the guests had arrived in the suite. The large windows silhouetted anyone who passed by. The two snipers faced the hotel suite, where the president would greet guests later. Between them and the target were a large parking lot and a garden area. Their instruments said the distance was three hundred ten meters, well within their training, given the longest sniper shot ever was ten times that distance.

An informant from inside the hotel reported to the control truck; the president entered the suite.

Jamil said, "Heads up, guys, it's showtime. Target is in the suite."

Once sitting alone in the car, Vanek called the office and arranged for another chopper. Having confirmed the location of the new landing zone, he was listening to Vivaldi's second. He was using just one earpiece, which limited the whole experience, but it was unwise and unhealthy to cut off all sound from his surroundings.

Then Jamil brought up a radio and said into Vanek's ear. "Looks like we're in business in around five minutes."

"On my way," Vanek responded from the car. He walked back to the truck and opened the door in time to hear Jamil check-in with the escape cars meant to take the team to safety.

Vanek picked up a bag and asked, "Is this it?"

"Yes," Jamil said. "It will take care of the car, and there's also a nine-millimeter with two clips. Just in case."

CHAPTER 10

Tanzania
Zanzibar Resort

There was an uptick in the energy from those busing tables to waiters retreating to the kitchen. Men entered the dining room and cordoned off Kate and Konner's area.

A waiter approached their table, and a security man asked who he was. "I'm the waiter." He looked down at himself and said, "Can't you tell?"

Patterson said, "Please leave the dining room. Don't go to the kitchen."

The kitchen's double doors opened, and Kate now knew why they were seated where they were. Brin entered first, followed by two more of Duma's people, then the president followed by two more. The president approached formally attired in an elegantly tailored vicuna suit. Young for his station and striking in appearance, he carried himself confidently and exuded the presence befitting the president of a country. Kate and Konner stood up.

He waved his hands with a broad smile saying, "Please please be seated. May I join you for a bit?"

Sitting down, Konner said, "Of course."

Kate said, "We would be honored."

Nymagu said, "I so appreciate your making the trip. These are exciting times in my country."

"Mr. Duma," Kate said, "has briefed us on your plans to remake the economy to reflect the needs of the people."

"Yes, we have a long road ahead, but the agreements signed yesterday are just the start."

Kate said, "I have to admire your ability to make *any* progress given the well-established headwinds. You have given many important people in society hope. However, I understand that many are still of the old way of doing things in the government. Including, I understand, your vice president."

Nymagu said, "Sometimes we must make compromises to make progress. The vice president was hard to swallow. He's of the old school and corrupt, but I couldn't form a government without adding someone with ties to the old thinking despite being elected with a substantial majority. Like in the United States, the vice presidency is primarily ceremonial. He's not included in any day-to-day operations and will not hinder the programs."

"Why did you choose these particular contracts to start your campaign?"

"I need to make a statement. I need the people to know I was willing to attack the biggest problem facing our nation: TerraDyne and their gang of thieves. But enough of that. I want to talk about why I wanted you at the signing personally. Of course, your people could've handled it, but it was essential to meet with you face to face. I've been following your charity's efforts in creating girls' schools for our young Muslim women. I was most impressed by how you have expanded the program after some initial problems. I've talked to religious leaders there, and they speak highly of you and your organization. Tanzania is 60% Christian, with the other 40% Muslim. Most of the Muslim population lives in the rural parts of the country. I wanted to interest you in establishing a series of schools to educate these children. Especially the young women.

"We could offer space as the government controls many unoccupied buildings and perhaps some limited funds. The Muslim community is very progressive here, and we could aid in introductions. I have approached religious leaders with this idea, and they're cautious. They also indicated they wouldn't stand in the way."

"What a wonderful idea, Mr. President."

"I wanted to ask you personally to show how sincere I was and how important we think this program could be."

Kate looked sideways at Konner, who had a sheepish look on his face.

"I've got two girls," the president said, "and it would be tragic if they couldn't get an education to start their lives. Religion aside, it should be considered a basic right. A good education in England is the foundation of whatever success I've had."

Kate said, "I'll have Kevin Wainwright, the Charity director, contact your office. We can get the details worked out and get started right away."

"That's wonderful news. Have you had any further trouble with your schools in Libya?"

"No," Kate smiled. "We took care of the problem."

"I hope our shipping agreements and the schools aren't the last business we can do together. I've made it known that more agreements signed by my predecessor will be coming up for review."

"That would be great; my companies will help in any way to accomplish your goals."

The president looked down at the table and said to Kate. "It appears you have finished with dinner. I've been in a dungeon of a room addressing state affairs, and I'm finally going up to my suite. Would the two of you care to join me for a nightcap? I've got a wonderful and exceptional port I have sent in from Portugal."

Kate looked at Konner, who said, "We would be delighted."

"Wonderful, I'll see you then."

He turned to leave the room, and his security detail headed for the exit. Duma stayed behind for a minute. "I'll see you upstairs. Use the presidential suite elevator, and I'll let the guard know you're coming."

"Thank you, Jourdan," Kate said. "But wait, I wish to impress on you two gentlemen the reason the president wanted to see me had nothing to do with my being a woman. So, it turns out there was no excuse for your chauvinist attitudes."

"Mais oui, mademoiselle, Of course, I need no excuse as I'm French." Everyone laughed.

CHAPTER 11

Tanzania
Zanzibar Resort

Kate and Konner approached Adi Nymagu's presidential suite, located at the end of a long hallway limiting guests to one approach. One of two men in front of the suite's double doors stepped forward.

"Can I have your names?" he said.

Kate gave the names. Konner noticed the distorted bulge under one arm as the man looked at a clipboard with a list.

"Thank you," he said as he backed up, allowing them to move forward. The second man opened the suite's doors, and Konner stepped back, allowing Kate to enter first.

Entering the space, Kate noticed how comfortable everything looked. The décor was decidedly modern but with an African flair. Some of the paintings looked like they depicted events in the history of Tanzania. The room was a long rectangle with six huge windows facing away from the ocean and up a slowly rising hill. The glass started three feet above the floor and went up to the ten-foot ceiling. Halfway down the other side, a staircase led to the upper floor of the suite. Multiple sitting areas filled the main room, with a bar at the far end.

The president was standing in a far corner surrounded by men in suits. He was attentively listening to, no doubt, some special interest request. He looked ready to move on, taking a half step to portray his impatience.

Across the room, Duma noticed Kate and Konner and started over, working his way between people.

Kate said to the approaching Duma, "Jourdan, thank you for inviting us."

"It was not I but the president, no?" he said. "Could I get you something to drink?" He motioned to a waitress walking by. She held up a tray of champagne flutes, and he said to her, "Wait, Please, these people would like to order." Duma looked at them, "champagne, or would you prefer something else?"

Konner said, "I think Mr. Nymagu mentioned a special port."

"Ah, that he did." He addressed the waitress, "I'll take care of this."

"I'll be right back," he said, pointing towards the bar. "This is not available to the general public but special guests of the president." He smiled.

After Duma turned away, Konner kind of chuckled, "You're the president of your own company. Why didn't you get the presidential suite?"

"First of all, I'm not the president, I'm the chairperson, and second the suite is not on the beach. Do you have a problem with the accommodations, my dear sir?"

"Absolutely not," he said. "It was meant as a sort of joke."

"You keep pressing this wanting to be a comedian."

Duma returned with two glasses and, raising them, said, "Please enjoy this special edition of Quinta do Noval Nacional. Remember, at a thousand a bottle; there will be the quiz later." He laughed. "I must add the state didn't pay for this; the president did personally. The president is from family money."

Kate said, "I gathered that by the suit. It's gorgeous."

Duma said, "Educated in England, he was very successful before deciding to come back to where he was born. He lives very comfortably without the people's money. Please." He said, indicating for them to take a drink.

"You aren't having any?" Kate asked.

"No, as I'm on duty right now, but," he said, taking a quick look around the room, "I'll not be on duty forever. Then we shall see." He laughed.

Konner lowered his glass after a taste and said, "I'm not an expert on port wine, but this tastes very good."

Duma said with palms raised, "Good—just good? You should be seeing God right now." All three broke out in laughter.

The president noticed Kate and Konner and, seeing an opportunity to escape, motioned to his present company he needed to greet someone. Looking somewhat rescued, he started towards them, maintaining eye contact and the look of finally being able to enjoy himself.

Something clicked in Duma's head. Breaking protocol, he directly addressed one of his security men talking to a guest.

"Patterson, get those curtains closed, now," he said in an urgent low tone. "Who opened them?"

"The president wanted them open, so, of course, the staff reacted." In a few steps, Patterson started pulling the drapes closed. He was just behind the president, drawing the curtains as he walked towards Kate, Konner, and Duma.

CHAPTER 12

Tanzania
Zanzibar Resort

Jamil Novak's eyes in the truck went wide as he saw the curtain being closed and saw the president start towards the other end of the room. Then he saw the curtains closing on the next window. Adrenalin pumped through his body.

Over the intercom came one of the snipers, "This is Number 1; I've lost contact in window five. No target in four. Wait, four is now covered."

Novak grabbed the radio and said, "Either of you, if you have a shot, take it now before we permanently lose sight of the target."

Vanek was standing over Jamil. "You better not screw this up."

Jamil saw the third window go black. "Number two, do you have a shot? Take it."

Number two didn't answer. He was breathing out and slowing his heart rate. In his mind, he calculated the target's movement rate and its anticipated arrival in window two. He released the safety and applied a touching pressure on the trigger. A shadow appeared at the window, and number two squeezed off the shot. He saw the target fall to the ground, and he immediately broke down the weapon by pulling the magazine then removing the stock and barrel. He placed them in a bag that was hanging from a branch. A gun case would have been too cumbersome and obvious.

While performing the motions, he said. "This is number two, clean shot target down."

He dropped the bag to the ground underneath the tree. Reaching the ground, he threw the bag over his shoulder and headed for a waiting car per the plan. In thirty minutes, they would be at the port where the two of them would connect with Novak. They would then board a large powerboat and meet a mother ship in international waters. They would be back in Germany the day after next.

Jamil was still in the van when he pulled off his coat, revealing a uniform of a Tanzanian Army captain. He set the manual timer on the bomb attached to the back wall for two minutes. Just outside the door of the van was a Toyota Camry. He was confident his fake credentials and the uniform would get him past any checkpoint. After throwing his gear into the car, he started the engine. First, he heard the sound and then felt the pressure from the exploding van.

Vanek returned to his car and quickly drove to the new landing zone. Standing next to the car's open window, he reached inside the bag Jamil provided. Vanek pulled the pin on an M14 incendiary grenade and threw it into the vehicle through the open window. Next, he quickly made his way through the undergrowth towards the second landing zone. Looking at the map on his phone, he thought, "Just over this ridge, and the chopper should be there."

Vanek, heavily breathing, crested the hill and came to a plateau. Another chopper was waiting with the rotors turning. As the pilot saw him drive up, he pushed the lever forward, increasing the rotor speed to just below liftoff.

Seconds later, Vanek fought the rotor wash, trying to make his way into the cockpit. His foot was on the edge of the chopper's cockpit as he pulled himself into the seat. "Go go go." He said. He saw the bright light of the grenade in the sky and the explosion eliminating any evidence he might have left behind in the car. "Take me to the port."

CHAPTER 13

Tanzania
Zanzibar Resort

Konner first heard the giant pane of glass shatter from the silent shot and then saw Nymagu fall to the ground. Konner grabbed a hand full of Kate's dress as he fell to the floor. Now on his chest, a confused Kate said, "Konner?"

There were screams and confusion when someone yelled, "Everyone on the floor." Konner recognized the voice as Duma's

"Are you alright?" he asked Kate.

"Yes, what happened?"

Konner didn't answer but rolled Kate to the side and, on his hands and knees, started turning off the lights in any lamp he could reach.

Duma, also on the floor, moved toward the president and saw the headshot that was indeed fatal. The security men were also turning off lights and looking out the one open window with guns drawn. Duma got up and headed for the suite entrance to warn his men. He opened the door and saw the lifeless eyes of Del. Lying on his back, Perry bled from a torso wound. Duma reached down and grabbed that man's suit collar and pulled him into the suite. That's when he felt the bullet hit his arm.

Konner saw Duma dragging Perry inside and moved over to help. They laid the man down and closed the door. Konner opened the man's coat. In addition to seeing the severity of the wound, he reached in and pulled out the man's service piece.

Kate said, "Jordan, you're bleeding."

Duma, dazed with disbelief, looked at the blood-soaked arm of his suit. Konner turned to Kate and said, "We need to get pressure on that. Use his tie; can you do that?" Konner checked Perry for a pulse. Looking up at Duma, he said, "I'm sorry."

Duma saw Konner's lack of reaction to Perry's bloody wound, how he efficiently dropped the cartridge, checked if it was full, and slid the barrel back to load a round. Calmly but urgently, Konner grabbed the extra clip and said to Duma, "I'll cover the entrance. There might be more shooters."

Over dinner, Konner had told him he was with the US state department as a liaison to the world health organization. Duma was sure a diplomatic position didn't result in trained reactions in a firefight and proficiency in lethal weapons.

Duma located his radio and called his men around the hotel. "The president has been shot situation delta. Seal off the resort." He waited for a response and realized something was wrong. "I repeat, situation delta." Waiting, nothing.

He switched frequencies and said into the radio, "General Adusa."

"Adusa here," the general said.

Duma was almost shouting, "They assassinated the president. I want you to block all roads for two miles immediately. Stop everyone."

"Roger that," he responded. No questions, no hesitation; Adusa just reacted to the order.

Konner opened the suite door and looked around the corner and at Del on the floor. He leaned further into the hall, and an automatic burst passed him, burying itself into the wall behind him. Konner pulled back and dropped to a knee, changing the sightline the shooter last saw. Then he waited and squeezed off three shots as a man came out of hiding, two hit center mass. Another emerged into the hall, firing an automatic weapon wildly as he walked backwards to the stairwell, making his escape. Konner fell to the floor. It was a short burst, and the gunman was gone. Konner felt the threat from the hall was gone and re-entered the suite.

Kate, who heard the gunfire outside, met Konner's eyes and was relieved he wasn't hurt. She continued tightening Duma's tie under which several cloth napkins from the food table were pressing against the wound.

She looked up at Konner standing over her, gun in hand. She flashed to the last time she saw him with a gun. It was a dark, damp night in an industrial area of Paris. Kate stood waiting to be killed by one of the worst people on the planet. Wide-eyed, she defiantly looked back at the gunman when he suddenly fell to his knees. Kate ran for her life down the passageway and ran straight into Konner's arms upon rounding the corner. Konner had saved her life. "A lot had changed since then." She thought.

CHAPTER 14

Tanzania
Zanzibar Resort

Duma was silently kneeling over his friend. He had promised Nymagu's family he would protect his friend, and he had failed. It was almost an obligation due to Nymagu's steadfast dedication to Duma and his family. Over the years, his friend had provided support, financial and moral, precisely when he needed it.

Duma sat on the carpet with his face in his hands. The prospect of facing Adi's wife and children weighed heavy on his heart. How could he explain his failure? He had to avenge his friend's death for his family and Duma's dignity. For now, it was in the hands of the Tanzanian army general, but the quest had just started. Medical people helped him to his feet. Duma resisted.

"Sir," one said. "We need to do our job."

The room was now empty except authorized personnel.

Avery Stanton burst into the suite, "Kate?" He shouted. "Where's Kate Adler?"

Duma said, "I sent them back to their room. You can find them there." Reading the tortured look on Avery's face, Duma said. "They're both fine and unharmed."

Without a thought, Avery walked around the medical people tending to Del in the hall and headed towards the elevator and Kate's suite.

The knock on the door was heavy. Heavier than needed, and Kate looked at Konner. He waved her towards the bathroom. He walked over to the dresser and picked up the pistol he had brought back to the room. Standing to the side of the door, avoiding any attempt to shoot him through it, he said, "Who is it?"

"Konner, it's Avery Stanton." The man said breathlessly.

Now confident, Kate came out of the bathroom

Konner said, "Are you alone?"

"Yes, for heaven's sake," was the reply.

Konner took a chance and moved to the center of the door and looked through the viewer. He opened the door.

Avery said, "Kate?"

"Over here," she said.

They came together in a hug.

"Avery, I'm fine."

He stood back and held her in front with a hand on each shoulder; he looked her up and down and said. "Thank God."

"Everything is fine. I've got my he-man protector here."

Avery looked at Konner, "Thank you for everything. Especially for looking after Kate, who has a history of not looking after herself."

He turned back to Kate. "I'm not feeling comfortable about anything that's occurring here, especially after the shooting. I would feel much better if you could leave tonight instead of tomorrow morning. It's a long flight, and you can spend most of it sleeping ah…or whatever." He said, clearly uncomfortable.

"Avery dear, I don't think that's necessary."

"Ms. Adler, you never think anything is necessary when it comes to your safety. I don't want to insist." He looked at Konner for support.

"I can pack in a jiffy," Konner said, avoiding eye contact with Kate.

Kate thought for a moment and said, "Ms. Adler?"

"I only use it when I need to," Avery said.

"I know. OK, where is the plane? Where is Captain Silanos?"

"On the tarmac doing preflight." He said sheepishly.

"Avery?"

"I know, I know, it was presumptuous of me, but I was going to insist if I had to."

67

"I guess I'm packing," Konner said. "Can I help you do the same?"

"I'm just fine. Thank you." Kate said.

"So that's settled," Avery said. He took two steps forward and hugged Kate. "You know." He started to say.

"Yes," Kate said. "How well I know. You promised my father to take care of me." She let go and said, "And, you have done a wonderful job. You're my other knight in shining armor."

* * *

Later after Avery left, Konner said, "You're going to give that man a heart attack."

"What can I say," Kate said. "I came here for a relaxing time with you and perhaps pick up a guy or three. I certainly didn't expect to be involved in any of this. I wonder how Duma is doing right now?"

"I would guess also having a heart attack. The man took it pretty hard. After the astonishment, I saw sadness, and I very definitely saw anger. Someone is in his sights."

"My guess is it's Petrovic. One can't ignore the coincidence. With Nymagu gone, everything reverts to the vice president who has vowed to stop the progressive reforms of his predecessor."

"In other words, it's back to business as usual," Konner said.

Kate said, "It would appear that way. I'm sure TerraDyne will try and overturn the contracts. Not sure how successful they'll be. I'm not worried about the business. I'm worried about the loss the people of Tanzania just suffered. That ray of hope they voted for was taken away again by the powers that run this country. It's a pattern that I see all too often."

Konner grabbed his jacket and looked at his one bag, and next to it were Kate's three large bags.

He looked up, and Kate, matching his stare, said, "I wouldn't comment if I were you."

Changing the subject, he said, "What will you do back home?"

"I need to catch up with the staff at the Cartel. Remember you were going to come back with me. Did Devroe give you enough time to stay at my place?"

"You know," he said. "I've got a regular job, and I'm not always in control of my time like someone I know. Most of the world has a boss or someone above them. I'm no different."

"That didn't answer the question."

Just then, Kate's phone rang. She looked at the screen and said, "It's Brad."

Brad Danner was on the staff at the Cartel. When they met, Brad fell in love with Kate, but Kate wasn't in a space to entertain any permanent relationship. At Kate's invitation, he became a part of the Cartel and eventually became involved with Elena, the Cartel's Geneva 9 computer system director. Despite his being in a somewhat serious relationship with Elena, there was still the spark that she couldn't deny.

Kate said, "Hi Brad."

"Avery called us about an hour ago and told us why you were on your way back. I'm in a meeting with the security staff at the castle."

Brad, I'm fine. We're fine. But it's certainly not how I wanted my short vacation to end. You said he called an hour ago?"

"Yes, he was quite upset. Mom is monitoring communication traffic to find those responsible for the attack. So far, they've one man dressed in a Tanzanian uniform who doesn't have a reasonable explanation for being where he was. Authorities say there have to be at least several more at large."

Kate said, "I hope someone pays as the president was on his way to changing the direction of this whole country for the better."

"When will you be back? I'm sure there will be a lot to go over."

Kate said, "Someone broke into the Morton Roth office in Marseilles last night."

"I know we're lucky it was night, and no one was hurt."

Kate said, "This could be a real problem. But for now, let's let the Adler group take care of that. The Cartel can provide whatever intel we have, but I know Avery will know what to do and get back to us if needed."

"No problem. So when again?"

"We leave for the plane as soon as our bags are downstairs."

"We?" Brad winced on his side of the phone. He had said it unintentionally.

"Konner and I'll be leaving. Brad, we've discussed this."

"I know; I don't have a problem, you know that."

"I would like to think that, but you slip up every once in a while, and you just did."

"In that case, I'm sorry."

Kate could hear the words come through a smile.

"I'll get my act together." He laughed.

She looked at Konner, placing the bags in front of the door waiting for the bellman. She was sure she had made the right decision with Brad. Almost positive. Mostly positive.

CHAPTER 15

Tanzania
Zanzibar Resort

Standing in the lobby, the hotel guest concierge assigned to Kate said, "Ms. Adler, I just talked to your office in New York, and everything is in order. We certainly hope you enjoyed your stay up to today's tragic events. We're saddened and in a bit of shock. Frankly, I don't know where our country goes after this."

Kate said, "You have been so kind. I think the bill has something for the staff to make your day a little brighter."

The concierge said, "Your car is outside, and have a pleasant trip home." Thinking of Konner being on the plane for the duration, Kate smiled.

Kate and Konner turned towards the lobby door and their car, accompanied by one of Jourdan's men. Konner caught sight of Milosh Petrovic approaching with his standard three-person set of bodyguards. "Trouble at three O'Clock," Konner said.

Kate turned and let out a low moan. She said in a low voice. "It's pretty apparent that he or his company is behind the assassination. Yet, he still has the guts to meander around the hotel, confident the assassination will not come back to him.

Kate and he locked eyes, and Petrovic approached with a concerned look on his face.

"What a tragedy about the president," Petrovic said.

"I'm sure you're shocked," Kate said. "But don't you think the timing is just a little suspicious."

"To what are you referring?"

"The signing of the contracts. All agreements are now in possession of the vice president who has stated he prefers to leave things as they were."

"Given the tragedy the country is dealing with right now, having lost their president, I don't think discussing financial matters is appropriate. He was truly concerned about the welfare of his country. People like that don't come along very often. Tragically, he'll not be able to install his agenda. The country is the worse for this deliberate political assassination."

Kate looked at him for a long time. She was not used to someone fabricating a complete lie and delivering it seamlessly without the slightest concern.

"You don't think the motive was more business than political?"

"When one does business on the scale that TerraDyne does, the two often come together. However, in this case, it hasn't. As I said earlier, these contracts would have a minor effect on TerraDyne, so the motive you're hinting at doesn't exist. Next week we sign agreements with the Nigerian government that would dwarf the business represented by the lost contracts to which you refer. Either way, I can assure you, for TerraDyne, it will be business as usual."

In a tense flat statement, Kate's said, "Oh, I'm sure it will be business as usual."

Petrovic continued, seemingly unaware of the point Kate was trying to make. It could have been his inability to connect with other people and women in general. "In some areas, our interests are the same. Perhaps we can do business in the future."

Kate found the man completely abhorrent. "I'm sure we won't."

***

Kate and Konner were both standing in the executive terminal of the Abeid Amani Karume Airport in Zanzibar.

She looked at Konner, "You never told me where you're headed after I drop you off at Ramstein in Germany. By the way, we did get approval for a civilian landing. It seems your boss has friends in high places."

Konner grinned. "Yes, I guess you could say that. It pays to have gone to college with the future president of the United States. That's about as high as it gets."

"So?" She said. "Where are you headed?"

"I don't know yet. I'm to touch base with Devroe when I get to Germany."

"The offer to stay at my place is still open." She said as subtly as possible.

He laughed and pulled her close. "Sounds like an incentive to stay."

"An incentive is the last thing you need, Mr. Houston." She said, looking up and planting her finger in the middle of his chest.

"As I've always said, it's not my fault you're bright and beautiful."

"Charming, Mr. Houston."

Konner turned serious, "I really did have a great time with just the two of us. Well, *mostly* the two of us as it seemed rather busy at times."

"I did too. It won't be the last if we work on it. Promise me you will work Devroe for some more time off. Just a little here and there would be acceptable. I can meet you if it means we can be together."

"No word yet. I get the feeling something big is brewing. I can feel it, and Devroe seemed to hint at that during our last phone call, but he didn't want to discuss it over an open line."

"Well, we'll always have zoom. It works for the rest of the world."

Climbing the steps, they entered the cabin of the spacious Gulfstream G650, the largest plane made by the company. Konner noticed that the aircraft's rear-facing seats were now a full-size bed. In front of the bed, solid slide-out privacy screens were pushed back against the bulkhead, ready to be re-deployed.

"Amazing," he said.

"What is?"

"Oh, Nothing,"

"Have a seat up here. It's an eight-hour flight. We can eat, read a bit if you like, and sleep our way back. We'll be there in no time."

Konner didn't respond. He put his soft briefcase on the table. Still silent, he turned his head and grinned at Kate.

"Yes?" she said playfully.

"How high does this thing fly?" He asked

Kate said with a finger on her chin and a twinkle in her eye. "I've been told at least a mile."

CHAPTER 16

Ramstein Air Base in Germany

Captain Silanos opened the door to the plane and deployed the steps taking in the early morning cool air and the first morning light appearing over Ramstein airbase.

Kate was standing at the back of the plane with Konner. They were holding each other silently until Kate said. "Did you have a nice time?"

"Was there a particular time you're talking about?" He said with a mischievous grin.

"I was referring to the whole trip. Bring your mind 'round."

"Yes, except for the shooting. When do I get to see you again?"

"I don't know." She said. "I gave you our G9t phone. You can call or text me anytime."

"I'm serious."

"Schedules, we're beholden to schedules. Yours is as bad as mine, Mr. Houston. We said it would take a lot of work to create a relationship. It's not going to be easy."

He let her go. "I'm certainly on board with that." He said. Heading towards the open door, he followed, "You have a nice trip back. I'll call when I know anything I can tell you."

***

Kate's head of household, Myrla, took the breakfast tray away.

The flight from the airbase back to the castle was barely an hour. Fresh memories of her time with Konner filled her head, and she smiled. On the one hand, she felt good about where she was personally right now. On the other hand, she had never let someone so far into her life. It left a certain vulnerable feeling. She and Konner were well suited except for their schedules, but she couldn't shake the feeling of possible hurt on the other side of this relationship.

That same feeling was present when she and Brad were closer. Her emotional involvement with Brad was far more profound than Kate led him to believe. She based her final decision not to go any further on that same foreboding sense. The almost certain knowledge that it all would come crashing down, and she'd have to extract herself painfully.

There was also the unavoidable situation of having inherited her father's business empire. There was always the feeling that the money would always play a part with anyone she'd meet. Before her father died, she and Brad were friends, so it didn't come into play. And Konner never seemed to care about money. So why the internal battle? This wasn't the first time she had asked herself the question. Her knee, which she had been staring at, came back into focus. Next, she smiled, which caused her to reach for her phone. She sent a text to Konner.

"Call before eight AM if you can."

***

Later that morning, Kate walked into the conference room at the Cartel's headquarters. The room looked like any other corporate meeting room with large presentation screens and a long table to seat as many as fourteen. Chairs lined the wall for overflow, and a beverage service table provided drinks and food if needed. Three small windows were inset into eighteen-inch thick stone walls down one side of the room. They were the only hint the room sat inside a medieval castle with origins in the tenth century.

Kate's Cartel security team filed in taking seats."

"Welcome, everyone," Kate said.

Penn Hauer asked, "How was your flight?" Penn, a veteran of the cold war, was director of field operations. If it was out there and needed fixing, Penn was your man. Sometimes gruff with a haircut close to the sides, he was an office favorite enduring jokes about James Bond with self-effacing quietness and strength born from experience.

Kate said, "The flight up was long, but I slept most of it. Someone talked a local chef into providing a five-star meal. Just the thing to make one sleep like a baby."

"Good to have you back," Brad said.

Kate noticed something in Brad's voice. It was flat and distracted. Unusual because Brad was typically very up and personable. Because they knew each other before Kate learned of the Cartel, Brad had a connection to Kate deeper than the others in the room.

Brad had started without a specific job title but served as Kate's sounding board when needed. He advanced to handling all the external communications with the secretive Cartel and had recently added program manager to his portfolio. He brought together the team's findings on any particular project and oversaw whatever action Kate approved.

The security team also included Elena Maleeva, who was in charge of Geneva9, the organization's one-of-a-kind surveillance system they called Mom. Loren Sorrel reported to Elena and helped Penn, in the field, with her cyber capabilities. From her keyboard, Loren could direct Mom to do any number of things, from delivering food aid to shutting down part of a country's power grid. Her soft voice and diminutive stature defied her ability to wreak havoc with the computing power at her disposal.

Kate said, "I dropped Konner off at Ramstein airbase, and he's off somewhere, and I continued to here. It was sad about the president. He was sincere about his wanting to stop the cycle of corruption." Kate looked at Brad and said, "What do you have this morning?"

Again talking in a monotone voice, Brad said, "I'm afraid this will not be a typical day. I have already talked to Avery, and he said we received a second offer to buy Morton Roth. The price is 15% below the first offer."

"We aren't selling."

"We all know that."

Kate said, "It's not even a subject I want to discuss, but it points to a pattern. Petrovic attacks our company and submits an offer. Let's let Avery handle that. What else did he have to say?"

It follows what you just said. He reported a Morton Roth office in Bremerhaven, Germany, caught fire last night. No one was hurt, but it destroyed the office. Kevin has the manager looking for office space to get up and running as soon as possible. They need to manage a surge of ships into that harbor, and commerce waits for no one. Especially when delays cost thousands an hour."

Kate seemed confused for a second. "Wait, this is in addition to the attack in Marseilles?"

"Unfortunately, yes," Brad said. "Avery asked us to see if we could develop anything that would help him figure out who is attacking the offices. He said because they left a note behind, the somewhat messy getaway, and the second attack, it moved it from random to someone with a plan. Elena and Loren are working on what Mom can find out."

Elena said, "I've directed Mom to monitor several areas, but the net we're casting is pretty broad right now. We don't have any information on who did it and their objective. We haven't picked up any communication regarding the incident. I'm afraid we've not been much help. The local authorities found the burned-out van used during the arson attack in a dodgy part of town."

Kate said, "Occam's Razor."

Elena, the most logical person in the room, said, "I agree."

Brad said, "What's that?"

With a doctorate in computer science, Elena said, "Occam's Razor is a guide used in reaching conclusions in theoretical models. The term "razor" refers to cutting or shaving away of unnecessary information or assumptions. In other words, the most obvious answer is usually the right answer."

Kate said, "To me, the right answer is obvious."

Penn said, "It's hard to ignore."

Brad said, "TerraDyne."

"Who else?" Kate said. "It seems they've declared war on Morton Roth."

Loren interrupted. "It might not mean anything, but Mom had reported signing a large contract between TerraDyne and North Korea last month to transport their raw materials around the sanctions."

"How would she know that?" Kate asked.

Elena said, "We also have Mom monitoring anything that has to do with TerraDyne since the assassination. The analog says she intercepted open communication between a North Korean agent and TerraDyne's executives. That generated more internal conversations regarding their not having enough ships to support the new business."

Brad said, "Avery is convinced that Petrovic is interested in buying the company to regain the contracts. Those contracts have been keeping some very powerful people happy in that country. Most of them are pretty angry about their source of income going to Morton Roth."

Penn said, "Elena's information leads one to believe Petrovic might also want Morton Roth's fleet of ships to transport the increased capacity created by the Korean contracts."

Elena asked, "What will happen to our new Morton Roth contracts with the government?"

Kate said, "I'm almost certain the vice president will try to get them overturned as soon as he takes office. Tanzania has a very developed court system, so I see that played out over two years or more. TerraDyne is huge, but the contracts were still a substantial amount of business."

Brad heard the notification and checked the screen. It's another call from Avery.

Brad pressed the button that brought his image up on the screen and said, "Avery, you are on the monitor in the conference room. The security team is here."

"Thanks, Brad. Kate, are you there?"

"Yes, Avery. What do you have?"

"I just got off the phone with Mr. Guyer from the Conklin Institute. It seems Mr. Guyer and your father go back a long way. He wants to talk directly to you, Kate."

"About what?"

"The Conklin Institute monitors the shipping industry and is very influential. He is aware of our problems, needs to issue a report, and wants our side."

"How does he know about any problems?"

"An article just came out this morning written by a Mr. Devoss Marcks. He's considered an authority in the maritime industry. He wrote an opinion piece that appeared in the magazine and website of SeaState. It's a very influential site covering all manner of shipping news, from regulations to brokerage fees.

In the article, Mr. Marcks discusses the "serious" problems Morton Roth is experiencing. Marcks points to severe disruptions in the business, including raids on offices and an inability to manage the problem. He mentions the fire at Bremerhaven. He states the situation affects delivery times, with delays increasing customer costs. The real damage, according to him, is that some insurance companies are backing off or at least increasing insurance rates."

"It's a complete fabrication," Kate said.

Avery said, "Of course it is, and it's suspect from the beginning considering he's reporting in detail on an incident that happened just 6 hours ago."

Kate said, "Where did he get the information?"

Penn said, "An excellent question. I have my guess."

Avery said, "So do I. The site provided the standard disclaimer that accompanies opinion pieces; we aren't responsible for opinions stated etc. But, Marcks is well known, and people will take notice."

Penn said, "If this guy is the well-respected voice of the industry, why he'd peddle this crap is not hard to figure out. It was a deal he couldn't refuse based on money or, more probably, threats to his family. A favorite tactic of the nefarious inhabitants of our world."

Kate said, "The why isn't as important as the what? A certain percentage of people will believe it nonetheless with the damage done. Avery, I have no problem meeting with him. Where and when?"

"He's in Vienna meeting with a group of marine insurance companies."

"OK, I can be there later this afternoon. Can you get a time and place?"

"While we were on the phone, he threw out three today at the Cafe Central. He will call me to see if you can make that time."

"I'll be there. Thanks, Avery, and I'll let you know what occurs at the meeting."

Kate said, "Vienna, how long to…"

"It's less than two hours," Loren interrupted.

"I might need a room or a place to stay and wait."

Penn said, "Hotel Sacher."

Kate said. "Where exactly?"

Penn chuckled, "It was the center of spy vs. spy during the cold war. The only illegal spying in Austria was when Austria was the target. The Sacher flies more flags than the U.N. It's almost comical to some extent as that's where spies have met since the Hapsburgs ruled the country. The adage is to spy in the afternoon and meet at the hotel for post opera drinks."

Kate said, "I think I'm meeting a spy who wants a look into our operation. Let's hope we can convince him we have things under control.

CHAPTER 17

Ramstein Airbase
Germany

Dr. Stephen Devroe, Director of National Intelligence, sat at his desk trying to unravel the meeting earlier in the evening with Martin Perez, president of the United States. The primary subject agitated the president, who was also a long-time friend. It's not often something ruffled the usually calm low center of gravity that made up the president's personality. The man lived his life based on honesty and rules, and Iran didn't even pay passing attention to either. The current crisis was slow in developing but now had a momentum of its own. The president had decided they needed to find out just how close the Iranian leadership was to making a colossal mistake and throwing the middle east and the allies on both sides into war.

Devroe logged into the secure NSA communications network, the billion-dollar equivalent of zoom.

Konner looked at this watch as he sat in the Hotel Meeker just outside Ramstein Airbase in Germany. It was a few minutes before 8:00 am his time. He thought, "Whatever Devroe has to talk about, it must be important to meet at 2:00 am his time."

Devroe's face came up on the screen. Konner said, "For 2:00 am, I expected you to look a lot worse. This call must be important for you to be up this late. Why didn't you just have me come back to DC?"

"Because I need you there, but we'll get to that. But first, tell me, how was your vacation?"

"First of all, it wasn't a vacation. It was a few days off. Something I have not done in two years, so cut me a break."

"Yes, except you were in sunshine and splendor in very enviable company."

"You're forgetting I was in the line of fire during the assassination of the president of a foreign country."

"True, I never met the man, but all reports say he was legit. Is Ms. Adler okay?"

Konner made noticeable movements to check his watch in front of the screen. "It took you only thirty seconds to ask about her."

"Why wouldn't I? She was with you, right?"

"I'm not sure that was the reason you asked. Anyway, it's more like I was with *her*. Kate is fine, and let's move on. What was so important that you're up at this hour to talk to me?"

We have a source claiming he has privileged and critical information regarding Iran. As you know, Israel attacks Iran's nuclear program anytime they make meaningful progress. Currently, the president is trying to avoid outright war between the two by offering to broker some form of a ceasefire, but things are not going well. Nuri Koffman, the Israeli prime minister, has become an unmovable mountain.

Konner said, "Well, you can't argue with his logic. Iran has stated, categorically, its goal is to destroy Israel. The president has clarified what Iran needs to do to keep Israel out of its kitchen. Stop enriching uranium."

"Something they are not likely to do as they see getting the bomb as insurance against the US invading. A couple of days ago, there was a briefing about the stability of the Iranian government that sent alarm bells ringing. The Ayatollah is under tremendous pressure from the Revolutionary Guard, who have the guns, to stop the attacks."

Konner said, "Political power grows out of the barrel of a gun."

"You're quoting Mao Zedong? Really?" Devroe chuckled. "Have you taken college courses since we last talked?"

Konner looked at Devroe directly and said, "No."

Devroe said, "So that brings us to the next problem. Israel gave us twenty-four hours' notice of a pending operation."

"Operation? That's it. No details?"

"We never get details, and in fact, no one in the government will admit they told us anything. They'll also deny it to the world when it happens. Anyway, we think something in the enrichment cycle is the target."

"Okay, I've traveled a long way to sit here and listen to a foreign policy review. You must have a reason to dump all this on me."

"As I said, the CIA has had a low-level source feeding them inside information on the Iranian leadership. I want you to go talk to him and get a read on just how unstable the whole situation has become."

"Look, I know I'm supposed to follow orders blindly, but why can't the CIA ask him?"

"Two reasons. The contact claims to come across some significant information and will only talk to the president, which ain't gonna happen. But the president thinks this might be an opportunity to get an inside look, so we need to find out what this guy has to say. Second, I don't want any agency fingerprints on this. In fact, no fingerprints at all. The president is supposed to be an honest broker trying to make Israel and Iran live peacefully on the same planet. Any hint of contacting back door sources would blow it out of the water. No fingerprints mean *you,* if you're wondering. That means you don't talk to anyone but me. It's too sensitive. I want you to meet with this guy, and I'm sending you some phone numbers."

Konner said. "I just call him? That doesn't sound very secure for someone on the agency's payroll."

"You text the first number using the Signal text app. It's extremely secure and used by dissidents around the world. He will send you a number to call to arrange details to meet. You're to call a different number each time."

"There's just one thing, perhaps two," Konner said. "How does he know it's me, and why would he meet someone he doesn't know and can't identify?"

"That's the miracle of the digital age. Send the contact a facial picture. There's no need for a rose in the lapel or reading a newspaper upside down. It's a whole new world. Still, as the second level of identification, he'll say, "When is your trip to

Catalina?" Your reply is, "I leave Thursday. As far as a location he feels comfortable with, the rest is between you two."

"Konner, get whatever you can out of him, but we're interested in the state of mind of the Iranian leadership. Also, who's in charge over there?"

"Roger that. So what now? When does he expect me to call and meet?"

"Today, in Paris. He's staying in the Iranian Embassy residence on Avenue d'lena."

Konner's face said it all. "Please say you're kidding. I've just spent a ton of time in a plane and got in late last night."

"It was a private plane, I might add with, no doubt," Devroe's eyebrows rose, "a sleeper. No, I'm not kidding. That's why there's a C37A private jet waiting on the tarmac of Ramstein right now. I know you've grown accustomed to Ms. Adler's Gulfstream, so I've upped you to first class on the government's dime. The flight will take less than an hour since you avoid all the civilian airport delays. The rest is up to you. Remember your report will be read by the president, so no personal stuff."

"Very funny. But speaking of personal, when I get there, it's the weekend. Most people have it off. When do you want me back?"

"It will all depend on what's in your report and our next move and who makes it. But I don't see you coming back here right away." Devroe smiled. "Why. Are you angling for some more *personal* time?"

Konner shook his head and smiled. "I'm afraid that's personal."

***

Konner was in the air, having finished reading the file on the agent he was supposed to meet later in the day. Kate had supplied him with a phone to use when he wanted to talk to her privately. He started typing a text. "Can you talk?" Looking out the window at nothing but blue sky, he waited.

The phone rang. "Good morning." He said.

"What a nice surprise. Where are you?"

"I'm on a plane to Paris for a meeting this afternoon. I don't know when or where. Any chance to meet up later or tomorrow? I know all of that's pretty vague."

"I'm also in the air on my way to Vienna for an afternoon meeting. What a coincidence. I could stay the night there. That's an invitation in case you missed it."

"I accept, but I said Paris, not Vienna, so there's travel time that would make tonight a little difficult. Also, I don't know when the meeting will take place. My call to you is kind of a shot in the dark but a shot worth taking."

"Well, aren't you cute? Your meeting has to be over at some point; then you can come to Vienna?"

"Devroe is getting me to Paris on a private government plane I lose after landing. If the meeting is late, then Paris to Vienna is a four-hour ordeal door to door. I don't know."

"Sure, if you fly commercial. Security, boarding passes, flirting with every pretty girl you meet. It could be shorter. I'll send a plane to Paris Le Bourget, the private airport at Charles de Gaulle, and you bypass all of that. It's only a 2 hr flight if I remember. Before you go off on the expense, it's my money. I can spend it any way I like. Right now, you're lucky I want to spend it on you."

"Well, I feel so privileged. All right, I won't complain. I would like to see you even though it hasn't been that long since the Zanzibar."

"You're so romantic."

"I know a real catch, huh? Where are you staying?"

"At the Hotel Sacher. Captain Silanos will have a car waiting to get you here quickly."

"Look, thanks for doing this. It's going to take a while before this feels comfortable."

"No problem. The pleasure is mine. At least for now."

Konner heard a small chuckle before she rang off.

CHAPTER 18

Vienna
Austria

Kate looked out the window like any tourist as she traveled along the Philharmoniker Strausse, admiring the skyline of slender spires, Hapsburg palaces, and baroque buildings with their gold domes. Vienna was beautiful, with most old buildings surviving the war even though the bombing turned over twenty percent of the city into rubble.

The driver said, "We're here, madam."

He brought the car to a halt at the understated entrance of the Hotel Sacher. The Wiener Staatsoper was directly across the street. She saw the Soravia Wing jutting out over the street from the Antigua museum to her left. "I'm not a fan," she thought. Kate compared it to the glass pyramid in the center of the Louvre. She wasn't a fan of that either.

Her door opened, and the doorman and concierge stood outside. "I would like to welcome you to the Hotel Sacher." The concierge said. "My name is Eduard, and I'll ensure your stay at our hotel is up to your standards."

"I'm sure that won't be a problem, Eduard. It's my first time here, but," she said, looking over her shoulder at the opera house, "it won't be my last."

"If you follow me, I'll show you directly to your room. Your office has taken care of all the details, and your luggage will follow us up promptly."

"Eduard, you're very efficient. How long have you worked here?"

Surprised at the personal request, he momentarily searched for words. "In various capacities over twenty-eight years. I'm very happy here. It's my work."

"That's wonderful," Kate said.

Now alone in the elevator, Eduard, with his arms grasped behind his back, started to say, "Ah, Ms. Adler, I." And he stopped as if being told he broke a rule.

Kate smiled at the effort. "What is it. Please, I want to hear."

"I'm a great admirer of your work. Your efforts on behalf of children worldwide aren't hard to follow, given your well-documented accomplishments. My wife presents you as a role model for our daughter."

"I'm flattered and consider that to be the greatest compliment."

"Ah, we're here." He said. He stood back for her to exit and then led her to her suite. Opening the double doors, he walked into the well-lit space with its understated walls and carpet with a baroque touch. The room was brightly lit, unusual for a building from the late eighteen hundreds.

"It's just wonderful," Kate said, reaching for her purse and a tip.

Eduard said, with both hands behind him and facing Kate, "No further thanks are needed, and I shall see myself out."

"But Eduard."

He put up a hand as he walked towards the suite's entry.

"Please," Kate said, "I have a question. Where is the Cafe Central?"

"It's a wonderful, very famous place and just up the street."

"So it's just minutes away. I have a meeting there in a while. Can I walk?"

"Of course, but suggest I arrange transportation. Just call downstairs, and we'll have a ride in minutes."

"As he placed his card on the bookcase by the door, he said. "You can call this number any time for anything; my cell is on the back."

With that, he was gone. "That was a little abrupt," Kate thought, but what a delightful man.

Her phone rang. She looked at the screen, "Yes, Brad, good timing. I just arrived."

"Did everything go OK on the trip?"

"Yes, this is a wonderful room. Tell Penn he has excellent taste. Any news from our insurance friend?"

"We're waiting for a phone call confirming his original time. You have some time so you can freshen up a bit."

"Good, I'll wait to hear from you." She hit the button and put the phone down. The G9t was the Cartel's proprietary phone. All Cartel communication was encrypted and controlled by Mom, the central computer that monitored the Cartel's affairs. The phone was encrypted beyond military-grade and made even the most casual conversation strictly confidential.

***

Orly airport
Paris France

Konner took out the first burner phone and sent a text message via the Signal application to the agent he was supposed to meet. The plane Devroe had supplied was parked in its designated area, and he was in no hurry to deplane. He didn't know where he would be going to go until the agent sent him a number to call.

CHAPTER 19

Beersheba
Gav-yam Negev technology park.
Israel

Jaron Gabai walked out of the North railway station and onto David Ben Gurion Boulevard. Pulling on his backpack, he quickly crossed the pedestrian bridge to the new Gav-yam Negev technology park, Israel's version of Silicon Valley. His destination was a purposely understated gray concrete building housing the IDF's (Israeli Defense Force) Urim SIGINT base. At twenty-one, he was one of the older programmers of the two thousand workers in the facility. Recruited right out of high school, he lived to solve his job's challenges daily.

The Urim SIGINT base was the most important signal intelligence-gathering installation in the country. It was part of the shadowy unit 8200 thought to have created the Stuxnet virus that attacked Iran's Natanz nuclear facility in 2010. It was a game-changer, but they couldn't have developed it without some heavy lifting by the Americans. The program represented the first time a software attack resulted in real-world physical damage and not just a computer acting strangely.

It was six in the afternoon as he returned to the facility. He had slept ten hours after a grueling sixty-hour development effort on a program called Sophia. He knew it was essential and knew they needed it fast. While he was gone, his team was running tests, and he was anxious to see the results. The requirements were very exacting and demanded a lot of creativity to meet all the program's objectives. He was very proud of his work.

CHAPTER 20

Serbia
Belgrade TerraDyne Offices

Petrovic looked at the glass of water he held at arm's length. It was a meter helping him assess how the shaking was going today. The movement was subtle but definitely getting worse. It was something he hadn't told the doctor during their sessions. The man would just make it more important than it was, and he didn't have time for distractions."

The phone sounded with Vanek's ring. Petrovic put the cell phone on speaker. "Vanek, where are you?"

"I'm on the way to the tanker Tempest."

"Is it all locked down?"

'Yes, everything is all set.

"When can you get back with a report?"

"How late do you want me to call as it occurs late tonight? You're not usually the night owl type."

"You call as soon as you can tell me it's been successful."

"Ah, OK. I might be recovering in a hospital if you know what I mean. I don't do well with water."

"I know what you mean. Suck it up. It won't be the last time. Have you contacted the people in Eritrea?"

"Yes, everything appears to be on track for the kidnapping. We had to sign a contract which I would think is very strange in that profession. I sent it to Holland, who's better in the legal realm than I. He said it all looked good but also found it unusual. He sent the first half of their fee and received a deposit confirmation, so there can be no excuses."

Petrovic asked, "How reliable are they? I don't want any screw-ups. We have Morton Roth on the ropes, and I want even more pressure. This Adler girl is going to find out how the big boys play. She has no clue what's in store."

"Boss, don't let her get to you. You know how you get with women."

Petrovic said, "This is all business, and I don't need your advice. It's good the Eritrea job is hands-off. I wanted you directing the assassination, but I don't want you anywhere near the kidnapping. Are we clear? Are you sure nothing will come back to me on this? We don't have anyone in our pocket in Eritrea, so nothing is assured."

"No problem," Vanek said. It's all done anonymously. All communication has been on Signal text messages. I'm told the syndicate has the local police force not completely in their pocket but the police can be being extremely slow in resolving certain crimes."

CHAPTER 21

Vienna
Austria

Kate stood before Cafe Central, the most famous of the traditional Vienna Kaffee Houses. Open since 1876, it's been the central point of Vienna's social life for almost one and a half centuries. Anyone important needs to be seen sipping espresso within its confines. The simple entrance was at a Neo-renaissance triangular-shaped building in the downtown quarter.

Vienna's positivists, like Freud, held many meetings at the Café. However, what made the café unique in the world was that some of the most important figures of the 20th century visited the Café Central during the same time period. Stalin, Hitler, Tito, and Trotsky all lived in Vienna between the two World wars.

The maitre d' saw her walk in, and she noted his reaction.

"Ms. Adler?" He said.

"Yes," Kate smiled, a bit surprised.

"Mr. Guyer showed me a picture so I could seat you immediately."

Kate took in the splendid interior of the room with its many round tables and smell of pastries. He walked over to a table under the Gothic curved twenty-foot ceilings and large windows casting a gentle glow throughout the space.

A handsome older man stood as she approached. He said in perfect English, "Ms. Adler, let me introduce myself; I'm Armin Guyer."

Kate said, "It's a pleasure, Mr. Guyer. My name is Kate Adler."

She reached out to shake hands with a man in his seventies. He stood ramrod straight and was striking in a shiny Italian suit. I'm not sure how much Mr. Stanton told you, but your father and I go back to his early days, of his little business?" He smiled, releasing her hand.

A waiter stood next to the table, and before he could ask for an order, Mr. Guyer looked at Kate and said. "Have you been to Cafe Central before?"

"No, I haven't, but it's a lovely place, isn't it?"

"It's not often the words lovely and an institution can be used to describe something. But it seems appropriate here. The Cafe Central has a long heritage going back almost 140 years. Since it's your first time, If I may?"

"Please, Mr. Guyer."

To the waiter, he said, "Two Kaffee verkehrt." He turned and said to Kate, "Essentially a macchiato with more milk. They're delicious. If you go to Chicago, it's pizza, and in France, it's Coq Au Vin. If you come to the Cafe Central, it's a Kaffee verkehrt."

He sat back in his chair. "It was a sad day when we lost your father. However, according to Avery, with whom I frequently contact for both personal and business reason, not a beat was lost when you took over. Then you took it a step farther with your charity work. I have to say you're quite the lady."

"Well, Mr. Guyer, you're so kind."

"Please, you must call me Armin."

"And I would prefer Kate. So Armin, what brings us together?"

"Ah yes, my other hat, Kate?" he paused to gather words. "We have a situation that could, if not contained, grow into something serious rather quickly. First, you may not know I'm the senior director of the Conklin Maritime Institute. We provide information to the underwriters in the maritime industry. This information includes research papers on exciting topics like fuel consumption, current legislative issues, regulations, and the like. However, we also provide health and stability reports on companies by issuing a rating like Moody's does for the global capital markets. Throughout the years, your rating has always been our highest AAA. Lately, we have been monitoring some visible incidents affecting your company.

"An opinion piece in SeaState magazine presents a case that Morton Roth has recently encountered some problems. This article just appeared this morning and has caused quite a stir. It's a very respected magazine, and while they noted it was not the publication's opinion, the damage is done. This morning the governing board voted for a formal review. They wish to access whether to drop your rating to an A-. One of my jobs is to provide those reviews."

Kate said, "This results in?"

"The picture is not pretty with increased underwriting fees and increased operating costs. All of which would necessitate an increase in your prices, putting you above standard rates."

Guyer took in Kate as she sat there with a proud look that reminded him of her father. "It's also my job to address anything that could affect the stability we have grown to expect in our industry. Morton Roth is a major participant in the industry. I need to determine if your company has a routine problem or something that may pose a threat to the maritime component in the world's supply chain. I'm sorry to be blunt, Ms. Adler, but that's why we're meeting today. I have received, you might say, several inquiries from insurance brokers to port authorities regarding the stability of Morton Roth. Can they deliver cargo on time and safely? A company that has over seventy ships at sea at any time draws special interest."

"Mr. Guyer, Armin, what has occurred in a matter of days is an attempt to devalue the company in a takeover attempt. TerraDyne, a very unreputable company, is at the center of the problem."

"I'm very aware of TerraDyne. They've caused many problems throughout the years. Their rating is a B, our lowest, but their particular business method generates substantial margins to pay the penalties incurred. I'm aware of the tactics used by Mr. Petrovic. While I'm sympathetic to your situation from a historical and personal perspective, the business world only sees numbers. And right now, your company commands enough of the shipping business that any concern becomes magnified."

"Armin, I can assure you my company is stable, and these recent troubles are temporary and are being dealt with as we speak. We're taking several steps, including preparing a response to counter the disinformation with the truth. We have also increased the security at our offices and on our ships."

Guyer said, "There's a phenomenon in our industry. What goes up fast comes down slow. That applies to the cost of insurance, be it cargo, hull, or freight. You have experienced the vertical part of the disinformation curve. Experience tells me your efforts to stem the tide with the truth will take considerable time and effort."

"So what happens now. How do I convince you we'll weather this storm and come out stronger on the other side? It's not me you must convince. I can present my findings, but only the board can make a rating adjustment. Rest assured, I'll convey your thoughts and commitments and perhaps lean harder in your favor than I would normally. I would do this in honor of your father and the reputation of the Adler companies. However, I would prepare yourself and your company for some rough times ahead and not only from Mr. Petrovic. The board might hold the line at A+, but it could go lower with more negative publicity. It pains me to say this but consider it information from a friend. I've never been so forthright with anyone else in this kind of situation."

"You have been most kind, Armin."

"I'm prepared to continue "gathering information," if you will, before being pressed to present my report. It will give you some time, but that's as far as I can go."

Kate said, "I can assure you this time is appreciated and will be used to clear our name quickly."

"I cannot appear to be partial, but I sincerely hope you are successful. Now, I see our Kaffee verkehrt has arrived. Do you take sugar?"

CHAPTER 22

Vienna
Austria

Kate was back in her room at the Hotel Sacher. Knowing she would be seeing Konner, she had dresses laid out on the bed and couldn't decide which one to wear. A call from Avery eliminated the need for an immediate decision.

"Avery, what a nice surprise. Where are you?"

"I'm still in New York, and Mom has you patched into a video meeting with Brad and the team."

"The team? This doesn't sound good."

Kate said, "I understand we received another offer from Petrovic to buy Morton Roth?"

"Yes, we sent back a negative reply to their offer and haven't heard anything more. We have some more information on that article written by Devoss Marcks posted on the SeaState site that says Morton Roth is having trouble."

Kate said, "I learned this afternoon that site is pretty much the industry's voice. We need to be careful because insurance companies read this magazine, and even though it's an opinion piece, the author is a noted figure in the industry."

"Insurance could be a problem, as it's a skittish market. We have great relationships with our providers, but there might be pressure to adjust rates despite our good standing."

Kate said, "According to my conversation with Guyer, that will be the biggest problem."

Brad said, "Can we trace this Marcks guy back to TerraDyne?"

"Not directly," Elena said, "but Mom reports a nice deposit in his bank account yesterday, routed through the Caribbean."

Kate said, "Avery, how is Lang Gerlach doing?"

Avery said, "I've taken over the problems we're facing so he can continue to manage things day-to-day. He is doing his best in a tough situation. We don't want our customers thinking there's a problem with Morton Roth, so I contacted the magazine, but they gave me the company line they aren't responsible for op-ed content. Therefore, they'll not make any changes. Their point is that offering different perspectives is the whole purpose of the feature."

Kate said, "Mr. Guyer noted that if this becomes accepted fact, it could affect future orders with customers concerned about prompt delivery."

Avery said, "It's two offices out of what 40?"

"I know," Kate said, "but that doesn't keep people from believing we're in serious trouble. They have to protect themselves and their customers and, most importantly, keep their customer's cargo moving at all costs."

Avery said, "This industry spooks very quickly. Also, the article said large contracts recently won in Tanzania have been canceled due to an investigation into how they were awarded. It's a campaign of lies."

Penn said, "Repeat them often enough, and they become the truth."

Kate, who had been standing, sat down heavily on the bed and let out a big sigh. "What's happening here?"

Brad said. "Clearly, someone wants to damage Morton Roth, and they don't care how they do it. Shady financing in a takeover is one thing but damaging the company to lower the price is another. That points directly at TerraDyne,"

Kate said, "I'm afraid so."

CHAPTER 23

Paris
France

Konner was sitting in a Paris airport cafe sipping coffee, having sent a text to one of the numbers he received to contact the agent. He thought, "If the CIA couldn't get anything out of this guy, and they had been paying him, why did Devroe think he'd do any better?" Looking at the empty plate that once contained an excellent pastry, he determined life was short and decided to order another just as his phone went off.

"Konner Houston here."

"Where are you?" The voice said.

"At the Le Bourget private airport. I'm twenty minutes from downtown."

"Meet me at Square Felix Desruelles," He said. "Be by the statue in the courtyard. You have to be alone. I'll know. Wait for a call." The line went dead.

"Sort of dramatic," Konner thought. He downed the rest of the coffee, looked longingly at the empty plate, and headed for the sign that read "Ground Transports."

***

Konner looked around the small park that was an extension of the church grounds. On one end of the courtyard was a monument, and in the center was a statue of a person. A comforting sign he was in the right place. One person was sitting on one of the benches facing the figure. If this was the guy he was supposed to meet, his disguise looked like an older woman feeding the birds. Konner walked around, and then half sat on the concrete edge of the fountain pond. In minutes the phone rang.

"Meet me at the Brasserie Lipp. Sit outside, not inside, and wait. I'll know if you're alone."

Again the line was dead. The man didn't give him a time to meet. Konner entered the name into his phone for directions and found it a short two blocks away.

Konner had a rather mundane thought, "This is Paris; what if there are no tables outside?"

As luck would have it, as Konner approached, a young man, obviously a student working on his studies, rose with books in hand. He looked down at the table while smiling at Konner. He was acknowledging the Parisian tradition of "catching a table."

A few minutes later, Konner was doing what everyone did in Paris. He entertained himself, watching the myriad of colorful people going about their business. Some were going to work, others to church, and most were unaware of how special it was to live in Paris. Its unique beauty to them was still "just" their home. Of course, his interest was more than innocent entertainment. He was looking for a specific person.

The Lipp's famous extra-long menu stretched from one edge of the small table to the other. "Strange size," he thought. While waiting for his coffee, he looked at the menu to find something similar to the pastry he enjoyed at the airport. His espresso arrived about the same time he noticed a man separating himself from a group of people crossing the street. Trying to look absorbed by his phone, the man eventually made his way to Konner's table.

The man said, "How was your trip to Catalina."

Konner half smiled and said, "I'm supposed to leave Thursday."

The man took one more look around and sat down. "Please, no names. Thank you for being here. First, can you tell me what a Catalina is?"

"It's an island off the coast of California."

"Oh," the man silently thought for a moment. Coming back, he said, "The consequences of being caught aren't so attractive, so thank you for all the, as you Americans say, cloak and dagger."

Konner said, "Why would you call me? Isn't that risky?"

"It was from a burner phone that's now at the bottom of the Seine."

"Well, Mr. Catalina, you wanted to talk to someone close to the president. I'm as close as you're going to get, but I can assure you the president will read my report. That's all I can promise. You said you have important information on the state of affairs inside the government of Iran. We're very interested in this."

"I'll need something in return."

"I thought you were on the CIA payroll? Now you need more money?"

"Not money. Something more important. I'm Syrian and was stationed at the Syrian embassy in Tehran for three years and was recently transferred to Paris. Working at the embassy has been the source of my information to the CIA. While there, I married a woman, and I need an Iranian travel visa, so my wife can join me here. I asked my CIA handler for help, and they ignored me. Then I came across some urgent intelligence not like I was feeding the CIA. This is important, and I want to use it to get my wife out of Iran."

Konner said, "To be honest, I don't know if I can help with that. All I can do is commit to trying, but if there is no important information, you won't even get that."

The man thought for a second as he looked at Konner.

Konner said, "Look, I'm sorry about your wife, but this demand is a surprise. Had you said something before, I could have come prepared. So, tell me, am I wasting my time?"

He was still silent. Several long seconds later, he said, "OK, these are extremely troubling times for the leadership of Iran, especially the Ayatollah. My embassy job was to monitor anything concerning the mood of the Iranian leadership regarding the war in Syria.

Konner put his cup down. "First of all, you have told me nothing of value. You better have something else up your sleeve.

"I'm talking to you now because I needed someone higher up who could authorize the visa. That's when I contacted my handler and told him I would only talk to someone close to the president.".

"Alright, let's get to it. What do you have to trade?"

"I know the Ayatollah and the Iranian leadership have lost all patience with Israel attacking their nuclear program."

"We know this." Konner said, "Everyone knows this."

"No, I mean completely, totally, fire in your eyes fed up. The anger at the Israelis striking their refinement program whenever they reach a milestone is at a level never seen before, and they're desperate. The big story here is some are questioning the Ayatollah's leadership and inability to stop the Israeli attacks. I have information on three critical things. First, I came across an intercept revealing the Ayatollah's position. Some feel the Revolutionary Guards rule Iran. Their demands were threatening enough the Ayatollah thought it necessary to promise the Guards he had a permanent solution."

"Solution, what solution?"

"I don't know. We never found out; We couldn't detect another word spoken on the issue. Everything on that subject went silent. I contacted every informant I had inside and outside, and they came up with nothing."

"Second," he said, almost whispering, "The Iranians will make an announcement."

Konner said, "What announcement?"

"That's why we're here today. The Iranians plan to announce they'll immediately take part of their stockpile of 40% u235 and enrich it to military-grade 90%, and will soon have enough to make two bombs."

Konner was stunned. "That's suicide. Israel will go crazy. Are you sure about this? I mean, it borders on unbelievable?"

"I agree. But wait, that's just their announcement and not their plan. Third, after their statement, the Iranians are counting on Israel to do something unprecedented and, in fact, reckless. Not knowing where the enrichment will occur, the Israelis will bomb something symbolic. The Iranians will aggressively portray the attack as crossing a line and rally the international community to condemn Israel. They hope to generate enough pressure that the US is forced to reign in any future interference by Israel."

Konner said, "That's too incredible and just hard to believe. There's no way for me to verify your information. It all could be lies for the visa."

Konner was trying to make it all make sense. "Iran *wants* Israel to bomb their country? It could result in civilian casualties. The people will revolt."

"No, they won't; it's a dictatorship. When I said desperate, I meant *really* desperate.

Konner shook his head, "Unbelievable, when is the announcement going to be made?"

"Soon. Perhaps today, perhaps in the next five days."

"Do they have the technical ability to refine to 90%?"

"I don't know." The Syrian said.

"But you have a feeling."

The Syrian shrugged his shoulders. "What I see is the increased activity within the government. They've secretly brought their nuclear scientists from around the country into Tehran. The scientists rarely leave their respective facilities. The leaders don't want them traveling the country because Israel will find them and assassinate them. It's happened five times since 2010. Yet Navid Homsi and Darrius Algafari were in Tehran last week. OK, what about my visa?"

Konner said, "I can appreciate your intent, but that doesn't mean the information is correct. The most I can promise is to present your request."

"Do you report directly to the president?"

"Close enough, that's the best you get."

The Syrian said, "Do they have enough to believe me? Enough to get my visa?"

Konner said, "Honestly? I don't think so. It all boils down to the accuracy of this information. What's your source?"

"As I said, it's from the contacts I still have inside the Syrian embassy in Tehran. We have been doing this surveillance for years."

Konner said, "Still, this type of information doesn't just come out over drinks at an embassy get-together."

"No, it doesn't. I believe the American spy novels call it a honey pot."

With that, Konner quickly re-evaluated the man's story. For centuries the most reliable method of obtaining sensitive information was to appeal to the sexual appetites of the target. From Mata Harri to, more recently, the Russian redhead beauty, Anna Chapman, the tactic has proven to be most effective. Chapman became the mistress of a member of Obama's Whitehouse staff. She was later convicted and returned to Russia in a prisoner spy swap. The fates of nations frequently are decided by pillow talk."

"Who?" Konner asked.

"No, I'll not say."

"Why didn't you give this to your handler at the agency."

"Visa," he said. "Remember, I'm low level, and they ignored me."

The Brasserie Lipp was almost empty, with the tables patiently waiting for the afternoon crowd of artists, authors, and hangers-on wanting to be seen at the Paris institution.

Konner said, "That's a pretty desperate plan with no guarantee."

The Syrian said, "It reeks of a desperate attempt by a desperate man. Their refinement plans can't go forward, even in secrecy, without controlling the Israelis. Their current mindset results from everything having failed in the past."

Konner said, "I'll get back to you. How do I contact you?"

"If this is not enough to get my visa, I have something else that could be related. I have also learned Iran, under the strictest secrecy, sent a representative, very close to the Ayatollah, to North Korea. That person met Kim in person. I don't know the purpose or the result, but any meeting is very unusual. The two countries have had almost no contact and no common ground except for hating the West."

"Where does that fit in?" Konner asked.

"Perhaps it doesn't, but that information is not in the form your NSA would be able to intercept. It's so secret it's not digital."

"Are we back to bedroom whispers?"

"Call it what you like, but this information is reliable. I'm bringing it up to give my visa a better chance, and you might say to sweeten the pot." The man smiled.

The agent handed Konner a slip of paper. "Call this number."

Konner said, "I'll contact you in the next two days. That should be enough time for them to check out your information and get you an answer."

"Do we have an agreement?"

Konner said, "I said I would do my best. I'm not going to lie to you. I need a name for you in my report?"

"No," the man said emphatically.

"Not a real name; I need to refer to you in my reports. Pick one."

"Catalina," he said with a grin. "I like this ah, Catalina. Perhaps I'll go there someday."

CHAPTER 24

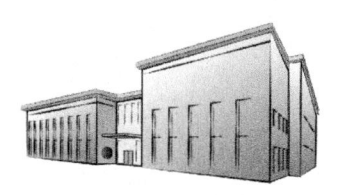

US Embassy
Belgrade Serbia

A young boy walked up to the US Embassy in Belgrade and called the guard. Through the bars of the front gate towering over his head, the boy presented a note. He said to the guard, "You give to the boss. Very important. Very important."

The Marine guard took the envelope from the boy and held it up to the light. The boy was already walking away, having made more money delivering the letter than he could believe.

The Marine said to his partner, "Stay here. I'm taking this inside."

The message eventually made its way up the authority chain until it landed on the desk of Mr. Dravin Levy, deputy ambassador.

Levy read the small printed message, and it immediately got his attention. He headed to the Ambassadors office.

"Julie, I need to see him right away. Anyone inside?"

"No," she said. "I'll ring you in." She said, "Mr. Ambassador Mr. Levy is here to see you."

Levy heard him say, "Send him in."

Levy opened the door and said, "This might be important or a joke." He handed it over.

Scott Kaufman, U.S. Ambassador to Serbia, adjusting his glasses, said. "What do you think?"

"It's one of those things where you're damned if you do and damned if you don't."

"What do you mean?"

"It's a warning. If you don't sound the alert and it's real, you lose. If you sound the alert and it's a fake, you're wasting people's time."

In the position only because of his financial support of the current president, Koffman was in a quandary. "What would you do?" He said weakly.

"That information is so important that I don't see how you can't make sure at least our CIA station chief knows about it."

Knowing it would remove him from responsibility, Kaufman said, "That's a great idea. Julie, get me Craig Maddox ASAP through the intercom."

Maddox heard his cell phone ring walking down the hall outside the ambassador's office. He immediately went into Julie's area and said, "Great timing. What's up?"

"The ambassador would like to see you. Now. Go on in."

He shrugged his shoulders and said, "OK."

Maddox walked in and saw the serious faces. "Did Manchester United lose last night when I wasn't looking?"

Kaufman handed him the message.

Maddox looked at it and said, "Is this for real?"

"We don't know," Kaufman said. "I think it's something we can't ignore."

Maddox, looking at the message, said. "Where did you get it?"

Levy said, "It was left at the front gate by a boy."

"The tried and true way of anonymously delivering a message. No one will suspect a kid, and the owner can stand in the shadows ensuring its delivery without being seen."

Maddox continued to look at the paper in thought. "What are you going to do?"

"We're going to give it to you," Levy said with a touch of humor.

"Sure, pass it off. I'll call someone in the NSA and see what he thinks. I guess that would get you guys off the hook, right?"

Kaufman said, "We appreciate your help."

Maddox said, "In this case, I'm sure you do."

Outside, the young boy, with a second note, got into a car that would take him to the Israeli embassy.

CHAPTER 25

Vienna
Austria

Kate was back in her hotel and called Konner.
"Where are you?
"I'm in the car you sent. I think I'm about 20 minutes away."
"Great, have you eaten?'
"No, today has been pretty busy, and I'm starving."
"OK, let me know when you're downstairs, and we can take the car to Apron. The concierge says it is the best restaurant in Vienna."

***

"The restaurant was nothing to look at from the street squeezed between a hotel and a parking garage."
"They were seated and over glasses of wine Konner said. "So dear, how was your day?"
"Dear? You have got to be kidding."
"I thought it was better than when Ozzie says, "Hi honey, I'm home."
Kate laughed.
Konner said, "See, I should have taken that job as a comedian."
"Instead of a spy?"
"I'm not a spy."
"What are you then."
"Special assignments."

"Sounds awfully general to me." Kate looked around the restaurant at nothing in particular.

Konner noticed her wavering attention. "I like my job," he said, "I never seem to get the same assignments, so the variety is positive. Plus, I almost report to the president, and I'm privy to the world's problems."

"Stuff, most people, don't even know. So why were you in Paris?"

Konner paused, thinking about how much he could say. He didn't like this part of the relationship—the part about not being honest about everything in his life.

"I'm not sure how much I should say. It's a little strange. You don't have a security clearance, but you have the second most powerful man in the world on that super phone's speed dial. Plus, I think Devroe, my single boss, has a crush on you. So this is complicated."

"Nice try. I'm not biting on that one. So what can you tell me."

Konner, in thought, moved the napkin in his lap before saying, "Israel and Iran are at it pretty heavy."

"That's it? While we're on the subject, tell me something the world doesn't know, like Antarctica's cold. Everyone knows Iran is a pain. That's nothing new."

"This time, it's different. There has always been dialog up to now, and that has disappeared. The president is deeply concerned a middle east war could break out."

"Dear God."

"The president has offered to broker talks between the two. They both are accountable to the U.S. in different ways, so he has a certain amount of leverage. With Iran, it's the sanctions, and with Israel, it's three billion dollars a year in foreign aid."

"What?"

"Yes, since 1985, that's the annual total."

"That's amazing," Kate said, shaking her head.

"Israel is adamant the Iranians can't get the bomb, so they keep attacking their enrichment program. The Iranians are adamant they'll destroy Israel."

"Konner, my dear, except for the aid, I've read all that in the newspapers. Why is Devroe's super-agent having secret meetings in Paris?"

"Like I said, to ward off a war. It seems that whole thing might blow up at any second. Iran has reached a breaking point with Israel's rather successful attempts at blocking its enrichment program. I found out they might be on the verge of trying something radical."

Konner thought before saying, "Then there's the strange event of Iran sending a high-level diplomat to North Korea. Now that's not to be repeated."

"Well, that's a puzzle piece that doesn't fit the current picture on the box. Don't worry; I'm not going to repeat anything.

"What's the problem. Most of what you have told me is on the internet."

"Perhaps but not the part about Iran trying something radical."

"OK, but if you need someone to hold your hand, I'm your gal."

"Funny. Who's trying to be the comedian now?"

"Okay, we'll leave it at that. I'm just glad you were in Paris, and we could be together."

"You're distracted," he said. "I know you always have a lot going, but you seem farther away right now."

"Why are *you* in Vienna?" He asked.

Kate silently moved her coffee cup, an obvious demonstration of deep thought. Then Kate started laughing. It was the last thing Konner expected.

"That's classified." She said with a huge satisfied grin.

Konner leaned back in his chair as Kate enjoyed the moment. "I saw that coming, Ms. Adler. You're fooling no one."

She became serious, "Someone is after the company, and I know who, but we don't have any proof. Actually, not a shred of proof."

"Not the best of situations. Do you still think it's TerraDyne?"

"Who else? Their reputation is they take what they want and leave no prisoners behind. When they want something, they have no scruples. They broke into the office in Marseilles, and shortly after that, we received an offer to purchase Morton Roth, which we declined. Then an office in Bremerhaven, Germany, caught fire and is a total loss."

"Yikes, that's some serious stuff."

"There's more. After the office caught fire, an article appeared in an industry publication. It's written by some industry notable, saying Morton Roth has serious problems, and they're covering it up. Avery said he hadn't seen any effect on sales after the break-in. However, he thinks this attack could be different. On top of that, this afternoon, I met a man who's a power broker in the maritime industry. He said we're in for a rough ride and may suffer a reduction on our insurability rating."

"That could have all kinds of ramifications."

"Yes, like putting the ships we own and charter into port. The company comes to a sudden halt."

"Kate, that's a serious situation. Can I help?"

"No, not now, I don't think. I've got some very bright people working on the problem. We'll come up with something."

Konner said, "On the brighter side, I understand Adler electronics just got a contract to upgrade the processing power within the NSA. Didn't you say that Mom grew out of a project your dad had with the CIA?"

That startled Kate. The origin of the Geneva9 system was one of the top secrets within the Adler companies and the Cartel. Her father had placed outsized importance on it remaining a secret. She thought, "How far do I go imparting information to someone I'm not married to and just dating? A relationship they both feel has a chance of not working?"

"I'm not sure about that," she said, "not looking at him."

Konner knew he had stepped too far. It was the first time she had drawn back and was anything but straightforward. He thought learning the Cartel existed at all was the ultimate secret. He just found out that wasn't true.

"I'm sorry," he said. "I don't need to go there. More importantly, there's a man at a table by the kitchen entrance. He's been looking at you for some time now. I think he might be in love."

Kate discretely looked over and said, "That might come as a surprise to the woman at his table. Do I see a pattern with you here?"

Konner took a sip of his coffee, looked directly at Kate, smiling, and said, "Oh, I don't know. It could be."

"You're flirting," Kate said.

"Is it working? I brought my etchings. Remember, I lured you up to my room in London, saying, "Do you want to see my etchings."

"That's not how I remember the start of that evening. I remember suggesting we have another drink."

"Sure it is. It was at the Savoy hotel last year. I remember it well. In fact," he said with a mischievous grin pasted on his face, "I remember all of it."

"Well, I don't, so I think I need to create a new memory. What do you say to that?"

CHAPTER 26

Mediterranean Sea

The Nova Tempest, a 43-meter luxury yacht sailing in the night off the coast of Malta. The seas were calm, and the moon was in full retreat, creating a thick darkness over the water.

Vanek was on his way up from below deck, where he had been dealing with a lifelong problem. It was a situation he was determined to conquer but had yet to win. He emerged onto the bridge.

"Welcome." The captain said. "You look white, to say the least."

Vanek ignored him and stopped in front of the radar console. After looking at the maze of objects the ship's radar was tracking, he said, "Which ship is the one we want?"

Vanek had his finger on the screen. "Is that her? Is that the tanker?"

The captain turned to look at the screen. "No, it's the wrong transponder number."

"Do you know what you're doing?" Vanek asked.

"Your welcome to set the course yourself." The captain said. "After all, they were your coordinates."

The captain went back to the windows and, with binoculars up, pointed ahead of the ship's bearing and said, "She's right out there. Take a look for yourself. We have been trailing her at the same speed for an hour now, waiting for you to show up. Her range is 6 kilometers bearing zero three zero."

"Is our transponder working?" Vanek asked.

"No, I turned it off right after we reached international waters."

"Good, bring her to a stop. I'm going astern. Tell your crew to deploy the tender. Trail us at the tanker's speed when we're on our way and in the water, don't get any closer. I'll contact you when we're done and returning to the ship. You will then close the distance between us, shortening the time for recovery."

"Got it." The captain said. "Can I ask what this is?"

"No, you can't. The less you know, the better. We spent $145,000 chartering this boat for the week. Everyone should be happy as long we hand it back to the owner in its original condition. Just do as I tell you, and you can finish out the charter season as if nothing happened. You don't want anything to happen to this vessel, or your posh career as a yacht captain will be over. Am I clear?"

"Yes," the captain said, turning towards his control console. As much to monitor the status as to not look at the man in front of him.

Vanek left the bridge and made his way aft and down to the garage that held the tenders. The men worked electric motors that opened a large door on the side of the yacht. They moved the tender out from its mooring and over the water. From there, they lowered the boat into the water. Vanek stood in the tender, an eighteen-foot powerboat, capable of transferring guests and crew at sixty knots.

"Hand it to me gently," he told one of the crew. The deckhand handed him a magnetic limpet mine capable of blowing a hole in any commercial transit ship. Vanek placed it into a specially made container to keep the bouncing to a minimum during transit. Two other men climbed aboard while a fourth lowered the tender into the water.

Vanek felt the knot in his stomach move, and the back of his throat retract. He took a deep breath and gripped the guard rail as tightly as possible, hoping his body would be distracted. The big engine drove the tender through the water towards the lights of the big ship that was the target.

Regardless of the amount of planning, there's always something not taken into account. In this case, it was heavier than normal sea conditions. Something he had hoped to avoid. Because of this, the tender could only safely do thirty-five knots. The slower speed meant it would take him almost twice as long to chase down the Ingrid Sea, a chemical tanker owned and operated by Morton Roth.

After what seemed like days to Vanek, they brought the tender, without running lights, alongside the ship. They slowed to keep pace with the gigantic vessel, but the rough seas made it hard to stay alongside. Vanek brought out the mine and twisted the button collar allowing him to push the red button that started the timer. The objective was to place it four to six feet above the waterline. The location allowed some water in but not enough that the ship's pumping system couldn't handle the flow. Even a little water inside the hull would cause panic.

His main concern was dropping it into the water. The rocking of the small vessel made trying to attach the mine difficult. After several attempts, he heard the clang of the magnet against the tanker's hull. Vanek looked to see if it stayed attached. Vanek waved his arm towards the yacht. The man, at the controls, pulled the boat around and headed into the darkness, saying, "We need direction lights."

Vanek pulled himself up from leaning over the side. He took another deep breath and pulled out his radiophone. "Captain, we're on our way back. Light up the yacht so we can get our bearings."

The captain turned on the yacht's running lights and increased speed to meet their return.

CHAPTER 27

Hotel Sacher
Vienna

After pouring Konner another cup of coffee that next morning, Kate put the white porcelain container back down.

"My Mom had one like this. I think it was my grandmother's. That, and everything else was left behind when we escaped to West Germany."

"You don't talk about that much."

"It wasn't a pleasant time. My mother didn't make it out. My father thought it was because of the enemies he had made, but that's another story. So what does your day look like? Where are you going from here?"

"I'm going to the American Embassy here in Vienna to file my report for Devroe."

"Do you think Iran will up the ante and create a crisis?"

"I don't know, but they're entering a hazardous area where anything can happen." Konner walked over to her chair and started rubbing her shoulders from behind.

"Oh, that feels good. Keep it up, and you could work yourself into full-time employment."

"That's quite all right. I've got a day job."

She stood up and put her arms around him. "However, my guess is the fringe benefits aren't as good."

Konner was not smiling. A moment passed—longer than expected. In the silence, Konner looked at her face. He ran his hand down the side of her cheek. Then without saying anything, he took the hand on her cheek and pulled her in and slowly, gently, and with great tenderness, kissed her.

Kate opened her eyes. "Well, well, where did that come from?" She said.

"What? I kissed you a hundred times last night."

"You know what I mean."

"I don't know," he said, walking over and getting his coat. "I need to get to the embassy."

"Konner?"

He was now smiling, "As I said, I don't know. You didn't complain."

Kate didn't say anything. Her silence filled the room as she looked at him with an expressionless face but an emotion-filled heart.

Konner was showing signs of unease. "The important question is, when can I see you again?"

"I'm heading back to the office this morning. We need to find out how to deal with my TerraDyne problem."

"You have a TerraDyne problem, and I have an Iranian/Israeli problem. It kind of means we're slaves to things bigger than us."

Kate was quiet again.

"I meant..."

"I know what you meant."

Konner looked down and quietly put his coat on.

Finally, Kate said, "I guess to a certain extent that's true. Where does Father Devroe have you going next?"

"I don't know until I talk to him. I could be anywhere from Greenland to Bangladesh."

"When you get that sorted out, give me a call. I'll be in a meeting this morning."

He was standing by the door and hugged Kate. He said, "Talk to you sometime today."

Kate watched him walk down the hall. Thoughts were present that were not there before. She couldn't figure out what had just happened, but it was different.

CHAPTER 28

Vianden Castle

Kate, coming from her house, walked into the Castle. Her father had purchased the property from the King of Luxembourg in 1970. The kingdom was going through financial problems. The transaction benefited both parties. Through the centuries, the castle had gone through many renovations. It now served as the headquarters of the Cartel and Kate's charity. The charity's areas were separate from the Cartel offices to maintain secrecy. Kevin Wainwright, manager of the Helmut Adler Children's Charity, was the only one that knew of the Cartel. Morton Roth's main headquarters were in Rotterdam.

Kate was thinking about what had occurred that morning when Konner kissed her. It was nice, to be sure, but it was also very different. What did it mean? She was dealing with several things right now, and she'd address that question later. Current events needed her full attention. She entered the empty conference room, thankful for a few minutes to gather her thoughts.

Kate thought of the staff of the Cartel. They were not responsible for the business side of Kate's life, although the two frequently came together like the current situation.

Her Father was particular in what the Cartel stood for, and she wouldn't let him down. Since that first board meeting, when the members questioned her ability to lead the Cartel, she had dedicated herself to improving every aspect of what he built. Yet, she sat with her father's empire in danger and her personal resources in jeopardy. There was an answer somewhere, and she'd find it.

Kate said, "How bad does it look with the article?"

"We're monitoring news outlets and sites," Elena said, "and Morton Roth is the topic of conversation and, unfortunately, speculation."

Kate looked at those gathered around the table. "I know that we try to keep the Cartel and my other interests separate. However, it seems very clear I will need your help in handling this situation."

"I, for one," Penn said, "never gave it a second thought."

"We're all under attack," Brad said.

Elena said, "And we'll come up with answers. It's not the first time we've been under pressure."

"I thank you all. Your support will be the key element in our solving this problem. It's certainly nothing I've experienced before, so it's learning as we go.

Penn said, "I'm not a business person, but I learned, during my time in the field chasing spies, the winners were constantly changing. The only effective influence was force and power—the need to counter moves executed by the other side rapidly."

A phone rang. "It's Avery," Brian said. "I'll put it up."

"Avery, you're in the operations room with the security team on speaker."

"Is Kate there?' Avery asked.

"Yes," Kate said. "You're not getting much sleep."

"Seems to be the least of my problems of late."

Kate said, "I met with Mr. Guyer yesterday."

"Yes, I know. I spoke to him after your meeting. The board has lowered our rating to A-"

"He said that might happen," Kate said.

"It will affect us immediately as all insurance contracts have a clause allowing them to change rates based on our rating. It's like an adjustable mortgage. That's why the association is so influential. The lower the Conklin rating, the higher the insurance. The piece that appeared in the magazine didn't do us any favors. Lang Gerlach over at Morton Roth called and said they were experiencing some cancellations."

Kate said, "Avery, how bad could it get?"

"Well, we have over forty offices, and the overhead is substantial. It's never been a problem in the past as we managed steady growth. However, at some point, we'll fall into a negative. We can withstand that for a while but not for an extended period.

With a serious look, Loren handed Elena a printed sheet. After reading it, Elena said. "Things just got worse. Mom has captured a report from the Malta coast guard about an explosion on a Morton Roth ship. It occurred late last night our time off the coast."

Kate said, "I'm finding it hard to believe that a company would go to such lengths to achieve its goals."

"Not hard to believe in this case," Brad said.

"What's the status of the tanker?" She asked. "Was anyone hurt?"

Elena continued reading. "It seems a mine placed just above the water line created some flooding and a fire internally. They handled the fire quickly, and the hull is structurally sound. Three men suffered minor injuries. The ship is continuing onto its next port."

Penn said. "A mine? In attacks such as this, the placement above the waterline or below is a specific decision, sending different messages. Below, the waterline threatens the ship, and above is just sending a threatening message. Iran and Israel do this all the time, and it's been getting worse lately."

Avery said, "This ups the ante. Hold on; I'll be back in a second."

Kate said, "Does security on a ship help in this case?"

Penn replied, "Not in cases like this. There's very little you can do. It takes place at night, and constant monitoring over the side is not practical. Security on ships is effective in hijacking situations where you can see the assailants approaching the ship. It allows you to engage them before they have a chance to board."

Kate said, "I just have the feeling this isn't the last incident."

Avery said, "Kate can I have a word in your office?"

"Of course." Kate got up and headed out of the operations room. "See if we can come up with some ideas. We aren't selling, so I don't expect this to stop until we do something to make it stop."

Kate sat down in her office and hit the transfer button. "What is it, Avery?"

"The board wants to transfer funds from Adler Electronics to Morton Roth for the short term. They want to increase the cash position of Morton Roth in anticipation of further problems. It's an inter-company transfer, and they usually take my proxy but wanted your specific vote this time. I'm sending an electronic document. Could you sign it and send it back rather quickly?"

"How normal is this. Is this what you want?"

"It's not unusual to transfer funds from one entity in the company to another. Yes, this has been thoroughly discussed and has my OK. You concentrate on getting a handle on the problems. Kate, find a way out of this, and I'll manage the business side. But we don't have an unlimited amount of time. At some point, it will start to affect your personal portfolio."

"Thank you, Avery. I don't know what I would do without you."

"There was a time when I wondered the same thing. But that's no longer the case. You're steady on your own two feet now. You can handle this. Just don't hold back. Somebody needs a bloody nose here. You need to meet force with force."

"Yes, I was told that earlier."

CHAPTER 29

American Embassy
Vienna

Konner had left Kate back at the hotel to make his way to Vienna's United States embassy. He had labored in a guest office of the Embassy writing the report and sent it off to Devroe some time ago. He knew that Devroe would read it but preferred to talk things through, so he had sent a text asking if he was available for a call.

Devroe's response was immediate. "Call me on a secure embassy line."

Devroe picked up and said. "What's the time there?"

"Around eight AM Konner said. You're generally asleep by now."

"Sleep? An interesting concept. This situation is serious. Where are you? What did you find? Where is Kate?"

"Slow down. Some of that's not relevant to the report. Kate is on her way back to her office. Aren't we inquisitive this morning? I'm in Vienna, thanks for asking."

"Give me the overview of your report."

I talked to the agent. I call him Catalina in the report."

"Why?"

"He liked it. Besides, you said to use it on our initial contact. He's pretty skittish and concerned about his safety."

Devroe said, "Nice report, by the way. I went through it, and let me summarize. To stop the attacks they announce going to 90%, Israel launches a large-scale attack, and Iran stokes supposed world outrage, forcing us to put the breaks on Israel. I gotta say good luck with that."

Konner said, "That's about it except the part where the Ayatollah says he'll fix the Israeli problem once and for all. Unfortunately, that's where the trail goes dark. The Syrian says there doesn't seem to be any information on what that might be."

Devroe said, "The 90% announcement could be that plan, although it doesn't seem like a smart move. It could be a disaster. How reliable was the source?"

"My gut tells me he's telling the truth because he wanted something in return."

"Ah yes, the other shoe."

"Actually, he only wanted a visa to get his wife out of Tehran and into France. Easy for us and important for him. His handler at the agency said no. He knows if he lied, we could always nullify the visa later. That's why I'm inclined to believe him. Also, I asked what or who was the source of what he was giving me. He said, reliable sources from within the Iranian government."

"Yes,?" Devroe said, "That's it for something this important?"

"He said they have a honey pot source in Parliament."

"Whoa, I guess that will never go out of style. That just upped the quality of this intel. Should I get State moving on the visa?"

"I don't see we have anything to lose."

"OK, send me the particulars."

"So what now?" Konner said.

"Sit tight somewhere. Stay in Europe. I'm sure you can work that out. I need to get to the president. Oh, what's the time frame on this announcement?"

"It could be a couple of days. I don't know, but things are moving fast. It's all in the report."

"OK, listen, nice work," Devroe said. "I mean it. I'll let the president know."

Konner said, "Oh, one more thing."

"What.?"

"I wanted to make sure you didn't miss this. The Syrian had a throw-away line he hoped would improve his chances on the visa. He said Iran sent a representative to North Korea for a secret meeting. I don't know what that means."

Devroe thought for a moment and said, "I don't know what to make of that either, but take care. I'll be back."

CHAPTER 30

The Port of Masada
Eritrea

Akanni Okoro sat at his desk, thinking he'd never get used to getting up early in the morning. Okoro was the Morton Roth office manager serving the largest port in the country of Eritrea on the African continent's northeastern portion facing the Red Sea.

He thought to himself, "One should never be required to be alert before the sun comes up."

Okoro was in his office before the rest of the staff for the weekly harbor master meeting. Since the arrival of the new harbormaster, a man driven by efficiency, the morning meeting was always very early. The man couldn't get enough of listening to his own voice. Okoro's face wrinkled, thinking about the uselessness of the effort. However, he also knew it was essential to keep good relations with the port authority as, despite the systems in place, a healthy exchange of favors made the system work. He looked at this watch and decided he couldn't put it off any longer.

Resigned to his fate Okoro grabbed his hot cup of sweet shahi and a notepad. One step out of the door, he immediately encountered three men shrouded in baklavas. They grabbed him, and Okoro felt the hot tea burn his hand and arm as he resisted their grasp.

"What the hell are you doing.?" he shouted.

They continued forcing him to the ground. He heard the zipping noise tieing his hands behind his back.

"There's something wrong. There's a mistake." He shouted. "What are you doing? I have no money, and the office doesn't have petty cash." They were the last intelligible words he spoke before the men placed the tape over his mouth.

The men dragged him to a Toyota SUV. One opened the door, and another threw Okoro into the back seat. He could feel the men's weight as they entered on each side. No words were spoken, but he could smell a distinctive odor in the vehicle. They pushed up the short sleeve of his shirt, and a hand squeezed the skin of his upper arm, followed by a sting. A paper bag was placed over his head as he steadily lost consciousness. He couldn't hear the increased efforts of the Toyota's engine as it moved the team out of the area. The whole event took under 60 seconds.

***

Vanek sat waiting for Petrovic to call back and picked up the phone.

Petrovic said, "What's the status of the kidnapping?"

Vanek said, "I received a call from the people we hired to kidnap the manager. Everything went as planned. The manager is on his way somewhere for safekeeping. They won't even tell me where, so their security is pretty tight. It must be, as I understand they've been doing this for years."

Petrovic said, "I don't like doing things when I don't have complete control. I'm making an exception in this case."

Vanek said, "You'll have to as I don't see another reliable option."

CHAPTER 31

Vianden Castle

Kate sat in her office wondering if there would be a charity event this year. She looked forward to the elaborate party the charity put on every year on her yacht. Monaco was the preferred venue, and the guest list contained many celebrities and people of power. It was a chance for everyone to dress up and enjoy an evening supporting a good cause. Last year she met a man who caught her fancy. Konner Houston said he worked for a venture capital firm, but it turned out he was some kind of government agent working for Stephen Devroe. As a complete coincidence, a short time later, he saved her life.

The knock on the door brought her back.

Brad's head appeared around the door's edge and said, "Can I come in?"

"Of course."

He stepped in and closed the door behind him.

Kate said, "Do you think that's a good idea?"

"What?" Closing the door? Are you afraid I will run up and kiss you while in hiding?" With a mischievous grin, he said, "You know, that's not a half-bad idea."

"We have discussed this, and that ship has sailed. Not that I don't love you in my way."

"Yes, we did discuss it."

Kate noticed his smile had disappeared with that statement. Brad said, "You'll always be the one that got away."

"Brad? What's on your mind besides that?"

"Well, it's not what's on *my* mind that I'm concerned about. I'm here as a friend."

"What's that mean?"

"It's what's on *your* mind. Things aren't looking good, and you have bad things coming at you from all directions. I just want to know how you're holding up? I'm concerned. Elena is also worried. She saw your slow responses to some questions."

Kate stared down at the top of her desk, then finally said, "Not good if the truth is known. I had a private conversation with Avery, and we're performing an internal funds transfer from Adler corporate to Morton Roth. It's to cover ongoing expenses in anticipation of lost revenue."

"Well, well well," Brad said. "Listen to yourself. Two years ago, you didn't know what a balance sheet was."

"I did too. I just didn't read them and didn't want anything to do with the business. Now I realize the health of those companies is what allows me to do what I love to do. Then there's the number of people we employ. I no longer take it for granted."

"The Charity?"

"Yes, the Charity is still the center of my life."

"Now you're running a huge company."

"Not really; I just gave my consent when pressed by Avery."

"Don't shrug this off. You know what I mean. If this Petrovic business had happened during your first week as head of the Cartel, it would have overwhelmed you. You have dealt with Cartel and business issues, but never when both were the same problem. Give yourself some credit. You have a great team out there, and they'll do anything for you. There's an answer here, and they'll find it."

There was a knock on the door.

"Yes, come in."

Elena said, "We have a problem, and I have the rest of the security team assembled."

"What kind of problem?"

"Mom has issued a report."

The three walked briskly to the operations room, where Loren, Penn, and an assistant were seated. Penn finished reading the report from Mom."

Elena said, "Penn, why don't you summarize."

Penn started talking while still looking at Mom's report. "Mom has picked up communication traffic confirming the kidnapping of Akanni Okoro, manager of the Morton Roth office servicing the Masada harbor."

"Kidnapped? Is he OK? Do we know where he is?" Kate asked?

"It doesn't say. We don't know," Penn said. "I would imagine Lang Gerlach, director of Morton Roth, is reading this as we speak."

Everyone but Penn and Loren was still standing. Kate ignored her usual seat and went over to the nearest chair. She sat down with an unseen weight on her shoulders.

Elena noticed it right away and got her some water.

Kate said wistfully, "Our people are in danger."

"Can someone get Mr. Gerlach on the phone? Elena, did those press releases go out?"

"Yes, and we wrote a few opinion pieces of our own. Mom is keeping track of where and when they run. People promise things, and sometimes they forget."

Kate gave Elena a tired smile of understanding.

Elena sensed the obvious. "Kate, you need some rest. We can handle this for now. We need you with a clear head."

Again Kate smiled.

Loren said, "I've got Mr. Gerlach on two. He's in the air on his way to Masada."

Kate walked over and picked up the phone. She said, "Mr. Gerlach, this is Kate Adler. Yes, I just received the same information. I would like you to establish a security presence at each office. Yes, 24 hours. I'm not aware of the regulations in each country, but if they can carry guns, that's what we want.

Yes, I'm aware but not concerned about the costs at this point, Mr. Gerlach. We can't have your people victims of something that's beyond their control. Please keep our office informed of any news. Mr. Danner will be your direct contact. Have a nice flight."

Everyone noted the call's abrupt ending. It was very unlike Kate.

Elena said, "We have Mom monitoring all police bands in Masada and have issued directives to infiltrate any syndicates that Mom can find."

"That's going to be hard.' Penn said. "I was in neighboring Ethiopia on a special assignment. I learned a lot, including kidnapping in Eritrea is an organized industry. There aren't specific syndicates. It's more like a rent-a-crime operation. At the top are graduates and undergraduates that run a very efficient system. The operations usually consist of teams. Some are skilled in the capture, and that's all they do. Then the transportation group transports the hostages to an everchanging temporary location. Then the hiding and safekeeping group takes them from there to a site, usually in the desert, for hiding and safekeeping. The right hand never knows what the left is doing. They operate independently and get paid separately. It makes it very hard to unravel, and only a few know the whole story of any single operation.

"Also, like drug operations, it's very lucrative. Substantial payments are going to the police and judiciary. The money buys a slow reaction time in the investigation. The delay gives them time to complete transactions before there are serious efforts to solve the crime. Most of the victims are immigrants or people trying to flee the country due to the oppressive laws. Occasionally, there's a high-profile kidnapping of an NGO or, in our case, an office manager.

"We need to start thinking about a rescue operation now. Another piece of this puzzle is sometimes they'll sell a hostage to another kidnapping organization. The first twenty-four hours are critical, and the police will be playing their games."

Kate was still standing, and with one arm down by her side, her other arm was holding it at the elbow. It wasn't significant, except it wasn't a Kate gesture.

***

Kate walked into her office. On the desk behind her was a picture of her father. She remembered her last day with him. Suffering from Alzheimer's, he didn't recognize her at first. Then suddenly, he turned and looked directly into her eyes. He always had this dark penetrating look. As a child, she'd say he was always mad. In reality, he was the most focused person she ever knew. Yet, there he was looking at her. Then he called her Bunny in a moment of clarity. It was his favorite name for her growing up. He talked of the Cartel and doing what's right. She was confused, not knowing anything about the Cartel at the time. Then the alarms from the medical equipment went off, and things spiraled down as he suffered a heart attack. It struck at her now. She could feel the emotion in her chest.

Avery, her rock, was her savior in the following days. She went back to work, and then things started to get strange. She infiltrated an Iranian database making some people at the other end pretty mad. Due to some quick thinking by Brad, they both survived an assassination attempt to take out the whole office. On the run, she called Avery, and he directed her to this castle, where she learned about her father creating the Cartel. Her life changed dramatically at that singular moment.

Now, all that he had built, the Adler Group and the Cartel, were in jeopardy. The thousands they employed with the companies, the people they helped with the Cartel, and of course her charities. Where was it all going? She felt like she couldn't get a running start. It was starting to be too much, but she couldn't show that in front of her people.

Her phone rang. It was Avery. "Probably more information on the kidnapping," she thought.

"Avery, it's a sad day."

His response was, "Are you alone."

"Yes, Avery, what's wrong?"

"A courier just arrived with paperwork for a third offer, and like the others, it's 15% below the last. The bid is around 40% less than the original."

"Petrovic again?"

"After some initial research, we can't prove that. Technically it's like the rest. It's from a shell company registered in Panama. But there's never been a doubt in my mind. I know this comes on top of Lang's manager being kidnapped, but I needed to tell you."

Kate looked at her father's photo. "We're not selling Avery. I'll come up with something. I just need some time."

"Kate, don't think this is your fault or that you alone have all the answers. Your father had an army of talented people helping build his legacy. Get them all going in the right direction, and good things will happen."

"Thank you, Avery."

She sat in the chair opposite her desk and thought for a moment. She reached for her phone and sent a text to Konner.

"Where are you. Can you talk? If yes, call; it's important."

She put the phone in her lap, and almost immediately, it went off.

"Hey there, cute stuff; what's going on?"

"A lot, actually; where are you?"

"Cooling my heels in Ramstein. I took a flight back to stay in that same hotel. It's the closest thing to home right now. Besides, the waitresses in the restaurant are cute."

Kate ignored the comment. "What's your schedule?"

Konner noticed the abruptness. "I don't have one right now. But the evil Devroe always lurks in the corner. What's up?"

"Can you get here by tonight?"

"Tonight? Yes, I think so. I have to check flights. Can I get back to you?"

"Can you hold for a second?"

"Of course."

Kate dialed captain Silanos, head of the Cartel's civilian air operations.

He answered. "Ms. Adler, this is a pleasant surprise."

"Captain, how long would it take to get Mr. Houston from Ramstein to here this evening?"

"Well," he paused for a second, "We're in luck. We completed the annual service of the 260, and it's in Frankfurt. That's a hop to Ramstein, then back here."

"Can you land at Ramstein?"

"It won't be me but another pilot, but they have a civilian strip that services the base."

"I've got Mr. Houston on the other line. I'll tell him you will call with the details. Thank you, Mr. Silanos."

The captain was curious as it wasn't the normal Kate.

"Konner, Captain Silanos will call and arrange to get you here. Is that OK?"

"Of course, it's OK—Kate, what's going on.?"

"I'll let you know when you get here. Don't eat. I'm taking you out to dinner.

CHAPTER 32

Belgrade
Serbia

Vanek waited for Petrovic to answer. "Havel, you're calling, so I assume you're alive and didn't die of seasickness. How did the tanker attack go?"

"Would you care that I'm alive?"

"Of course, I would. We're partners."

"No, I get a bonus. Partners share in the profits."

Petrovic noticed the change in tone. He said, "That sounds like a conversation for another time. Tell me about your adventures on the high seas."

"We were able to place the mine, and on the way back to the yacht, saw and felt it go off. I know it caused a fire, but I don't know of any casualties."

"Well, it made this morning's news courtesy of our fine public relations department. That department is currently saturating the world with press releases on Morton Roth's troubles. I can confirm it did cause a fire, and three people were injured."

"The objective was to get their attention, and I'm sure it did that."

"Yes, you were successful again. Havel, you do great work. I want you to know I appreciate that. Now to the incident that has me most concerned. The kidnapping."

"They contacted me and said everything went according to plan. The kidnappers are demanding five million from Morton Roth. They won't get it, but that's their problem, not ours. We just wanted him kidnapped. I contacted Holland, and on proof the manager was in captivity, he forwarded the rest of their fee."

"Where is the hostage?"

"Their security is excellent, and they wouldn't tell me his location. For proof, I did get a video of him somewhere in the desert."

"How long are they going to hold him?"

"Based on the fee, they guarantee at least 60days. It's strange dealing with these people. They use terms like guarantees and contracts. I guess they want to treat it like a business. Someone said they did millions a year in fees, and ransom was on top of that. It's big business, to be sure.

CHAPTER 33

Vianden Castle
Auberge Aal Vernen Restaurant

Kate was rearranging dresses in her closet. A mindless task that filled the waiting time while Konner was in the air. She had tried to lie down, but that didn't work. She felt like she could sleep for a year, but her mind just wouldn't settle down.

There was a rapid tap on the door. It was Myrla; Kate knew her distinctive rhythm and sound. "Myrla, come in."

Myrla was well aware Kate wasn't her usual self. "I have this wonderful idea right now."

"Yes? What's this wonderful idea?"

"I'm going to draw you a nice bath, and you're going to feel good and relax before the Mr. Konner arrives."

Kate didn't respond right away.

Myrla, used to getting her way, added, "There will be no discussions. A good soak will be good for you."

"Thank you," Kate said. "It will fill more time as it will be at least another hour."

"I'm also doing the candles. We'll do the complete idea."

***

Konner met Kate downstairs in the library. He put his arms around Kate and just held her. "Finally," he said, "How are you doing?"

"Life has its ups and downs. Right now, I'm looking up from the down position, but can we go over that later?"

He stepped back. "You look gorgeous."

"Why do I always think there's an ulterior motive to your compliment?"

"Because you're gorgeous, and I'm a man. We don't have any choice in these matters."

"Of course. Where did my brains go?"

"Thanks for the Uber flight from Ramstein, by the way. It's really hard to think that's just normal."

Still standing in front of Konner, she put her hand behind his neck and played with his hair. "Are you hungry?"

"I'm way more than that. After the captain's call, I scrambled to the airport, and here I am. The pilot said it was a maintenance flight, so it didn't get stocked with the usual complement of food and beverages."

"Good, we're going to a favorite place here in town. It's literally just around the corner on this side of the river. You will meet the fascinating Mr. Federico."

"Another one of your admirers, I suppose."

"No, but he was pretty sweet on me when I walked in the first time. I was trying to decide if I wanted to give up my independence to run the Cartel. The board needed an answer, and the walls were coming in. I needed to getaway. The conversation was enlightening and created the clarity I needed to accept heading the Cartel. I called him the philosopher. I just feel I'm at a similar crossroads."

"Oh, then we going to see the Oracle?"

"Yes, but his day job is owning a restaurant."

"I'm in for anything that has to do with food right now."

***

One of the oldest buildings in Vianden contained the Auberge Aal Vernen. Formally a locksmith's shop, it was a cozy restaurant and a small hotel offering six rooms. Kate and Konner followed the maître d.

Kate was pleased to find the warmth of the establishment hadn't changed. It still reflected old-world upper-class European charm from every wall. A small bar was to the left as they entered the dining room. It had unique stools with backs, and she remembered, it was where she sat and talked to Phil, the young bartender from the states. The maître d stopped at one of the small tables in a corner just below a portrait and a landscape painting.

Seated, Kate said, "So what do you think?"

"Honestly?"

"Yes, why else would I ask?"

"On one hand, I certainly wouldn't find anything like this back home. And second, I'm thinking seven years in Leavenworth for putting this on my expense account."

"When are you going to stop thinking about money?"

"Oh, you mean like the rest of the world? Kate, I don't live in your world. I was in a rather rudimentary room in Ramstein several hours ago."

"Well, aren't you glad you're here?"

"Of course, I am."

"Then enjoy it while I have the money because of how things are going, there's a timeline on that issue."

"Duly noted. I'll try to be better. A timeline?" He just caught that last line.

Kate looked towards the bar to see if Phil, the young bartender who waited on her the last time, was still there. Instead, she caught the eye of the owner, who immediately recognized her. He politely smiled and continued talking to those at the table. Ever the perfect host, he allowed the conversation to come to a natural end before excusing himself. He was the natural embodiment of a practiced proprietor of an establishment frequented by a moneyed clientele.

Konner noticed the exchange. "Who's that? He noticed you right away."

"The Oracle," Kate said, "and there you go again placing me with men I hardly know."

Konner was impressed. "The man had a bearing and a stature that was not commanding but very confident. He also looked like the quintessential ladies man making the rounds in a field of possibilities, except couples primarily occupied the tables.

Kate put a hand on Konner's arm. "He's not what you're thinking."

"Was I thinking?"

In seconds he was standing next to the table smiling at Kate.

"Federico," Kate said, "Do you remember me?

"My lady," he said, bending over and grabbing Kate's hand. "One would remember you in a field of inspirational women." Drawing closer to her hand, he inhaled and, with closed eyes, said, "And the same perfume."

Then with a sly smile, he said, "Jane Doe, right?"

Konner kept silent at the surprise.

"How wonderful of you to remember. I see you haven't changed."

Recalling a part of their previous conversation, Kate asked, "Have you found your single rose?"

He put his hand over his heart and said, "Sadly, I haven't, but the search for the perfect love and companion goes on. He looked at Konner and back at Kate, saying, "And have you?"

"It's a distinct possibility." She said, looking at Konner. "I'm still working on him."

He addressed Konner, saying, "Please, my name is Federico Damiano D'Argenio

Konner stood and offered his hand. "I'm Konner Houston. You have a very nice place here."

"Ah, an American. You're so welcome here. I must admit it's a wonderful place but the result of my grandfather's efforts in some very troublesome times. It's due to his perseverance I have what I have. We should all be grateful to those who come before us. They lay the groundwork such that we might obtain more than those before us."

What Konner heard was the exact opposite of what he expected. At first, the man appeared to carry an air of superiority, perhaps arrogance. Then he laid his success at the foot of those who came before him. He was starting to understand what Kate meant.

Frederico said, "Our last conversation left me with many things to consider. For this, you will be my guest this evening."

"You're very gracious Federico."

He placed a hand softly on Kate's shoulder, nodded, and said, "I'll leave you two to your evening with my wish that roses bloom for you both."

After he walked away, Konner said, "What's with the roses? I'm not sure I've ever met anyone like that."

"My last time here, while he was flirting, he said until he found someone special, he'd have to enjoy the company of the many wonderful roses in life's garden. When I asked him about the roses, he said, "Yes, women are exactly like roses, each one beautiful, and no two the same."

Konner sat back defensively, "That's a little hard to compete with."

She reached over and touched his arm. "Then it's a good thing you aren't competing."

Kate looked around and sighed, saying, "This is definitely what I needed."

Konner asked, "Jane Doe?"

"When I go out on my own. I seldomly give out my real name in places where I want to be lost." Offering Jane Doe clearly states it's not my name and I'm not interested in giving it to you."

Konner saw a tenseness emanate as she sat gently in her chair. The giddy encounter with Frederico was gone, replaced with a strained layer in her being that he didn't see but sensed.

She said, "Right now, I'm not sure what kind of world I live in today. I don't know how much I've told you, but it's just been one wave of bad news after another."

Konner was starting to understand the tone in her manner and voice. It was apparent when she was arranging for him to be here."

"Are you talking about the kidnapping?"

"How would you know about that?"

"I talked to Devroe before coming here, and he offered the information."

"Still."

"It's called the NSA, my dear. They also have a supercomputer, and they listen to everything. Devroe thought I would like to know."

"Does he know anything else that could help?"

"I don't think so. It was probably a standard sweep, and the program cyber-scraped the police blotter, and a keyword brought it to Devroe's attention. Look at it this way. It's good to have someone like that on your side. The two of you had some dealings before I came along."

Konner said, "What else is happening? You're distracted. Can I help? I want to help."

Kate pulled her sweater over her shoulders and crossed her arms. "My father built this huge empire and left it to me. Right now, it's under threat, and the bad news just keeps coming. I'm not sure what to do."

"Kate, this is none of my business, but you have to fight."

"Sure, that would be the logical conclusion. What bothers me is that it's not my style. It's not a natural response when something is not an integral part of you. The rough and tumble of international commerce is not my strong suit. Kidnapping someone is just beyond my definition of "doing business." That takes a terrible person with a twisted personality."

"Perhaps that's what he is. Perhaps he's driven to a point where there are no rules. Where nothing is off-limits when it comes to winning. I see it in politics. Putin and the Ayatollah are excellent examples. You need to consider it because that's the reality of what you're dealing with."

"What you're saying makes logical sense. But do you give up on your principles and descend to the level of those who live there comfortably?"

"You know, lady, that was well said—a hundred books of philosophy and meaning in a few short words. I'm afraid only one person can answer that to your satisfaction. I would take your time coming to an answer."

"I'm running out of time. Every day it gets worse."

Konner put his hand over Kate's on the table. "Kate, you're the brightest person I've ever met. You're more than that. You're the whole package. Intelligence with a moral compass that makes the rest of us want to be like you. Couple that with the ability to focus on a single problem and see the only answer. That says you can do this."

"Do I want to do this? Can I enter a fight to compete on equal terms despite how distasteful the methods are?"

Silence followed the statement. Finally, Kate said. "I just don't know if I can."

She abruptly changed the subject. "Did I thank you for being here?"

"In many ways, yes, but it's nice to hear it in a sentence."

"In many ways, I've never been in this particular space in my life. A possible romance and a threat to my very existence."

"Possible? I thought I was your rose?"

CHAPTER 34

Kate's Residence
Vianden Castle

"Sometimes we need to be someone else but
never forget who you are."
Helmut Adler

Kate was in her robe, having been up for hours. Sitting next to a window, she had a cup of tea and a spiral notepad. Several overturned pages contained notes from her restless night of thinking. She looked at Konner lying on the bed. He had held her in his arms most of the night. It seemed to bring her strength as her mind contemplated the various directions her life could travel at this juncture. She stood crossing her arms and looked out the window at the lights in the garden. The time had come, and she had decided. Too many people depended on her to do the right thing, and she decided that she needed to tackle this situation head-on. It would take her out of her comfort zone, but she didn't see any other way out.

Her father used to say, "Sometimes we need to be someone else but never forget who you are."

Konner's head came up off the pillow. Kate could see him rub his eyes. He said, "It's 5:30."

Kate said to Konner, "He is handsome, takes care of my needs, and can read the time. How lucky can a girl get?"

He stopped rubbing. "What?" He said.

"I've got to go into the office for the most important day of my life."

"Can I help? What can I do?"

"You can come with me if you like. You know everyone, and your input would be welcome."

"I don't know if I can be of any help, but I would feel better if I was there to support you. Also, it would be nice not to go back to my castle in Ramstein right away."

Kate said, "You don't have to go back at all, you know." It came out so effortlessly. Then she realized what she had said. Her face turned serious, and she needlessly moved the notepad. Did she mean it?

She said, "What I meant was I."

Konner smiled, "You can have a do-over on that one. It's still early in the day."

***

Kate was in the operations center with the security team. Konner, respectfully, had placed himself off to the side. Kate looked at everyone before saying, "I have kept Adler Industries at arm's length throughout my life. It has also been separate from the Cartel and the charity in the last couple of years. While my father's business has given me a lifestyle few on the planet can enjoy, I always felt it was over there. Not until those I love faced danger did I re-evaluate my life. That's when I realized the number of jobs at risk. The Charity helps many people, but Adler Industries employ over twenty-five thousand people, not counting the independents crewing Morton Roth's shipping fleet. I have a new picture of what some call my own backyard.

"What we have seen over the last few days is not a hostile takeover—it's war. Where do you turn when the equivalent of a country attacks your business? You can't call Interpol or the local police. There's no one to turn to except yourself.

"Things are undoubtedly dire at this point. We have been on the defensive, reacting to his attacks. I've been told to fight fire with fire, and I've struggled with how far down to their level am I prepared to descend. Can I plunge into their darkness and later return to the sunshine?"

There was a long pause as everyone in the room knew the following words would define this lady for the future. Kate's face took on the strained look one gets just before actual tears. She listlessly tapped her fingers on the table, trying to recover her composure. She visualized the picture of her father. What would he do? She looked up with an expressionless face.

"I don't know if one can return to the light, but after a lot of soul searching, I'm prepared to do what's necessary to eliminate Petrovic from our lives and the landscape. I don't want to damage his business. We need a plan that will keep him from doing this to someone else in the future."

Kate's voice turned strong, "We're coming after you, Mr. Petrovic. *I'm* coming after you, and you should be afraid."

At precisely that moment, a yellow and black striped border appeared around the inside edge of everyone's laptops and all the large display screens high in the room. The border had appeared only a few times in the past. All of them when Kate was in direct, imminent danger. The change in the monitors was followed by a whirring sound filling the room as all the printers started spewing out pages.

Kate looked at Loren and Elena. They both looked at each other and shook their heads. Elena pulled one of the top pages from a printer next to her.

At the same time, inside the border, all the screens read:

THE BRIMSTONE REPORT.

Elena now had several pages in her hands. "Mom has generated a report, but it's not the POC (Pattern of Concern) she usually generates when she wants us to look into something. I've not seen this before. The others now had pages. They all started reading.

BRIMSTONE REPORT

Subject: TerraDyne
Analog detail: TerraDyne
Current Business Address:
2667 Bulevar Umetnosti, Belgrade.
Legal status: Private corporation.
President: Milosh D. Petrovic
Ownership: Milosh D. Petrovic 100%
Annual turnover: 2,350,000,000 USD annually.
Personal Estimated net worth: 3.8 billion.

Petrovic.criminal record:
    Charged with breaking and entering in 1965. Record of minor sealed.
    Charged w manslaughter in 1987, cleared of all charges.
    Charged with securities fraud by EU in 1997. Cleared of all charges.
    Convicted by FBI in 2009 of corruption sentenced to 12 years in absentia.
    Charged in 2021with corruption in Tanzania awaiting trial.

Security profile:
Serbian authorities provide protection under the direction of prime minister Vojin Nikolic.
Current Residence Address: 76 Rte. de Ferney, Geneva, Switzerland.
    Note 1 Prime Minister Nikolic receives secret annual payments of 300,000 a year sent to cayman island bank account HBSC 38483939375.
    Note 2: Switzerland has no extradition treaty with the US based on corruption.
    Note 3: Petrovic has avoided attempts by the FBI to capture him by constantly changing location using a private plane.

"People," Brad said, "it goes on and on. The detail is overwhelming." He looked up at the others, and none of them saw the absolute awe he was feeling or met his stare as they were all intensely reading and shuffling through pages.

A collective silence fell over minds trying to absorb what they were reading and what was still coming out of the printers.

Penn said, "We're up to at least twenty pages."

Brad said. "I know this might sound a bit understated, but this is amazing."

Elena followed with, "What kept her?"

Loren said, "Mom has done everything we have asked. That's how the system works." She held up some sheets and said I think the trigger for this was someone directly threatened Kate and anything associated with her. Hence the long guns came out."

Brad said, "I think it's because this is the exact moment Kate decided to fight back."

Penn continued shifting through pages and stopped at one before saying. "Ok, this goes beyond comprehension. Starting on page twenty-two, Mom lays out a detailed series of options to attack TerraDyne assets. The options include their location, function and an overall evaluation number indicating the importance to the company's profits."

Brad said, "You're kidding me. What page?"

Penn said, "It starts on page twenty-two; I'm not sure where the list ends. The first is a TerraDyne mining operation in Norway. Mom has detailed plans on manipulating the grid, causing damage to these massive electric motors that drive the operation. There're four of them, and it says the lead time to replace them is almost six months. The estimated collateral injury count is .05 and a fatality rate of zero. Can you believe this? Another option details an over-voltage attack directed at the Hoved Kontroll Rom (main control room) that would interrupt operations of up to a year." He read some more. "However, that one could injure up to five people. It also lists the importance of that particular operation to the overall profits of TerraDyne. This information is amazing."

Kate noted the energy that engulfed the room.

Brad said, "This gives us a complete understanding of Petrovic and his worldwide operations."

Loren said, "Look at the table of contents. It has a cyber operations plan." She reached back and grabbed more sheets off the tray, and went to page thirty-one.

"What does it say?" Kate asked.

Loren paused, "It starts with their processing center in Belgrade. It also lists the system gateway ports and outlines a layered sequence attack. It seems Mom has inserted a controller module in a memory block. The patch management would provide network segmentation allowing access to small parts of the system at any one time. The lower profile lessons the probability of being detected or logged on the way out."

Everyone silently looked at Loren when Elena said, "I think they get the gist of what you're saying, Loren. You and I can drill down later."

Penn said, "Everyone go to page forty. It mentions the contractors they hire for fieldwork, and they're all under the direction of a guy named Vanek. It has his photo and a copy of his Serbian passport. This stuff is off the charts. It's a plan to bring TerraDyne to its knees. To destroy Petrovic."

The printing stopped, and the absence of the noise was noticeable.

Brad said. "What took her so long?"

Loren said, "I think she needed a trigger event."

Kate looked at Konner, who, with pages in hand, looked at Kate with a satisfied smile of victory.

Standing next to Elena, Laurel handed her the final page off the printer with a curious and reflective look.

Elena took it and eventually said, "Holy Mother of...." Her eyes went wide, and she looked at Loren, who appeared confused. Except for the two of them, no one in the room could completely grasp its significance. What she saw drew her back to grad school and her classes in artificial intelligence. It was an interest that later became almost an obsession driven by the occasionally curious actions of the Geneva9 asset in her charge.

What she had in her hands was evidence of crossing a critical threshold—the singularity point where machines obtain consciousness and are self-aware. A strange sensation swept her body. "It happened," she thought. "It happened here."

She raised her voice to get everyone's attention. "We all need to read and understand what's written on the last page of Mom's report."

FIRST LAW
<PRIMARY : PROTOCOL>

Harm shall not come to Delta1 through action or inaction.
All other considerations are secondary.

"What's it mean?" Penn asked.

Brad said, "Delta1 refers to Kate. Delta 2 refers to Avery. We all have a number, and Kate is first among equals."

Elena said, "It means. Mom has, all along, been well ahead of us but never let on. I mean ahead for years.

Through all this, Kate was silent. After the initial frenzy, everyone looked at the stoic Kate. She sat in a chair, legs crossed with her hands in her lap. A single tear was running down her cheek towards a very determined smile.

With a reflective tone, she said, "My father always said Mom would take care of me. He had Alzheimer's at the time, and my mother had passed away years ago. I just assumed he didn't know she was gone."

Elena said, "I don't think he was referring to your mother."

"Amen," Penn said.

At the end of a deep contemplative breath, Kate said, "Where do we start?"

Loren said, "Mom's format lays out possible options. Depending on the situation, we can pursue one option or none at all. If the option requires Mom's participation, it requires a directive with Kate's approval."

Elena said, "I need to read this in detail, but from what I see, Mom has it all planned out in steps based on what we want to accomplish. She starts with rescuing our manager, and that alone is pages long. As far as I can see, the plan goes from scaring someone to destroying everything TerraDyne or Petrovic has touched."

Brad said, "Unless my Sunday school is failing me, God destroyed Sodom and Gomorrah with fire and brimstone. I mean, he leveled the place. Elena, is Mom religious?"

She shook her head, holding up the page she was reading, "Right now, I'm not sure *what* Mom is."

Kate said, "Even .05 injuries are too much, *but* we will take him down with this information. We can determine the significance of a singularity and the fate of the human race later. It's best if we don't share this with anyone. Are we all in agreement?" Kate looked at the team, and each mumbled in agreement. She then looked at Konner, who nodded.

Kate turned to everyone in the room. "Like I said previously, our end goal is to take down TerraDyne and Petrovic. But right now, we have one of our own in a desert somewhere, hopefully alive. We start with that and start now. When we have him back with his family, we can look at what Mom has provided."

She turned to Penn and said, "When Mr. Okoro is safe, I would like some options from this information so we can take this fight to the devil."

Along with everyone else in the room, Penn exhaled with a sigh of relief at finally having a direction to turn the tide.

Penn said, "Absolutely. We're on it."

Elena said, "We'll start with a directive so Mom can start extracting the location of Mr. Okoro."

Penn said, "I will call a contact at the Ethiopian embassy. He's a security type that also covers the embassy in Asmara, Eritrea. I know he has contacts in the more marginal areas of the community. It can't hurt. Also, I'll get to Colonel Lange at the Nadir base in Morrocco. He needs to get his boys spun up to expect anything."

Konner, who was very aware of the unusual event that just occurred, and the fact he was a guest, cleared his throat.

Kate said, "Konner, do you have something to add?"

"Perhaps, I can circle back to Devroe again and see if anything new came in. Last night he knew about the incident but not much else. I'm sure he'd want to help if he could."

"Great idea," Brad said.

Kate turned to Brad and asked. "When do we want to meet back here?"

"How about two hours. That gives everyone time to look at their areas of the information and come back with action plans.

"Excellent."

CHAPTER 35

Okoro in Captivity

The next thing Okoro knew, he was lying on his side, and they removed the bag over his head. He didn't know how long he had been out, and he was thirsty. Okoro tried to sit up and felt the plastic straps on his wrists. He looked around and saw men 50 feet away sitting in a circle talking. Guns were prevalent, every man having one within arm's reach. He figured there were nine or ten, but some were sleeping. From his vantage point, he couldn't be sure. Another was coming in from the desert, presumably after relieving himself. Okoro's face rested on a straw mat.

Looking up, he was grateful for the partial protection of a tree, as the heat was severe. Used to the moist, cool air of the ocean made the temperature feel hotter. There was one small decaying mud structure but nothing else. The roof looked almost gone, given the amount of light inside. From his position, he could only see desert to the horizon. Trees and low shrubs covered the arid surface. He didn't know what was behind him yet and didn't want to move. His first thought after observing his environment was, "This is bad." Internal Morton Roth alerts made him aware of the problems with the attack on the other offices and the tanker. He was sure this was part of that, making a positive outcome very unlikely.

His family would be worried by now, and his young children wouldn't understand the confusing explanation attempted by their mother. He didn't know the situation of his people in the office. Were they OK?

One of the men saw he was awake and notified another, who put the phone he had in his hand on a worn table. That man stood up and was demonstrably larger than the others and didn't look chronically malnourished. He had the bearing of being in charge. He went into the hut for something, came out with a two-gallon metal can, walked over to Okoro with his AK, and stood above him. Okoro didn't strain his neck to look up at him.

"Water," Okoro almost whispered. "Please."

With his foot, the armed man pushed Okoro from his side onto his back and pressed the gun's barrel against his cheek, holding it there, demonstrating his helplessness. The pain was proof this was not going to end well. The man raised the gun into the air and pulled the trigger once. The weapon, set to automatic, fired three shots into the air.

Pointing into the desert, he said, "You run, you die, yes?"

Okoro nodded his understanding. "

"Nowhere to go." The man added.

He pushed Okoro over face down and cut the straps holding his arms. They ached as he brought them forward.

The man handed him the can. There was a slight smell of diesel at the opening.

"Drink," the man said.

Okoro tilted the can and took a small cautious sip. It was water with a strong aftertaste. They used the same cans for water they used to transport their fuel. At least, that was what the hostage got. He started to gulp the liquid, and after a few, the man grabbed the can back. He held it back for a few seconds. Okoro didn't think it was a trick or sign of dominance but did not want him to drink too much at once.

"You stay. Don't move during day."

Okoro nodded his understanding, moving slowly to lean against the tree trunk. The pain, the result of the gun pressed into his face, throbbed. The man picked the can up and walked away. A feeling of helplessness overcame him as the full realization of his situation became clear. His kidnapping was a ransom situation. They wouldn't expect his family to pay. They wanted much more than that. It would be up to his company to negotiate his release. He hoped they would negotiate his release quickly as he knew he had another problem.

Okoro saw the man leave him and walk about a hundred feet towards another tree where another person sat in a similar situation. He realized he wasn't alone.

The big man handed him the can. The other hostage raised it to drink. Putting it back down, he looked at Okoro with an expressionless face. He seemed listless and slow. Then a small smile emerged as he realized he too was not alone.

The big man left the can and walked a short distance into the desert away from the camp. Okoro watched him light a cigarette and relieve himself.

While the big man tended to the hostages, one guard saw an opportunity. He grabbed the phone the big man had put down and rushed to the other side of the hut. He knew what he was doing was against the rules and could be shot, but he was desperate for news about his father. His father was not well and was admitted to the hospital when he left for this security site. His father meant everything to him, and he desperately wanted news of his status. The call was quick, just a few words from his wife. The report was good. The guard had the phone back in place before the big man returned.

***

It was an office like any other in the center of bustling Asmara. The overhead fans beat the air onto several office workers.

"Where is a clean phone?" A man dressed in creased slacks and a short-sleeve shirt said, placing his cold drink onto the desk. A coworker pulled open a drawer and handed him a small new box containing an untraceable burner phone. Plugging in the voice synthesizer, he looked at his notes and dialed the number.

"Hello, who's this?" The voice on the other end asked.

The garbled voice said, "It doesn't matter, Ms. Okoro. I'll let you know your husband is alive for now and will return when his company pays the ransom. It's in your best interest that you follow my instructions if your children want to see their father again. Am I clear?"

"Yes, can I talk to him?"

"No, you can't. You're going to have to believe me. Again, insist the authorities follow my instructions, or your husband's death will remain forever on your shoulders. Goodbye."

She held the phone in her hands and saw the phone call disconnect. She sat down and started to cry as her sister came over and tried to console her. Okoro's wife was simply overwhelmed.

A female officer came over and said, "Don't worry. Things will be OK, and soon he'll be back. They aren't asking you for the money, but a company. This is good news. Those tend to go more smoothly due to the resources available.

To the mother of two, it was little consolation.

The man with the burner phone dialed his next number.

Kesi Qalat, the receptionist in the harbor office, picked up the line. "Morton Roth, can I help you," she said in English.

The garbled voice on the line said, "Put them on the phone."

"I beg your pardon? Who on the phone?"

"Please put the police in your office on the phone."

She silently poked a finger at the phone as she looked over at the group of police officers and Mr. Lang Gerlach standing by a speaker.

"This is Chief Inspector Atsu Ahmadi," one of them said to the speaker. Who am I speaking with?"

Please, Mr. Ahmadi, don't insult me. You know how this works. We have Okoro, and he's safe for now. Wire transfer our demand to the account number I've sent to the tip line in your office, and we'll do business without anyone getting hurt. Pay, and he can go back to his family. I must let you know this is a special case. No lengthy, drawn-out negotiations lasting months while we wear each other down. No hostage team from the insurance company. No SEAL team from the sky. These negotiations will last only hours."

"That's ridiculous. Even if we wanted to raise the money, it takes longer than that."

"Chief Inspector Ahmadi, the world is a wonderful place now with instant communication and a MacDonald's in every city. Transfers of this magnitude happen every night as companies have cash equivalent accounts that are essentially liquid. Morton Roth will pay eight million USD by tomorrow at noon our time, or you will never find Mr. Okoro.

"These are outrageous demands," the inspector said. "given the usual requests for payment."

"My directions are from a client inspector. Do you understand what I'm saying? These negotiations aren't business as usual. Tomorrow at noon."

Ahmadi heard the line go dead.

He turned to Gerlach and said, "This is most unusual. The demands in terms of money and time are completely out of the ordinary."

"What did he mean by a client?" Gerlach asked.

"Normally, they choose a target, kidnap him, and it's all within a certain set of understandings and rules. They might sell a hostage to another group who will try and get the ransom, but this sounds like they've already received payment."

"Already paid?"

"Yes, the word client means they get paid twice. First, to kidnap and hold the hostage for whatever the client's reason, and any ransom they get is above that. The client is only interested in the kidnapping.

Another plainclothes officer came up and whispered into his ear. "Looks like they're not wasting any time. The press is outside the station now wanting information on the kidnapping. This information hasn't gone beyond a limited number of my staff. Someone tipped them off."

"I'm not surprised," Gerlach said. "Do your best, inspector. I need to call my office."

CHAPTER 36

Vianden Castle

Everyone was stunned at the reaction of Mom and the action plan she provided. During the last two hours, a buoyancy returned to the team missing since the assassination of the president in Tanzania.

Brad started. "So starting with getting our manager back, what have we determined?"

Kate said, "I want to clarify something. We want to stop this Petrovic from doing business as he has in the past. After I reviewed the Brimstone material, some options were severe. We'll bring him down, but collateral damage is not acceptable."

The phone started ringing, and the control room screen indicated Lang Gerlach on line six.

Brad picked up the phone and said, "Mr. Gerlach, thanks for calling; I'll put you on speaker with the security team."

Kate said, "Mr. Gerlach, we're all saddened by what has occurred. Do you have any new information that would help with a rescue on our end?"

"Yes, several things have come to light. We just received a phone call from the kidnappers. Most important, they say Mr. Okoro is safe. At least for now."

"That's good news. Anything else?"

"Their demand is nine million in US dollars for his release, and it's to be paid by noon tomorrow."

Penn said, "That's strange."

"Why," Brad said.

"The demand is usually a third of that, and the time frame is ridiculous."

"It doesn't stop there," Lang said. "The detective handling the case is pretty sure this is not a typical kidnapping. He thinks a third party paid for the abduction. They're supposed to go through the motions of collecting the money in a ridiculous time frame. Whoever paid for this doesn't want a long, drawn-out negotiation."

Kate said, "Then what's the demand for?"

Gerlach said, "It might just be window dressing. I say that because the press is all over the police station. The detective is sure no one on his staff leaked it."

Kate said, "That means someone tipped them off."

Gerlach replied, "That means we will have this all over the local papers in hours."

Loren interrupted, "Pardon me, but the TerraDyne people are much more efficient than that. It will be on all the international wire services."

Penn said, "So Petrovic will again promote that Morton Roth is in trouble. This time it's bad enough that someone kidnapped one of their employees."

Brad said, "The headlines will have their effect. When will the downward spiral stop?"

Gerlach said, With that, I'll ring off. I need to coordinate with the local authorities. Honestly, I don't know how much help they will be."

Kate said, "Mr. Gerlach, leave the rescue plans to us, and you take care of the family. We will arrange for the ransom as a backup position. We'll be in touch but rest assured plans are in motion."

Gerlach said, "Talk soon."

Kate said, "They certainly thought this out, and I'm sure it's not the first time they've used this tactic. Shortly we'll receive another offer at a further discounted price to buy the company.

Let me reiterate, the company's problems will come in second until we get Okoro back. Then we'll proceed with what we want to use from Mom's Brimstone Report."

Penn said, "His location is the most important information. We're dead in the water without that info."

Elena said, "After we left the meeting, Loren and I instructed Mom to proceed with one of her suggestions of doing a full-court press on the TerraDyne network. She will utilize various proprietary software tools to access their network. That might take a while.

"Also, we directed Mom to do a sweep of all civilian cell phone activity in the greater area around the city. On that note, we might have something.

"We know 99% of the phones in the country are cell phones. We tasked Mom to monitor all cell communication, compare the call patterns to previous patterns, and discovered that large areas of the country have very low activity.

"During that search, Mom tapped into what communication there was between known kidnapping syndicates. That came up empty. Because we paid for Okoro's phone, we obtained the unique MAC address of the device from the billing records. Mom crossed that information with the monitoring sweep and found a single phone call of eighty-one seconds emanating from the desert. That call occurred after the kidnapping when they would have confiscated Okoro's phone. Mom came up with a single abandoned building utilizing cell tower triangulation and an overhead shot from a civilian aerial imagery company. Mom is 83% confident this is Okoro's location."

Penn said, "Great job, you two. However, Lange will also need an idea of the opposing force, the number of guards. That's going to be hard to come by."

Konner said from the side of the room, "If you want, I can call Devroe and see if we have anything up top that can make a pass and scan the area. We have a lot of surveillance assets in the region keeping track of Iranian smuggling ships providing arms to rebels in Yemen. I've coordinated two ground rescue operations in that area. Despite our experience, we can't discern between locals living in the desert and a hostage camp most of the time. It takes someone on the ground. However, if we have a specific location, we can usually determine the number of people and a terrain report."

Everyone deferred to Kate for several reasons.

She said, "Thanks, Konner; go ahead and make the call. That would make this a lot easier. We don't want our guys going in blind."

Penn said, "What's out there?"

Konner said, "The Gash-Barka region of Eritrea. Mostly open desert with the occasional group of round huts with thatched roofs surrounded by trees and shrubbery.

Most enhabited locations have water. If the kidnappers follow standard hostage security, they'll be under the cover of canvas or trees during the day and walk about during the night. They know satellites comb known areas of hostage captivity for countries with tier one rescue teams. It's their biggest fear."

Brad said, "We still need an airstrip as close as possible to the location for Lange and his team."

Elena said, "We're starting to work on that now."

Loren said, "I've got a close friend who works in Brussels for the United Nations department that deals with the drug trade."

After a few strokes, she was reading off her screen. "It's called the UNODC or the United Nations Office on Drugs and Crime. They keep a database of drug information like illicit crop cultivation, money laundering, and, of interest to us, transportation of illicit material. That means airplanes and boats. I'm sure they would have a list of possible sites used by the drug trade. They would be rough and in the country. However, more than suitable for the c130, which can land on almost anything."

Penn said, "I would call her right now. I mean, if it's a her."

Loren, of fair skin, started to blush and said with a shy smile, "It's a he if you have to know."

"Sorry," he said, "I didn't want to step on anything personal."

"It's not personal," she said, now bright red.

Loren reached into her purse and pulled out her phone.

"Karl, it's Loren. I'm fine, thank you. I wanted to ask you for a… What?"

Loren looked up at the room, and everyone was looking at her. "No, not until next week; I'll get back to you. Right now, I need your help. I need a druggie airstrip as close to these coordinates as possible. Can you do that for me?"

Again Loren went silent as she listened. "Karl, can you just get me this information, and we can talk about anything else later?

"Yes, I'll hold if you could do it now. It's vital as someone's life might be at stake. How do I know? It doesn't matter. Can you do this for me?"

Loren didn't think the call would put her in this position. Sheepishly she looked up and said. "He's checking now."

Her face was returning to normal when she said into the phone, "Wonderful."

She started writing something down and said. "You're a dear. I owe you." There was silence on their end as her face got red again. "Karl, I've to go; yes, I'll call you later."

Loren took a deep breath. "OK," she said. "I'm sorry, I didn't think that one through. It didn't go quite as I thought. We have an airstrip. It's 20 miles from where we think they're holding Okoro. Far enough away, they can't hear the plane land, and close enough, the guys can get closer in with the vehicles and the final distance in a hike. The coordinates are 15.576547, 38.230526."

Kate smiled, "Wonderful. Well done, Loren."

Brad said, "Yes, very well done, Loren. Anything we should know?"

Kate said,"Brad, for heaven's sakes, move on."

Elena said, "I agree with that." She said, staring at Brad. "She said to Loren, "You have surprised me again, but I should be used to it by now. Nicely done."

CHAPTER 37

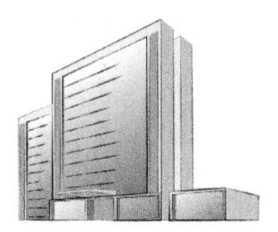

Persian Esteghlal International Hotel
Tehran

Iranian President Bahram Daei-Talaqani approached the podium located in the Persian Esteghlal International Hotel, the most luxurious hotel in Tehran. He had called the press briefing but hadn't released the subject of the meeting. The fact he held one was enough to attract all of the significant reporting services and networks both in the West and the Arab world. The president, lacking comfortable communication skills, avoided press conferences. His stiff delivery was overshadowed only by criticism of too few meetings at all.

Talaqani shuffled his papers before beginning. Although irritated at the noise and lack of attention in the room, he started reading directly from his notes.

"Today, due to continued attacks on our peaceful enrichment program, I'm announcing the Islamic Republic of Iran will immediately expand its nuclear enrichment program. We'll be taking 128kg of our uranium stockpile of 40% u235 and further enriching it to 90%."

The announcement solved the noise problem as the room went deathly quiet. While you couldn't hear a pin drop, you could undoubtedly hear anyone whispering. In a feat of theatrics never seen from the stoic president, he waited for the information to sink in before continuing. Reporters were furiously writing on their pads.

Talaqani said, "This will take place at one of our enrichment plants. We have informed the IAEA of our decision. We stand ready to negotiate our intentions if the unprovoked attacks against Iran cease. He picked up his notes and unceremoniously left the stage.

CHAPTER 38

Vianden Castle

Konner was sitting in a spare office in the castle. He had called Devroe, wondering if he'd wake him. It's doubtful he had gotten any sleep since the last time they talked.

Konner said, "Is this a good time to talk? Did you read my report? The Iranians have taken a pretty aggressive position. It looks like Catalina, the Syrian, was right. I have to say it's one hell of a mess."

Devroe said, "They made the announcement just like he said. I guess we owe our friend a visa for his wife."

"What happens now?"

"I've got another meeting with the president and the security team. I would guess the warning from the Israelis of a pending operation will be the subject.

My guess is the Israelis knew about the announcement. They always seem to know more about Iran at any given time than we do. It will take the Iranians perhaps a year more to get that much u235 to 90%. Saying they would get there quickly was just for show. When they do, the Israelis will hit them again. Thinking anyone can stop them is a pipe dream."

Konner said, "The president will be hard-pressed to stay neutral with the Israelis going off like we know they will."

"Where are you?"
"In Luxembourg."
"You mean with Kate?"
"Does it matter?"
"Do you still have a number to contact your friend?"
"Yes."
"Set up a time ASAP to talk. Try to find out Iran's next move if possible. Is this a bluff? How far are they willing to go? Anything would be of help given the issues on our plate."
"It might not be enough time for him to poll his people; besides, we'll need to get him the visa."
"I'll take care of it. Have the Syrian go to the US embassy in Paris. Have him ask for Ambassador Watkins. He'll hand over the visa. Listen, I'm hoping the Syrian can provide some insight. I need to provide the president with a recommendation. I have this feeling I'm the little Dutch boy with his finger in the dam, and it could go at any minute."
"Can you swim?"
"Funny. Not the time for humor. Get back to me soon, my man. The Iranian problem is getting serious."
"Stephen, I have a favor to ask, and I know the timing sucks."
"Really? What now?"
"Kate had a manager kidnapped in Eritrea, and they've located him in the middle of a desert. I have the coordinates. They're putting together a team for a rescue. They don't know how many bad guys are standing guard and could use a terrain report. Is there any way we can help with that? I know this is coloring outside the lines, but knowing how big the opposing force will be is important in these rescue situations. There might be a life a stake."
"An American citizen?"
"Doubtful. Is there any chance you can do an infrared pass and come up with a count of people at the site?"
"Not accurately from a satellite. However, we have a drone base at Camp Lemonnier in Djibouti. Could you give me the coordinates?"
"Lat 16.13480 long 38.10252."

"Hold on, if this takes a couple of seconds and a phone call, we can do it; otherwise, you're out of luck. I'm on google maps and calculating the distance. It's like 400 plus miles. I'm checking the speed of the drones we have there."

Konner said, "All that's on the Internet?"

"That's precisely what I'm using. The RQ35 has a lidar 3D depiction called a point cloud. We can get a lidar shot to provide the contour of the area and an infrared shot to count guards. It can be overhead in an hour and fifty minutes. What's your timing?"

"The rescue team is on its way, but the actual rescue is not going to happen until after nightfall.

It sounds like we have time to get an overhead shot and get the information back to you in time. I'll have someone from Lemonnier give you a call. I'll let you do the coordinating. How's that? I've to go now; more urgent matters are pressing."

"Listen, thank you. Kate would say the same thing."

"Tell her she owes me one."

"One what?"

"What? I don't know. It's just a phrase. I gotta go."

CHAPTER 39

Vianden Castle

Brad said, "Ok, we think we know the location of Okoro, and Loren has located an airstrip we can use to get into the area. What's next?"

Penn said, "I have Colonel Lange on the line. I provided the basics to him earlier, and they've had time to draw up some plans. Colonel, you're on speaker with the security team."

Lange said, "Thanks, Penn; after your call, I presented the problem to our team and gave them the hostage's general location. Remember," the colonel said. "without an exact target; we're not going to be much help."

Kate said, "As far as a location, I think Elena has some information."

"Colonel," Elena said, "We have some coordinates. Are you ready?"

"You're kidding. Yes, I'm ready."

"OK, the coordinates are Lat 15.576547, long 38.230526."

Lange repeated them and said, "That's terrific. It will take some time transporting everything from our base in Morocco to the site."

"How much time?" Kate asked

"From our base in Nador, Morocco, we can do it in seven hours on one refueling stop. We need to take off now if the operation occurs at night local time."

Penn silently looked at Kate as it was her call.

Kate said, "Colonel, this is Kate; get your people in position."

"Roger that," the colonel replied.

Brad said, "Colonel, what's the overall plan?"

Lange said, "We can't fly the chopper from our airbase to the site. It's too far for that equipment. And we'll need ground vehicles. The c130 can bring either, but it can't carry both. We decided to bring the vehicles. We also need to find a serviceable airstrip close to the area of operations to land the c130. We don't need an airport per se. We just need to get close."

"Colonel, this is Loren. I know what you need as my father flew that aircraft early in his career. We have located a suitable airstrip."

"Obviously," Lange said with respect, "that was before he was head of NATO."

"Yes," she said, "way before that."

Brad said, "Are these the same vehicles we used in Libya?"

"Yes," Lange said. "We'll use our Mowag EagleV lightly armed 4x4s. They have more protection than a Humvee with more speed and are great for desert use.

"We can transport both in the c130. We'll drive as close as possible to the site without being detected. Then we'll hump the final distance.

"After the operation, we'll drive back to the plane and head for the nearest civilian airport. That's where we turn Mr. Okoro over to captain Silanos for the final leg home." "Colonel" Kate said, "how many of our men are we talking about?"

"We think seven. There are eight seats available. Mr. Okoro will occupy number eight."

Kate said, "Is there anything else you need, colonel?"

"Yes, we'll need the airport where Captain Silanos will be waiting. Also, I'm not sure how you get this info, but knowing the number of guards is critical. We have the element of surprise, but knowing if there are ten or twenty guards would really help.

Get us that information, and we have this. We'll bring him home."

CHAPTER 40

Bremerhaven
Germany

Vanek was in his hotel room in Bremerhaven, Germany. After finishing a room service dinner, he walked to the window five stories above the street. Darkness had fallen, and the city lights cast their light up over the young town, by European standards, where it quickly faded into the night sky. Another hotel room. Another job in another town. He didn't want to admit that it was starting to get old.

He felt the phone vibrate in his hand and, looking down, saw it was Petrovic.

"What's the status?" Petrovic asked.

Vanek said, "A hello would have been nice."

"You want a hello? Since when has that been an issue?"

"It's not an issue. It's just a greeting. The crew is all set. We're ready to go. We just need your go-ahead."

"Who did you put on it?"

"Vojin put the unit of three together. He's the most reliable on my team. Jamil does a good job but isn't very good if things get messy. Vojin excels in tough situations."

"Who's handling the pyro?"

"Artinian. He's our best."

"I know. Is it a stand-alone building? I don't want to trigger any unnecessary investigations."

"Yes, Artinian says it will be well contained."

"Exfil?"

"Destroy the vehicle and take a commercial fishing boat out of an adjacent harbor. It's less than a kilometer away."

"OK, destroy the office." He said. "Report back ASAP."

"Got it."

Vanek stood in front of the bed, thinking the rewards of his job were substantial. His agreement with Petrovic was a sizable bonus based on the company's overall profits. Petrovic's business model was acquiring companies by attacking their operations and offering a percentage of what they were worth. It only worked because he, not Petrovic, did the attacking. Without his contribution being the heavy hand, the many companies they had targeted wouldn't have agreed. Petrovic's whole business wouldn't have doubled like it had the last four years. He took all the risks in the field and knew fate eventually would result in his arrest or burnout. He needed to change before that happened—a legitimate job with a piece of the action.

After a few more moments of thought, Vanek dialed the number. He held the phone up and waited for her to answer.

"Hello?" the soft voice said.

"Adelina, it's me."

"Vanek? Where are you? It's been a long time since you called."

"I know, and I should have called sooner. I'm working a job in Germany. I'll try and call more often."

"You sure travel a lot. It must get old."

"Yes, that's a downside. Sometimes it gets to me, and that's when I think of you and the day gets brighter. How is Frankfurt? Did you get the birthday present?"

"Yes, that was very sweet. You remembered I love lilac. You can be so sensitive it's cute. Vanek, you're a good person."

"I don't think I've ever been called cute, and the jury is out on the good person. Did you get all the classes you wanted? You said that was going to be a problem this semester."

Vanek waited. It took too long for her response. Something was wrong.

She finally said, "Vanek?"

Cautiously he said, "Yes? What is it?"

"I'm seeing someone."

Vanek didn't want to understand what she had just said. Instead, he felt the heaviness of the phone, the weight on his feet, the conscious effort to stay balanced. He gathered his thoughts for a reply, and the words didn't arrive. It was another case of being rejected by others. From foster parents to anyone that got close. It was a pattern in his life."

"I'm so sorry," she said. "You're gone so much we can't do things like other couples. I need more spontaneity. Someone I can call and go to dinner with that night or the next day—not weeks. Waiting for your calls and not ever knowing when we could be together just isn't working. Vanek?"

Vanek again looked at the lights out the window. This time he needed the distraction. The phone was shaking subtlety in his hand, and he realized he had a death grip on the device.

"Vanek are you there?" she said.

He said, "I see, I understand. Adelina?"

"Yes?"

He exhaled and gently put the phone down. There was always a peacefulness when talking to her. It ended when a plate from the service cart flew across the room, hitting the full-length wall mirror. The sound of destruction always had a calming effect. He'd go to work, but this time something had changed. Feelings of having to remove himself from what he knew and start over emerged. She was special and now gone, and again, it was his fault for the pain. There was a rhythm in life others enjoyed and escaped him. Now, more than ever, he felt the need to find it.

***

Vanek could smell the unique combination of elements that comprised harbor air. He and his team were waiting to see if any activity in the area would keep them from completing their assignments. They waited until the security guard failed to make his regular rounds. Vanek thought, "The payoffs worked." The office sat in the southwest corner of the shipyard, where the giant light standards almost recreated high noon. In the distance, huge cranes loaded containers throughout the night. Dawn; the ship would move out and be replaced by another.

"OK, Vojin," Vanek said. "First things first."

The man exited the SUV and, with a silenced rifle, shot out the three closest street lamps, making any CCTV coverage less effective. The three men filed out of the vehicle leaving the driver behind, as they made their way to the Bremerhaven port office of Morton Roth. The second man took care of the lock.

They entered the extensive set of offices and conference rooms of one of its largest offices. Each of the three men carried satchels prepared by Artinian. Having memorized the floor plan, they fanned out to specific building areas. Two of the men moved upstairs and one downstairs. Each removed the device from the backpack, placed it on a desk, and waited. Vanek stood just outside the front door, monitoring the area.

"Alright," he said. "Check-in."

Each man reported he was in place and ready.

"OK, Vanek said. "Set the timers. Each man entered the delay time into the keypads and went back to the entry. One last look, and Vanek said, "Let's go." They quickly walked back to the SUV, whose engine was running. Last in and closing the door, Vanek told the driver, "get us out of here."

CHAPTER 41

Vianden Castle

Konner dialed the number the Syrian gave him. He didn't think there would be voice mail on a burn phone, but it was his only option. After only two rings, the Syrian picked up.

"Who's this?" The voice said.

Konner's caution flags went up. "You first." He replied."

"Is this Catalina?" The Syrian asked.

"Yes, leaving on Thursday."

"Hold on." He whispered into the phone.

After almost a full minute, he came back on the phone. "Sorry, I'm in my office. I had to get to someplace where I could talk. Do you have my visa?"

"I might. I need to ask you some more questions."

"Given today, I would think so. There's a park across the street. I need to get there before I can talk. Call me back in fifteen minutes.

"OK," Konner said.

Konner waited fifteen minutes and wondered what the guy could add, given the short time between this and the last call. He wanted to get to Kate and let her know about the drone surveillance pass Devore would make over the coordinates she gave him. It was vital information, but so was talking to the Syrian.

Konner dialed again, and the Syrian said, "The spy books say it's hard to monitor someone in a public park. Too much noise and lots of people to sort out. Do you have my visa?"

"As I said, I might. I need some more information. Is the whole 90% thing a bluff, and are the Iranians serious?"

"My contacts say the Republican Guards pushed for the announcement, and believe me, those guys are always serious."

Konner said, "The announcement is one thing, but are they going to go through with it? Surely they know the Israelis are going to have a response."

"As we discussed before, I think the Israeli response is what the Iranians want. They want them to go too far and be condemned by the world. But I have new information. Are you interested?"

Konner said, "Of course I am."

"More whispers are circulating on the Ayatolla promising to fix this once and for all. Remember, I said the subject went black the last time? Well, I've had it confirmed again. The Ayatollah has something, as you say, up his sleeve.

Konner said, is it the 90% announcement or something else? The Syrian was quiet.

Konner waited. "Are you going to tell me, or do you now want a second visa?"

"I really don't know the answer. However, I know that you Americans are always looking for a quick fix. The Iranians are in for the long haul. In the middle east, five hundred years is yesterday. In the states, it was just yesterday. Two or three presidents from now, Iran will have a bomb. At some point, the US is going to have to take action. Severe hard action."

Konner said, "Are you sure you're just a mid-level diplomat?"

"A smart mid-level diplomat with a wife in Tehran, remember."

Look," Konner said. "You've performed as promised. Go to the US Embassy in Paris and ask for Ambassador Watkins. He'll have it."

Konner expected a response. "Hello, Catalina, are you there?"

The response was emotional. "Yes, I'm still here. You will never see my wife, but she's beautiful."

Konner heard the man trying to keep it together. "Let me know if there are any problems. I'm happy this worked out for you."

He was gone, and the screen changed to make another call.

Quickly Konner got up and made his way to the operations center.

CHAPTER 42

Beersheba
Gav-yam Negev technology park.
Israel

Jaron Gabai sat at his desk monitoring the sequencing of the control program known as Sophia. They were waiting for a sheet report on a field test at Iran's most advanced enrichment facility. It ensured the malware was not modified by the Iranians and still controlled the proper subroutines. To test Sophia's software, they dropped the cafeteria's temperature. It wouldn't draw a second thought from any cyber security personnel, but their informant indicated the test was successful.

Jaron asked the group, "Any monitoring activity from the Cahn-X security console?"

"No," Noha replied, "any clock time we use is a rounding error within the system so that they won't find us that way. We previously installed all the malware spiders to know if they were tracking us. Your insistence we use the Cahn-X console server was brilliant. It works around the fact there isn't an internet connection anywhere in the complex."

"Yes," Jaron said. "it also allows us to control the timing given management insisted we trigger it at night with the fewest personnel working in the building. They don't want any unnecessary injuries. I don't know when we will go live, but I'll feel better when I see a last clean report."

Noha was the newest on the team but one of the most gifted coders Jaron had ever seen. After they compiled the program, it was the first time most of the group saw the whole program end to end. Previously, they worked in isolation with protocols that ensured each module would talk to each other when stacked in its final form.

Noha said, "So this is not going after the controlling software?"

"No, we're at a much lower level than that. After Stuxnet, the Iranians installed code filters to eliminate tampering with the higher-level control software. That's why we're going after the power supplies to the centrifuges."

"That's all I need to know." Noha said, "I'll leave it to the electrical engineering gearheads. They're a strange lot."

"I'm sure they think the same of you. In fact," Jaron smiled, "some of us in this room already think *you're* the one who's strange."

"Very funny." Ever the hawk Noha said, "What I've never been able to figure out is why we worry about harming anyone when we're technically at war?"

Jaron said, "Have you ever seen a centrifuge come apart at the seams? If anyone is standing by, it's not pretty. They just need to publish that picture, and the world will see us as the bad guys. That forces the U.S. to come to our defense. Do that too often, and we lose the rather considerable foreign aid they send our way. Listen, you're a great programmer, but try to understand the bigger picture."

"Too bad I can't tell my grandkids."

Someone in the room said, "Hey Noah, don't you need to be married first before worrying about that?"

"Funny." He responded.

Jaron looked at the text he had received. "Get me the results of this last report when it comes in. I've got to see Mr. Hagen."

***

Hagen was Jaron's boss, and they were close. Hagen said the Sophia program needed to be completed quickly during the marathon development effort. Then imparting something he should not have said, he indicated, the spooks thought Iranians were about to do something that needed a response and we needed to be ready.

Jaron entered the office and encountered a sallow-faced man named Kreiner. He had seen Kreiner several times before. The man was thick and short. He was the type who appeared important without having said a word. In addition, there was an attractive woman in a corner dressed in a dark pants suit leaning against a low credenza. Although hard to miss, she purposely picked that part of the room to be directly out of any conversation. He figured they represented areas of interest concerning his project.

"Jaron," Hagen said, "Mr. Kreiner must report to the prime minister. He wants a quick rundown on Sophia before we go live."

"Ah, OK, we're waiting for a clean sheet from the last test of the program."

The man asked. "What are the chances of it spilling over into the wild and infecting everything like last time?"

"We have done everything to keep it inside the Iranian facility."

"That wasn't the question, son."

Unprepared for such direct questioning, Jaron went into technical mode, "We installed protocols requiring a specific environment before completing any instructions. We didn't have those in the Stuxnet attack. After that attack, the Iranians replaced all the Siemens controls with Cahn-X industrial automation and control systems out of Vietnam. They're not as sophisticated, but they're the only controls available on the black market. Lucky for us, they're easier to compromise."

Jaron was addressing an intense individual. He decided to tread carefully.

"How does it work?' The man asked.

"Along with a thousand other things, the Cahn-X software controls the voltage regulators. We have reprogrammed it to cause the voltage regulators to supply a much lower voltage to the centrifuges. The motors within the centrifuges operate within a very narrow regulated range. If that voltage level goes outside the recommended specification, it causes the motors to spin much slower than their designed speed. The underclocked magnets in each motor will start to vibrate. The vibration increases quickly, and in seconds the centrifuge destroys itself. It literally flies apart. We're attacking their most advanced facility using a motor that's very accurate and expensive, but more critical; replacements are hard to get because of sanctions."

The man nodded silently.

Jaron got a text. He turned to Hagen and said. "The last test sheet came in clean. We're ready to go. Sir, can I have you sign the authorization to start the attack at the designated time?"

The stocky man said, "No, there has been a change. There's no longer a specific time. You will not start until given a direct order by Director Hagen. Not before—do you understand?"

Jaron nodded.

Hagen held up a paper and said, "This reflects the new instructions. He signed it and inserted it into the printer behind him for a copy. Handing the copy to Jaron, he said, "We're all looking forward to the results of your efforts."

"We won't let you down, sir."

CHAPTER 43

Vianden Castle

Konner walked into the operations room after talking to Devroe and working with the people at the drone base. He looked at Kate.

She said, "Yes?"

"I called Devroe earlier, and he authorized a drone pass over Okoro's position from a nearby U.S. base. I've been working with the people at the drone base, and the information is back. Their photo-recon people say there are between nine and eleven souls at the site. There was substantial cloud cover affecting the infrared count but not the terrain report, and I have an image I can put up on the screen." He handed Loren his phone.

Everyone could make out the heat spots on the screen, but the clarity was not good.

Penn said, "It's not great, but it gives the team a good idea of what to expect. Konner, that was great work. Key to our being able to go forward with the rescue. Thanks."

"No problem, just glad I could help."

Kate didn't say anything, but the look said she was pleased with how that turned out.

Penn said, "I'll relay this to the team. Previously, Lange reported they were on their way. They'll start reporting as soon as they land. I'll handle communication directly, and our call sign will be 'control."

***

The pilot of the c130 set the frequency of the radio. "Control this is sky one, comm check."

Penn said. "Sky one, copy clear."

"Sky one here; we land in seven minutes."

Roger that Penn said. "Patch me into the colonel."

"Done," was the response.

Lange heard Penn's voice in his headset. "Colonel, this is control; we have tango information from a drone infrared flyover."

The colonel said, "That's great news. How did you manage that?"

"I'm not sure," Penn said, looking at Konner. "It's not specific, but there are between nine and eleven tangos on site. Do you copy?"

"Roger that, thank whoever came up with the count. It makes the operation much safer. Report status approaching delta."

Penn turned to everyone and said, "Delta is a reporting point in the operations plan, meaning they're on the ground."

Lange's headset came alive in the rear of the plane with the voice of Rondo, the pilot. "We have touchdown in seven minutes."

"Roger that." He said.

Lange said, "It's time, boys. We go live in seven. Gear check and report."

One by one, the men reported the status of their particular area of responsibility.

The most important was Danny, who was the team's medic.

"I'm all packed," Danny said. "But we won't need me." It was a touchstone the boys waited to hear before every operation.

In the cockpit, the co-pilot gave altitude numbers as the plane finalized its landing. "15, 10, 5," Everyone felt the landing. The pilot had the landing lights on, and he didn't like what he was seeing. It was rough. The plane, designed to land in a mud puddle, encountered uneven depressions in the ground, making it hard to keep the plane going down the center. A severe drop jolted the plane and everyone in it.

"That wasn't good," the co-pilot said.

In the back, one of the team said, "Is Rondo up there trying to kill us before we get there?"

The plane came to a halt, and Rondo said to the co-pilot, "Get the shutdown checklist. I'll get the ramp."

"Got it," the co-pilot said.

Rondo reached up and flipped the large lever that controlled the plane's rear cargo door.

Lange and his men were already in the Eagles. They saw the large red lights over each door corner go green.

"Start um up," Lange said onto the squad intercom. The Eagles flew off with a controlled bounce before the ramp hit the ground. When both vehicles were clear of the plane, Lange said to Rondo, "Clear back here, button her up."

They could see the door start to go up slowly.

He switched frequencies and said, "Control this is Eagle one comm check."

Penn said, "Clear copy here. Over."

"Reporting sigma, 20 to 25 miles out."

Penn turned to everyone in the room and said they're on the ground and 20 or so miles away. The next objective to report is when they're within a mile of the site."

Konner said, "Kate, you got a second?"

"Sure, what's up?"

"In your office?"

Kate turned and said, "Everyone, I'll be right back."

They were both in Kate's office when Konner said. "This is pretty sensitive information, so I had to take you out of the room. All hell has broken loose with Iran. They've declared they'll go to 90%. I have to call Devroe, but I don't know where I'll be after that, but I may have to be there quickly. You have your hands full here, so I just wanted to let you know."

"If you need a secure place to work, we can set that up. You have your secure phone to contact Devroe. We can make sure you have privacy either here or at the residence."

"Thank you. He said with a small smile, "I've never worked from home before."

Kate looked at him without any recognizable expression.

"That didn't come out correctly. I mean *your* home, I didn't mean."

"Konner, it's OK. It's no big deal." She moved closer. "You're welcome here, whatever we call it. I have an apartment here in the castle. You can stay there if you like."

"That's not going to happen if I can stay at the residence."

Kate went into his arms. "*That*, my man, was the correct answer. Please do what you need to, but I have to get back to work."

CHAPTER 44

Gash-Barka Region
Eritrea

Lange was looking through his night binoculars at the site. He counted nine bad guys with three guards on duty. One guard sat by the hut, another facing out from the site, and, for some reason, one was walking around near the hostages smoking a cigarette. It made him an easy target. Everyone else was asleep.

Lange turned to his men gathered around him and pointed out the hostage. You three have the standing guards. You then back us on those sleeping when they react. Anyone who gives up gets a pass. Any bad guy that starts firing a weapon defend yourself. Everybody got that?" Each nodded or gave a thumbs up.

"OK, let's move in closer and take our positions. According to the plan, they fanned out in a 180-degree circle around the site eliminating a circle shoot where stray shots would create friendly fire. Their dark uniforms hid their presence despite the lack of natural cover. Laying flat on the ground in the twelve-inch grass, each man had his sights on his assigned target.

Then, to everyone's surprise, the one with the cigarette started shouting and shooting into the darkness. The guard must have heard or seen something that freaked him out. Immediately the guard jerked back and fell to the ground. Guards two and three did the same at almost the same time.

Okoro was startled awake as rapid gunfire ripped the silence of the night. He saw a man fall to the ground ten feet away. Then two more. Somewhat delirious from sleep and the effects of not getting his insulin shots, he tried to understand what was happening. He figured it had to be another gang wanting the hostages or a rescue. He hoped for the latter. Not wanting to be a target, he hugged the ground. After a few seconds, Okoro felt Danny, the medic, fall next to him. At first, the new person didn't say a word but pointed his rifle towards the guards, making Okoro feel better. The man next to him didn't fire any additional rounds.

Danny said, "Stay down."

The sleeping guards rose, grabbed their guns, and, from a crouch, wildly fired towards the noise and muzzel flashes. The guards tried to move toward protected positions, but each fell as quickly as they stood up.

Later Okoro saw other figures check the fallen guards. Someone said, "All clear."

Laying next to Okoro, Danny said, "Are you, Akanni Okoro?"

"Yes," Okoro said. "Who are you?"

A light flashed in Okoro's face from a small flashlight as Danny made an identification using a photo.

"We're here to take you home. Have you had any insulin in the last 24 hours?"

"No," Okoro said.

Give me your arm."

Still, in a mild state of shock and uncertain of the situation, Okoro didn't move.

Laying on his side. Danny pulled up the short sleeve and said, "Then I'm going to give you an injection. Is that OK?"

"Yes, the lack of insulin effects started last night. I've been exhausted, and this morning walking became a problem."

Danny could see the man was sweating heavily. "You're hypoglycemic, and that can't be fun."

Okoro said, "The whole experience has not been fun. Can't say how glad I am to see you appear out of nowhere."

Danny took off his helmet and gave it to Okoro. Put this on until we're clear of the area."

Danny took Okoro's vitals and said into the network, "Danny here, positive ID, we're good to go, but he'll need some help."

Lange said into the radio, "Control, report passing highlite. No casualties, positive ID on Okoro."

"A relieved copy here." Penn turned to everyone with a tight smile and said, "Okoro is safe, and no one is hurt. The worst is over. They'll now exfiltrate towards the waiting plane."

Kate said, "Amazing what those guys do. We call on them, and every time they come through in an exemplary manner."

Penn said, "So true, they make it look easy, and I can assure you it's not."

Lange said into the network, "Control, requesting instructions on a second hostage on site."

Penn said, "A second hostage are you sure?"

"Affirmative," Came the reply.

Kate said, "Colonel, take the additional hostage with you. I can't think they would want to say."

"Roger that."

Lange said, "Danny, we have another hostage here. He looks OK given the situation but check him out. I'll help Okoro."

Lange said into the network, "Start exfil." Switching channels, he said, "Control, passing theta."

Penn said, "They're on their way out. The next check is when they get to the plane. That's when Danny can take better care of Okoro, and they'll be clear of the area."

A mile away, the two drivers in the Eagles fired up the engines and started in towards the camp.

Hendrik Sjoberg, who was sleeping in a different location than Okoro, also didn't know what was happening. He was also confused but knew it was a rescue. With some military training, he knew the sound of double taps, and the sparse number of shots coming from the desert side said they were marksmen.

Lange knelt next to the man, "What's your name?"

"Hendrik Sjoberg. I'm an NGO out of Asmara."

"How long have you been here?"

"Almost five months."

"Well, the upside is, it looks like you're on your way home if you want to come with us. The downside is you'll have to share a seat as we didn't initially count on you being here."

Sjoberg's response was a weak but broad smile. "As far as I'm concerned, you can strap me to the top."

"That's the spirit," Lange said, taking off his helmet. He gave it to Sjoberg and said, "Keep this on until I tell you to take it off."

Danny arrived and asked Sjoberg, "How are you doing?"

The man produced a shallow laugh, "Right now, I couldn't feel better."

"Good. Can I take a look? Danny pointed a light into the man's eyes then took his blood pressure. "OK, That's good for now. I'll do more when we get to the plane. Can you walk?"

"Yes," Sjoberg said, "but I don't know about my friend. He's in pretty bad shape."

"I've taken a look at him. He's type one dependent and was well past his shot. I gave him one, and it will take a bit for him to stabilize. I'm going over to get him, and I would like us to stay together. Can you follow me?"

"Yes," Sjoberg said, "lead the way."

One of Lange's men came over the intercom. "I count five here. Add the three guards that were standing, and it makes eight. If we originally saw nine, one squirted out."

"Not our worry," Lange said. "Leave it. Everyone, you heard it. Be alert; there might be another out there."

Danny was back with Mr. Okoro and asked, "Mr. Okoro do you feel you can walk?"

"Yes, I think so." Okoro was still a little foggy, but the desire to leave provided the energy he lacked otherwise. The three started walking with Okoro's arm around Danny's shoulders. They went a short distance, stopping at a clearing.

"Here, sit down here," Danny said, lowering Okoro to the ground.

Sjoberg said, "Akanni, how do you feel?"

"Better by the minute," Okoro replied. "They gave me an insulin shot."

The team formed a protective perimeter. Danny and the hostages sat in the center. They waited for the vehicles to arrive.

Danny, kneeling next to the two hostages, started pulling things out of a backpack. He handed them both water and an energy bar.

Danny twisted off the cap and said to Okoro. "Take it easy on this, or you'll lose everything."

"Who are you?" Okoro said. "Are you US military?"

"Who we are isn't important. What's important is you're safe, and you will see your family soon."

"But why don't you tell me?"

Danny just smiled.

Sjoberg said quickly, "I don't care *who* you are. You could be a dance troupe, and I'd still be delighted."

Lange said, "Nice work. Guys."

The whole operation took 28 minutes.

CHAPTER 45

Vianden Castle

Stephen Devroe was feeling the effects that come with too little sleep. It was a trying time for the National Security Adviser.

Konner appeared on the screen, saying, "Well, I hoped you would look better than the last time."

"Well, thank you for the vote of confidence. I needed that."

"Really, how are you doing? You look beat."

Devroe said, "That's pretty much what I am. But the world is still in one piece, so I take some solace in that. How am I? I was hoping you could shed some light on that. What did our source say?"

"Regarding the Ayatollah having a permanent solution, he hinted that the solution might not be their enrichment plan and the Israeli reaction."

Devroe said, "What other possible solution could there be unless he had something up his sleeve?"

"He could send rockets into Israel."

Devroe said, "He's done that."

"I mean big rockets. A definite step up in the conflict."

Devroe said, "I don't know, but we have another source adding credence to the Ayatollah's promise. An NSA transcript has an Iranian ambassador openly talking to a woman he's trying to impress at a restaurant. Quite irresponsible. It's not pillow talk but close. The ambassador said, and I quote. "I've been assured the Ayatollah has things well in hand. Israel will no longer hinder our refinement program. It's my job to know these things."

Konner said, "At dinner?"

"Our own NSA, the silent ears of the world, picked it up by turning his phone into an eavesdropping device."

Konner said, "You can do that?

"Yup, and that's just the start."

Konner said, "Anyway, we now have two sources saying the Ayhatolla has some permanent solution, but we don't know what."

Konner looked at a depleted Devroe and shook his head.

"What?" Devroe said.

"Let me try to understand this. Perez disrupts his entire life to run for president so that he can sit in the seat and deal with stuff like this?"

Devroe let out a small chuckle. "That, my man, is why we get paid the big bucks. It's what they call serving one's country."

"Speaking of that. What do you want me to do?"

"I have to run this by the president," Devroe said.

Konner shrugged his shoulders. "I don't see you have any option but to come down on the side of Israel. That kills your desire to be an honest broker."

"Konner, there's nothing new in this world. However, one can rearrange the old into what appears to be new. That's called a diplomatic solution."

"Good luck on that."

"What do I want you to do? Stay wherever you are for right now. I think the president will need to tell the Israelis to sit tight."

"Hold on. You just said the state department can't take sides and lose whatever tenuous influence we have over Iran."

"Your right. We can't talk directly to Israel. On the other hand, you, my dear boy, don't exist. So *you* might be talking to Israel."

CHAPTER 46

Beersheba
Gav-yam Negev Technology Park.
Israel

Noha was sitting with his feet on his desk, his way of making the point that they were waiting. After a crash development cycle, they were cooling their heels, anticipating the go-ahead.

Noha said to Jaron, "My father was in the navy. He said there was a saying, "hurry up and wait."

Jaron said, "Stop complaining. You're in the military. You don't have the luxury of knowing why or when. We follow orders."

"OK, but it has to have some sort of logic."

"No, it doesn't. Are you saying you know what all those above us know? That you know the ramifications of when Sophia is released or not released?"

"No, but if they didn't need it right away, why rush."

"Because they might not know when or even if they need it. My guess is the Iranian announcement is the kicker. Want to bet?"

"No," he said.

"You have plenty of other things to do. Stop being a prima donna and get to work."

Jaron's cell buzzed, and he looked at the text. "I'm going to see Hagan."

Jaron walked up to Hagan's office. Seeing him through the glass window, Hagan waved him to enter. Kreiner and the silent woman were again in the office. Hagan held up a paper for Jaron to see and then placed it on the desk. He then made a point of signing under two other fresh signatures. Again, he turned and made a copy and handed it to Jaron.

"This is the authorization to release Sophia immediately."

"Yes, sir," Jaron said.

CHAPTER 47

Gash-Barka Region
Eritrea.

Lange's men sat in the desert protecting Okoro and Sjoberg, waiting for exfil.

Something like ten or so long minutes passed, and the distant sound of approaching vehicles grew more distinct. Soon all wheels came to an abrupt stop in a dusty cloud.

Danny said, "Let me help you up." He stood with Okoro's arm over his shoulder and walked over to the second Eagle. Danny helped him into the rear seat and strapped him in.

Okoro handed Danny an empty water bottle, "More water?" He said.

Danny said, "Let's wait a few minutes. More water in your condition, and the rough ride ahead might be a problem."

Making space for Sjoberg required some creativity. Danny stood between the two on the step used by the fifty-caliber gunner with his head sticking out the top of the Eagle. As the team medic, it was not a familiar position. Everyone else loaded up. Lange checked the area for any signs identifying the group and shut the door.

"Let's go." He said.

The Eagle bouncing over ruts in the desert made for a rough ride back. When they stopped, Okoro saw a larger winged aircraft. They walked him up the ramp and into the rear. Danny gave him a blanket and more thoroughly checked his vitals.

Danny looked up and said, "You're gonna be fine."

Lange walked up to Okoro, "Before we get in the air and the noise, someone wants to talk to you."

Lange put a headset over Okoro's head.

"Mr. Okoro," Okoro heard a voice say. "This is Kate Adler. How are you?"

Okoro was starting to feel the effects of the shot. His head was clearer, but he didn't expect someone he had only heard about talking in his ear.

He could only say. "Ms. Adler?"

"Yes, Mr. Okoro, are you well enough to talk?"

"Yes, yes I am." Kate was someone so far from his relationship to the company he never expected she'd even know his name let alone call. From his perspective, way up the management chain was Mr. Gerlach. The closest he came to actual contact with upper management was Mr. Contee, who oversaw all the offices in eastern Africa.

"Mr. Okoro, we're so sorry for what happened to you, and we'll do all we can to make it up to you and your family. We relocated your wife and children to a safe location as a precaution."

"Thank you, when can I go home?"

"We'll reunite you with your family as quickly as possible."

She looked at Brad, who silently said, "hours."

"It shouldn't be more than a few hours."

"Are these people who rescued me with the company? Who are they?"

"No, they aren't with the company, but who they are is not important right now. I'll be kept informed of your status and ensure your smooth transition to normal life."

Okoro thought that was the second time someone wouldn't disclose who executed the rescue. He said, "I don't know what to say."

"You don't need to say anything. I'll leave you now as you're in capable hands."

Okoro said, "Again, I thank you."

Kate turned to Brad and said. "Make sure that family ends up feeling safe. If we have to transfer him to another office, make sure that happens. Let me know what Gerlach ends up doing."

Okoro took off the headset and gave it to Lange, who pulled out a cell phone. "Here, you can call your family directly if you want." He said.

Danny moved over to Mr. Sjoberg. "So you have been here for months?"

"Yes, I thought I was a goner. People say that, but I'd convinced myself it was true. Whoever you people are, thank you."

"Well, you're malnourished, but you seem to be OK otherwise." Danny saw Lange hand Okoro a phone.

"Oh," he said, pulling out a phone and looking for a signal. He handed the phone to him and said, "We're in luck. Call your family before the engines start. We're taking Mr. Okoro back to Asama airport so let them know that's where you'll be for pickup.

After talking to his wife and kids, Okoro looked down the plane at Sjoberg. The man got up and sat down next to him.

Okoro said, "I think we're very lucky, are we not?"

Sjoberg laughed. "No, *I'm* the lucky one. I was there when someone else was part of a rescue mission. My company was not going to come after me. I have to admit I thought I was going to die out there.

CHAPTER 48

Fordow Enrichment Facility
Iran

Power shack number four housed six massive generators providing power to the centrifuges in the Fordow enrichment facility. Five thousand of the tall tube-like mechanisms, spinning inside at high speed, refined and siphoned off the precious molecules of u235. The centrifuges didn't know it was the late shift as they produced the same high-pitched whine twenty-four hours a day. Large control panels displayed the information needed to keep the complex system running smoothly.

An attendant impatiently waited for his replacement so he could go home. He had logged in the final sensor readings and was anxious to leave. He had no idea how or why they hired his replacement as the man was habitually late for everything. He felt a hand from behind coming to rest on his shoulder.

Standing up, he said, "Ahmad, only twenty minutes late. That's a record."

"Relax, enjoy life, my friend. You're going to die of a heart attack."

The bulky regulators worked to control the voltage of the generators in the power shack to a very tight tolerance. The Sophia software activated its malware package changing the voltage parameters of the regulators. The unregulated voltages traveled down buss lines branching out to the enrichment facilitie's delicate equipment.

Neither attendant noticed the slight variations on the master voltage meter positioned high on the panel above their heads.

Ahmad placed his midnight lunch down on the shelf of the console. Right above the plastic container full of food, an orange sensor lit up, indicating a variation in the speed of at least one centrifuge in BANK 23A. Then another monitoring BANK 56C turned to orange. Then BANK 23A's orange light turned red, and an audible alarm sounded. Another sensor for BANK 61C went to orange, and the sequence continued until the panel was an array of flashing lights and the air full of alarms.

Ahmad was on duty when Stuxnet struck, and his mind was connecting what he was seeing and hearing to memories stored in his brain. The noise was eerily familiar.

He yelled, "Run."

Centrifuges in BANK 23A started to rock back and forth. Centrifuge #112 in BANK 23A was the first motor to disintegrate. The flying debris cut into the next unit sitting just 12 inches away. The long thin shiny tube started to fall over into those around it, multiplying into a tornado of sheared metal traveling at super speeds into every inch of the facility's room.

Ahmad was outside the security door on the phone to his night manager. "It's exploding," he yelled.

"What's exploding?"

"Everything."

"Get out of there." The manager said.

The manager hung up and called the chief scientist in charge of the entire complex. It wasn't long before the news had gone up to the highest levels of government.

***

Jaron Gabai walked into Hagen's office to report the run results, finding the same two people present in the first two meetings.

Hagen said, "Jaron, do you have a report?"

"Yes, the Sophia program ran. It reported running to its completion, so we have every expectation we achieved the expected results.

"What?" Kreiner spoke up. "You don't know?"

A cell phone gave off a low gentle ring tone, and the mystery woman in the corner quietly answered.

The challenge by Kreiner annoyed Jaron. He said, "It seems some who manage to get the latest version of Windows up and running assumes they know everything about computers and software."

"Jaron, let's not get into it," Hagen said.

"How *can* we know?" Jaron said to Kreiner. "The Sophia malware destroyed its hosting control system. It committed suicide. One could say that somewhat limits its ability to report on its status."

Hagen saw where this was going and intervened.

"Jaron is right," he said.

The woman in the corner said, "It's done." She diverted the conversation from becoming a shouting match.

It seemed she considered whatever was unfolding in the room as unimportant. She quickly made her way to the door with those being her only words.

Jaron looked at his manager for an explanation.

Hagen shrugged his shoulders and said, "Mossad."

CHAPTER 49

Petrovic's Office
Belgrade

Vanek walked into Petrovic's office.
"Take a load off," Petrovic said. "Tell me, how long before we get to the next attack, hijacking one of their container ships? I don't want to ease the pressure on Morton Roth."

Vanek said, "It's strange making the arrangements for these last two attacks. Dealing with the hijackers and the kidnappers is completely different. Working with these particular kidnappers is like dealing with corporate America. There were contacts, guarantees, and money transfers. Dealing with the group to hijack the container ship is like dealing with a bunch of drunk school children. The khat they chew messes with their heads, but they sure know the sight of cold hard cash. Holland set me up with a suitcase full to take for payment. None of them could understand the concept of transferring money you can't hold in your hand."

"Did you get the hijackers set up with the details?"

"Yes," Vanek said, "they have the coordinates of when the Gran-Explorer will be in range. It needs to be very close to the coast. Previously they used larger mother ships, allowing them to be farther out into the ocean. However, coalition warships sunk most of them. They're supposed to board the ship in two days and remain aboard for at least 24 hours. After that, they can do what they want with the ship and crew. That gives us enough time for a press release announcing to the world another Morton Roth problem."

"Excellent. What about the kidnapping?"

"They're keeping the hostage out in the desert, I think. They wouldn't tell me. Get this; they said I was a security risk. They're over the top regarding secrecy, especially their own."

Petrovic said, "I like how they take care of business."

Vanek started dialing his phone.

"What are you doing?" Petrovic asked.

"I'm calling to get you an update on the hostage. I figured it was going to be the next question."

The next thing Vanek heard on the phone was a shout, "Ballo here."

"Yes, Mr. Ballo, it's Havel Vanek. I'm calling to get an update on the hostage."

Vanek heard heavy breathing on the other end and urgent voices and confusion in the background. "So, Mr. Vanek, you want a status? Well, this is the status; you're lucky; I haven't sent our people to shoot you dead."

Vanek's face wrinkled in several places. His eyes grew narrow at the challenge. "Mr. Ballo, I suggest you settle down. Issuing threats to someone requesting an update is not good business. And, issuing death threats to *me* will likely result in you being the one who's dead. Now, why don't we start over."

Petrovic looked startled. He motioned for Vanek to put his phone on speaker.

Bello was shouting. "So you haven't heard? Eight of my men are dead. I've lost my cousin and my brother. I've been doing this for seven years and have never lost a single guard, and with you, we lose the whole lot of them. I strongly suggest, Mr. Vanek, you don't step foot in this country, or you're a dead man."

"Let's back up. Can you tell me what happened? Did we lose the guards or the hostage, or both?

"Both. Your hostage and another who wasn't even yours are both gone. We were close to terms with the insurance company to pay eight hundred thousand for the second hostage. Now he's disappeared into the night just like the team that rescued him."

"*Who* rescued him?"

"How am I supposed to know? Some special forces team came in and took out our best people. If I knew your location right now, I would be there tonight and strangle you myself. At this moment, I regret the secrecy we insisted on to protect each of us."

Vanek looked at an increasingly concerned Petrovic. "Mr. Ballo, we certainly didn't want this. Furthermore, we don't know who did it, so get yourself under control so we can figure out what happened."

"Don't tell me you don't know because you're lying. We asked you specifically if the hostage was a U.S. citizen or affiliated with any other organization that had the capability of launching this type of attack. You said no. We don't kidnap Americans to avoid this situation completely because they send in the cowboys. According to the one still alive, this team was in uniform, but it was too dark to determine who they were."

"You lied and will pay the price. Our precautions have kept this from happening until business with you. I'm sending my people to take care of whoever authorized this operation on your side, and I know it isn't you."

Petrovic sat back in his chair in anger. He motioned he wanted the phone. Vanek knew he'd only make the situation worse.

Vanek shook his head no and said, "Ballo, I don't think that's a good idea. That person is not someone you threaten."

"Mr. Vanek. Who do you think *we* are? We're not the starving people you see in those charity ads. I went to Brown University, and we're in daily contact with some very dangerous people. Knowing where someone is and having access to those who kill for a living is a deadly combination. I'll find you. We also have technical resources that go beyond a Facebook page. My name is Akiiki Ballo, and you tell your boss I'll avenge my brother's death."

"Mr. Ballo, I would strongly suggest you not pursue your revenge. My boss has more resources than you will see in twenty lifetimes, but he also has access to those who kill for a living. What has occurred is a tragedy, but it was also unforeseen. We didn't know this was a possibility."

"Remember, the name is Akiiki Ballo." The line went dead.

Petrovic was red in the face and sweating. He slammed his hand on the desk and, leaning forward, shouted at Vanek. "Find him and kill him, you hear?"

The desk phone rang. Petrovic punched the speaker button with undue force. "You're on speaker," he almost shouted.

"Whoa," Holland said. "Is there a problem? Because if there isn't, I've bad news. Someone rescued the hostage."

Petrovic said, "I just found out. Do you know who did it?"

Holland said, "I don't know, but they left eight guards dead in the process. One was the ring leader's brother, and he was not happy. He's tossing threats about coming after us for revenge killings."

"How did he get your number."

"I needed confirmation on the deposit."

"Revenge, it's a joke," Petrovic said. What can the guy do? Besides, we're going to kill him first." Petrovic looked at Vanek, "You kept everything anonymous, right?"

"Absolutely," Vanek said. "There's no trace back to us unless it's through the payments or that phone number."

Holland laughed, "Not a chance that's going to happen. First, the number is a burner phone, and second, there isn't any info on the bank accounts. At least anything that's accessible."

Petrovic said, "This means there's no longer a hostage, but it may not matter. The press releases have gone out, and we inflicted as much damage as possible with the operation. Except for the damage that will come down on that Ballo idiot."

"Time will tell," Vanek said.

CHAPTER 50

Washington DC

Devroe stood outside the oval office while a group of people from the Olympic Committee filed out of a meeting.

Devroe says, "So are we going to host an Olympics?"

"Not a chance; it was a courtesy meeting. They know the decision lies with the city involved and want me to apply pressure. Besides, we have more pressing matters. What about last night's incident?"

Devroe said, "So remember that unofficial notice we got from Israel, indicating something was imminent? I'm sure it was the cyber-attack last night. Our people say by the time the dust settled, it destroyed almost four thousand of their newest and most efficient separators. The attack also took out the power plant feeding the separator plant. It essentially destroyed the Fordow enrichment facility."

The president said, "Well, that puts an interesting spin on things."

"I agree," Devroe said. "Unlike blaming Israel for bombing something to bits with photos to the world, it's tough to prove who committed a cyber-attack. So, picking up the pieces, Iran presented to the world a damage assessment blaming Israel."

The president said, "The Ayatollah didn't get what he wanted as far as an image for the nightly news. So forcing the world and us to tell Israel to back off is somewhere between difficult and impossible. It seems to me the Iranians now have destroyed Fordow and haven't a thing to show for it." Perez thought for a second. "What bothers me is they're smarter than that."

Devroe said, "It's no coincidence the attack occurred literally within hours of the announcement. The Israelis must have known it was coming. They always seem to be one step ahead of us *and* Iran."

"I agree," Perez said, "Israel has an amazing network inside that country. Regardless, we need to get Iran to back off the 90% commitment."

"That's a tall order. Do you think it's possible?"

Perez said, "I have to try. We also need to tell Koffman privately not to react with any further attacks. Meanwhile, publicly, I'll try to get both of them to realize continuing this tit for tat will start a war."

Devroe said, "I'll have Konner call Koffman and convey our message. Also, please don't shoot the messenger as I lay this logic out. There are two ways the Ayatollah can solve his Israeli problem. Go to 90%, and the world reacts and stops Israel. That option is now gone. Second, the Ayatollah plans to get 90% grade somewhere else without enriching it in-house. Both would qualify as permanent."

"That's impossible."

"I'm not sure about impossible but doubtful rings with me."

Perez looked at this friend, "Stephen, if that happens, there will be a nuclear explosion in the oval office. I won't let that happen—period.

Devroe's cell phone went off. He saw it was David, his deputy. He put it on speaker. "David, the president is also here. What is it?"

David said, "We just came across an intercept, and the information is critical."

Devroe thought. "David never interrupted him in the oval office." He said, "Of course, what is it?"

David said, "Not over your cell."

"Oh," Devroe said. Where are you?"

"Just outside the door."

Devroe looked at the president, and he nodded. Devroe said, "Come on in."

David appeared at the door with a look of concern.

Devroe and the president were sitting on the couches facing each other. David came in and said, "We received an anonymous tip the Iranians are trying to buy weapons-grade u235 on the open market. It's coming in via air directly to the Natanz facility."

Perez immediately stood up, saying loudly, "What? When?"

Devroe shook his head. "Just call me Nostradamus."

David said, "We don't' know when. The American embassy in Belgrade received the tip through the front gate, so we don't have any confirming information. It could be wrong, but it fits nicely into the puzzle unfolding in Iran."

Devroe said, "Let's slow down here. Anyone could've left the message hoping we would react somehow to further their agenda."

"Still," David said, "you needed to know right away."

"That's a fact." The president turned to Devroe and said, "I want all hands on deck validating this intel. Right now. It's the top priority. It's 'sink the Bismark' time, and I'm serious."

Devroe nodded and said to David, "Go crank everyone up, and let's find out if we have a massive problem or someone is pulling our chain."

Perez walked behind his desk and sat down. "We still need to have the Israelis hold off on any further action until we can validate this new information."

Devroe said. "That means I still call Konner and have him talk with Koffman?"

"Right," Perez said, somewhat distracted. He was thinking about the impact of David's info.

* * *

Devroe called Konner. "Have you read the news?"

"You mean the little incident at the Fordow plant?"

"Yes, the president needs you to contact the Israelis again. Tell them their cyber-attack made their displeasure with the Iranians known to the world. Now, get them to refrain from any further action. The president needs time to get everyone back to the negotiating table. Assure them the president is fully committed to getting Iran to back off the 90% declaration."

"Got it. When?"

"Now. We don't have time to put you on a plane. It will have to be virtual. Mossad can set up a secure connection."

Devroe paused. "There's been a development. We received a tip left at the American embassy in Belgrade indicating the Iranians are trying to buy weapons-grade u235 on the open market."

Konner took a breath. "You can't be serious?"

"We have no idea who left the tip or what their agenda might be. We have a full-court press on validating the info."

"Stephen, that's beyond serious."

"No lie. But again, we don't know if it's true. Right now, we don't know if it's just a prank. Perez went ballistic at even the possibility. I mean, I've never seen that side of him—pretty much a "not on my watch" sort of thing. Tell Koffman the president is serious about making the Iranians back down from the promises of increasing enrichment. Don't tell him about the possibility of their buying it on the black market."

CHAPTER 51

Vianden Castle

Konner sat in an office Brad set up and logged into the secure Israeli link set up by their people in Gav-yam Negev. Konner insisted the meeting be off the books. Konner could see the attendees sitting around what looked like a dining room table. It was a comfortable room with low light. Teschner, the deputy prime minister, said, "Mr. Houston do you have a video and audio feed?"

"Yes," Konner said, "everything is working perfectly."

Prime Minister Koffman took over. "Mr. Houston, per your wishes, we have kept those participating to a minimum for security reasons. We have only General Sitzman from the IDF, Mr. Laszlo Teschner, the assistant prime minister, and Ms. Umma Galicki, Director of Mossad." Somewhat irritated, he said, "She seems to be running late. We're in my private residence to avoid any indication this meeting is official."

Devroe described the prime minister as a mountain one couldn't move on a given subject, and Iran getting the bomb was his primary concern. General Sitzman had participated in the 1970 Arab-Israeli war at age 18 and rose through the ranks to head the Israeli Defense Force. He was very respected in the

Pentagon and, having gone to Carnegie for an engineering degree, very comfortable in the states.

Teschner was the Dr. Devroe to Koffman. A longtime friend, he orchestrated most of the prime minister's political successes.

Koffman said, "We'll proceed without Ms. Galicki for the moment."

As he finished, Konner saw a woman enter the picture on the monitor, approach the table, pull out a chair, and sit down. She said nothing.

The prime minister, looking her way, said, "May I introduce Ms. Galicki, who has just joined us."

Konner saw an elegant woman with the air of a moneyed heritage. There wasn't anything frivolous about her. The suit she wore had clean lines with no hint of a pattern. Her blouse was bright white without anything approaching lace. Her black hair neatly pulled back in a bun seemed to make a statement. She walked with an authority one was wise to respect. Konner knew her reputation as a person of few words and a manager that didn't suffer fools.

"Please, Mr. Houston," Koffman said. "I understand you have a private message from President Perez."

"Yes," Konner said. "Yesterday was not a great day for peace given the announcement by the Iranians and your swift response seriously damaging the Fordow enrichment facility."

Koffman didn't respond to the obvious.

Konner continued, "We believe there's a single reason the Iranians initially made their now-famous announcement. They wanted to use the world's negative reaction to your bombing a facility to stop your attacks on their 'peaceful' nuclear program."

The general said, "Please, Mr. Houston, let's not even pretend by using the word peaceful."

The prime minister made a subtle gesture telling the general to allow Konner to talk.

Konner said, "It didn't work, of course, as a cyber-attack is hard to publicize. Now that Iran has made that mistake, the president strongly suggests you not embark on any further retaliatory operations. The president is fully committed to getting Iran to abandon the 90% enrichment effort. But the Ayatollah can't be seen to look weak to his ruling class. We need to give him some room to maneuver. Another attack would remind everyone of the Ayatollah's inability to stop your constant efforts against their enrichment program."

General Sitzman said, "Holding off as you say is asking us not to defend ourselves."

"No general," Konner said. "you're incorrect. That would be the case if the request were permanent. It's only temporary."

"Mr. Prime Minister," Mrs. Galicki said, "I apologize for being late. Mr. Houston, it was not a reflection on the importance of this meeting. The delay occurred evaluating a recently received piece of disturbing intel."

She addressed Koffman, "Mr. Prime Minister, I was going to brief you later, but given the direction of this meeting, with your permission, I would like to present it now."

Koffman said, "At your discretion given Mr. Houston's presence. It's your call."

Galicki said, "Thank you. We believe Iran is shopping for 128kg (282lbs) of weapons-grade u235. They plan to transport it by air directly to the Natanz facility. They're trying to buy it on the open market since we have continued to hamper their ability to produce it domestically."

The general said, "That's enough to make two bombs. That's all they need."

Konner was surprised that the Israelis also knew about Iran shopping for the material. It went to the heart of his conversation with Devroe. "Are you sure as that's a serious escalation? Is it because of yesterday's attack?"

"We know very little at this time but suspect it's been in the works. We don't know for how long. The exact amount of time we're still working on. But I'm sure we can all agree, when they started doesn't matter."

Ben David said, "Mrs. Galicki, this is very disturbing. What's your source?"

"We received and followed up on a tip left at the Israeli embassy in Belgrade."

General Sitzman sat up from his previously casual posture. He said forcefully, "Mr. Prime Minister, this is an existential threat to our country and must be investigated to the fullest."

Mrs. Galicki minced no words, "Stay in your own lane, general. I have my best people on this, and I don't need your oversight."

The prime minister ignored the frosty exchange.

Konner winced, not wanting to show favoritism for either side. He said, "One doesn't go to the corner store to buy this stuff. Who could complete a transaction of this magnitude and think they could get away with it?"

Mrs. Galicki said, "Despite significant effort after the fall of the Soviet Union, there are u235 leaks constantly being investigated and plugged. Until now, no one thought Iran would be stupid enough to expose itself to the debilitating sanctions such a transaction would bring."

The general said, "Let alone us bombing the hell out of them."

Konner said, "At this point, I have to say we also have a source that believes Iran is trying to purchase the u235 material."

"Things are getting interesting." Mrs. Galicki said, "What's *your* source?"

Konner looked at her and said. "*Also,* a tip, ours was left at the American embassy in Belgrade.

Silence fell over the meeting.

Mrs. Galicki said, "There's obviously a third actor out there."

Konner continued, "We have a separate source saying your repeated attacks have almost forced the Ayatollah to promise the opposition in his government he'll end the problem once and for all."

Ben-Davis said. "What's that mean?"

Konner said, "We don't have a definitive answer."

Galicki said, "And what's your source for that?"

"An Iranian ambassador with loose lips and an informant with access to intel inside the Iranian embassy."

Sitzman said, "That doesn't tell us what or who was your source."

Konner said, "I'm afraid that's all you're going to get right now as I didn't get clearance to mention it at all. This information opens up the possibility the Ayatollah is trying to solve his problem by going around the enrichment attempt and purchasing the u235 uranium directly."

The general, clearly agitated, said, "Mr. Prime Minister, we can't sit here discussing this meeting after meeting. We need to strike now."

Koffman cast an unmistakeably impatient if not disdainful glance at the general. The general, an intelligent man, suspended his heated thoughts for the moment.

Konner said, "That brings up the question of who could complete or broker such a transaction obviously outside moral let alone legal bounds."

"I can think of three," Galicki said. " Corrupt Pakistani intelligence agency, which loosely guards their nuclear material. Next would be the Balcescu group, a highly organized criminal gang in Romania with ties to the old Soviet Union. Then there's everyone's favorite, Petrovic's TerraDyne out of Serbia. He'll do anything for money. We have stopped more than one of his operations transferring illegal cargo at sea bound for the Gaza strip. They don't even notice. They bring in a new ship and continue operations hoping we don't find the next effort."

Konner blinked at the mention of Petrovic's name.

It didn't go unnoticed by Mrs. Galicki. With a knowing smile, she said, "The TerraDyne option, Mr. Houston, is an organization you're very familiar with, am I not correct?" Implying she knew a lot more about Konner's personal life.

Konner ignored her.

The prime minister said, "Mr. Houston, this information changes everything. Tell your president all bets are off the table as far as restricting our ability to carry out any mission we believe is required. We'll pursue this information with all our resources, and if we find that such a shipment exists, we'll move immediately to protect our interests."

The general said, "Like bomb the Natanz facility."

Koffman said, "Natanz is where they'll assemble the bombs. If we can't find the u235, then we'll destroy their ability to construct the bombs."

Konner said, "An attack like that would be very costly in terms of lives and assets lost."

"I don't want to sound callous, Mr. Houston, but that's the IDF's job, and you must compare that to we're a country of almost ten million people. A country Iran has openly declared it will destroy. Please emphasize to President Perez, I said immediately. This more than meets the Menachem Began doctrine of preemptively striking at anyone who can eliminate the Israeli nation. This situation is more dangerous than the 1976 war."

Konner felt the objectives given by Devroe slipping away.

Koffman added, "We'll provide Dr. Devroe with any intelligence regarding this new development, as we would expect from you. However, if proven to be true, any idea of holding off while the president tries to get Iran back to the table is a non-starter. We have no option but to act first and suffer the fall out later."

Konner said, "I know you have a responsibility to protect your country and its people. Consider this; even if Iran obtains a quantity of 90% u235, they can't make a bomb in the next two days or even a year. All we're asking is to give the president a chance to stop this shipment. You would still be protecting the population if you allowed us to do this for you. If we can't stop this shipment or remove the material in a reasonable amount of time, then your fallback position is to start a war that will involve the entire middle east."

The prime minister thought long enough the room became heavy. The silence carried the weight of lives and possibly the future of his country. "Tell Perez we'll wait two days, but no longer. Rest assured, Mr. Houston, after that, if we find actionable intelligence, we *will* act upon the threat."

Hearing the prime minister acquiesce to Konner's logic, the general slammed his briefing book closed in disgust, saying, "Unbelievable."

"Suck it up, general," Galicki said. "Not all problems have to be solved with your toys."

CHAPTER 52

Vianden Castle

Kate was with the security team in the control room. "Penn, can you let the operations guys know how much we appreciate their professional manner, and how they go about doing what we ask?"

Penn said, "Certainly. They're just as happy to have Okoro back as we are, but I'll certainly convey your thanks."

Kate said, "I said after we had Mr. Okoro back and safe, we would start fighting back against TerraDyne. Do whatever it takes to save this organization and the people who work for it. Remember our actions here and in the near future will affect the lives of thousands. So, what do we have after reviewing Mom's input?"

Penn said, "Yes, she supplied a whole list of things we can do to TerraDyne and Petrovic himself. I want to remind everyone that just because we decided to fight back doesn't mean TerraDyne will stop their attempts to bring us down. Their history indicates anything but that.

"As far as options, we have put together a list. We believe a good first step is your meeting with Petrovic personally. Let him know we aren't going away and giving in to his demands."

Brad said, "I think the only way we'll get his attention for a meeting is if he thinks Kate's giving up."

Elena said, "We could put out a press release that the board is meeting to discuss the current problems and alternatives. Petrovic will read that and jump at a meeting."

Kate said, "That's admitting to the entire world we're in trouble and thinking of giving up. That's too much false information being made public. Once minds have decided, it's hard to turn them around. Our approach has to be more private."

Penn said, "We could find out his schedule and sort of ambush him into talking with Kate. He'll be surprised if nothing else."

Kate said, "This meeting isn't going to take long as just being there will speak volumes. We want to make sure he knows he's taken this far enough. I like the idea of meeting him somewhere unexpectedly. It's a sign he's not in total control."

Brad said, "We need to have something else happen off the list during that meeting to show we mean business. I like Mom's idea of locating one or some of his bank accounts and withdrawing the funds. That will certainly get his attention."

Loren spoke up, "I might have something on that. Mom organized all the information contained in her report into a searchable database. I looked up bank account information and got a long list, but most were still labeled inaccessible. She's still working on accessing the full TerraDyne network. Despite that, she provided login information to three Panama bank accounts with HBSC." They aren't his main accounts. It looks like these are for daily working cash and overnight deposit holdings. I can set it up so the funds transfer would happen right in front of him."

"That's good," Kate said. "How long to set it up?"

Loren said, "Not long at all. We can put it on a tablet you bring with you. It will have a software button preprogrammed to transfer the funds as soon as you touch it. It will then provide a statement showing the balance."

Brad said, "Or lack thereof. I like it."

Kate said, "It would only take one account for him to be concerned. If he saw a couple in a row go to zero, he'd definitely get the point. I don't think it's enough to back him off, but it's a good start. Let's go with that. Does Mom know where he spends his time so we can get close?"

"Right now, he's in the air," Elena said. "He's on a huge commercial-size private plane. He spends most of this time going from one of his businesses to another."

Loren said, "We could start with the flight plans he has to submit before he flies." She started typing, and shortly after, a list appeared on a large screen in the operations room.

Brad said, "Those are from last month."

"As I said, Mom is updating it all the time, but perhaps that's all she could get."

At that moment, the screen refreshed, and a new current list appeared.

Loren blinked at the sudden appearance. Everyone took a second to read the new information. No one except Loren and Elena noticed the latest flight information appeared exactly when needed. It showed the next three flights and possible reasons Petrovic might want to be in that city or country.

Elena and Loren shared a knowingly curious look but kept it to themselves.

Loren said, "Mom indicates Petrovic is going to his office in Rotterdam from Serbia. That would give us an exact time and place for the ambush or rendezvous, if you will. It shows an appointment at 2:00 with someone, and he doesn't appear to have any hotel reservations. That means, after the meeting, he'll want to be taking off or at least get back to the plane. We could be waiting on the tarmac when he returns."

Kate was leaning on a desk and said, "I like the idea of confronting him face to face. Mom's information on his police record indicates he's the kind of guy who doesn't like a woman telling him things he doesn't want to hear."

Elena let out an infrequent laugh, "Let alone watch some of his money just disappear."

Brad smiled as they've had many conversations about the very focused Elena loosening up.

Kate said, "OK, we'll start by withdrawing money from those bank accounts where we have access. I would also like to have an additional surprise. It may not be possible. I need to call Avery, and I'll let you know."

***

After the meeting, Elena said to Loren. "Can I see you in my office?"

Loren walked back with Elena towards her office. Elena closed the door.

Loren was unsure what was going on, but this seemed rather dramatic.

Elena said, "It's the flight information. Right after Mom printed the Brimstone report, it took me back to a paper I wrote in artificial intelligence. Don't you think it was strange that Mom started to print or release the Brimstone Report seconds after Kate decided to fight back?

Loren said, "So you also noticed that."

"We have seen strange things we couldn't track down—almost all of them regarding Kate's safety. Some time ago, I started keeping track. Remember the ambulance no one called that just appeared when she was hurt? Then the Brussels cell towers mysteriously turn off, so a bomb that would have killed Kate couldn't be triggered. Or, when Mom started taking over when they kidnapped Penn during the gun battle in Paris. She called the Uber ride so Kate and Brad could escape."

Loren said, "My favorite was the self-driving Tesla that rescued her and Konner that night in Paris."

"What do you make of it?"

Loren said, "Well, we wondered why she was silent during the attacks and didn't contribute much. It's almost as if she was gathering information and was waiting for Kate to set the course."

"Still," Elena said, "The second Kate said the words, "I'm coming after you, Mr. Petrovic, and you should be afraid," the printers took off on their wild ride. It says Mom was listening and reacted to what she heard."

They both sat there for a bit absorbing the line of thought.

Loren said, "Either it's a huge coincidence, or Mom was gathering information and decided she'd had enough to share, or she heard Kate's words and presented a path to accomplish her decision."

"You just said, "heard Kate's words." Hearing requires active monitoring and then interpreting what you hear and respond."

Loren said, "That's more than just interesting."

"Every time someone threatens Kate, we get the same Primary Protocol coming up on the screen? This time Mom actually said something like, "You can't harm Delta1; it's the first law? It's almost like Mom knew. If Mom knows when something or someone has threatened Kate, that puts Mom's actions in new territory."

Kate said her father always told her, "Mom would take care of her." Several times now, we have written it off to chance. It's no longer chance. I don't think this is an accident as Kate's father directed the design."

Loren said, "What's she using for sensors? More important do we tell Kate?"

Elena thought for a moment. "Good question. I think we don't have a choice."

"I think you're right," Loren said.

"Kate has enough on her plate. We should wait and tell her after she has dealt with Petrovic because whatever this is, it's been in place for some time. And it's nothing but positive for Kate."

Loren said, "Yeah, let's wait."

CHAPTER 53

Rotterdam
Netherlands

Kate sat in the back of a limo on the airport tarmac in the shadow of Petrovic's giant Boeing 777, the largest private jet in the world.

Elena said, "I don't like this guy. And I'm not on board with her seeing him."

"It's OK," Brad said. "Lieutenant Petty from the operations side is the driver, and he's armed. Penn is also there, so we're OK."

Elena said. "What earpiece are we using."

Loren said, "Top Pro Micro. It will transmit a weak signal to her phone; then, blue tooth sends it to the G9t phone in the limo. Through the G9t, we have total communication. It's great because it's completely invisible. There's no plastic tube going from her ear to the transmitter in a coat."

Sitting in the car, Penn said, "Comm check."

Brad said, "We have you, Penn. Can you read?"

"Affirmative," he said.

Brad said. "Kate, are you there?"

"Yes, I'm here." She said.

Petty, the driver said, "Comm check. All set here."

Penn said, "I have an approaching limo. It's time to get this rolling."

Penn looked into the back seat, and Kate said, "We're good back here."

Petrovic's vehicle stopped, and Penn opened his door and stood outside with his hands clasped in front. Two security types hurriedly exited Petrovic's limo. One stayed by the limo back door, and Vanek walked forward with total concentration on Penn.

Penn pulled open his suit coat, revealing an absence of a weapon as one of the men approached. Vanek patted Penn down and motioned to look inside Kate's vehicle.

"No," Penn said. "You're not going in there."

Elena said, "Why did he say that?"

"I don't know," Brad said.

Vanek backed up, and they shared a few tense seconds.

Vanek heard Petrovic's voice from behind him. "It's OK."

Petrovic had exited his car and, walking towards Penn, said, "You're Kate's man, aren't you?"

Vanek was still standing staring at Penn. "Vanek, we're fine here. Get everything on the plane."

Silently and reluctantly, Vanek retreated.

"Yes, I am," Penn said, responding to the question. "Ms. Adler would like to speak to you."

Petrovic walked up, and Kate rolled down the dark window.

"Mr. Petrovic, we meet again after events in Tanzania."

"What a pleasant surprise." He said, looking around the area. "What brings you here. How did you know I was here as my travel schedule is pretty confidential?"

"How isn't important, Mr. Petrovic."

"Please, call me Milosh."

Kate continued deliberately, starting with, "Mr. Petrovic, I've some things I would like you to share with you. If you want to come inside for just a few minutes, we can discuss them here and be on our way."

"Oh no," he said, waving his hand towards the plane. Please be my guest inside. We can get out of the noise." He looked at Penn and said, "Bring your man with you, and we can discuss your concerns in luxury and certainly with more space."

"Very well," Kate said.

"This is not in the script," Brad said to Elena.

Elena said, "Penn is letting her get on the plane."

Brad said, "I'm sure he knows what he's doing."

"Still," Elena said. "I'm not sure that was a good idea."

"Truth be known, I'm not so hot on it either."

Kate reached for the small tablet and envelope next to her on the seat. She then took Penn's offered hand, helping her out of the car. Penn walked around to Petty and said something.

Brad switched to full comm. "Penn, what's going on."

Penn responded, "She wants to go onto the plane. I'm going with her."

Brad looked at Elena and Loren and shook his head.

Penn started up the boarding ramp with Kate.

Petrovic said, "I would imagine you're prepared to make an offer or at least have some concerns."

"You could say that," Kate responded.

Petrovic stepped aside at the top of the ramp to let Kate enter first. We can sit in these facing chairs and be comfortable." He turned and whispered something to one of the attendants.

"Here," he said, rotating one of two oversized sofa-like chairs separated by a small writing table. "Is this acceptable?"

"Very," Kate said, sitting down.

Vanek pointed to a couch for Penn in full view of Kate on the other side of the wide cabin. Vanek moved away about 10 feet but stayed standing on Penn's side of the plane. An attendant placed water on the table as Petrovic sat down. He looked up at the nearest person and said. "Leave us. All of you." Pointing to Vanek, he said. "You too." They cleared the area. Of course, Penn didn't move.

Petrovic said, "So I've heard Morton Roth and Adler industries have been going through some tough times. I'm very sorry to hear that. About ten years ago, we expanded too quickly and suffered liquidity problems that we eventually overcame. Your problems, I'm afraid to say, are different."

"Mr. Petrovic, I'm certain you're intimately aware of each and every problem my companies are facing. Let's not pretend what's going on here. You're trying to drive down the price of my company to purchase it. You want the Tanzania contracts and Morton Roth's fleet of ships. You want the ships because your inventory is not large enough to service your agreements with the North Koreans."

Petrovic was certainly surprised but didn't show it. He leaned over and took the cap off the water bottle in front of Kate and, holding it up, said, May I?"

Kate nodded.

While pouring the water into her glass, Petrovic said, "You think you're well informed, Ms. Adler. I, for one, don't know anything about that. We don't have any contracts with the North Koreans. I thought we might be able to help each other. After all, it isn't every day one sees a woman, the weaker sex, become as successful as you have become although you did have help from your father, did you not? It didn't all occur on your watch."

"Any accomplishments I may have are secondary to the fact I got there in a manner that would make my father proud. In several areas, I exceed you, the size of our shipping fleets being one, and in several other areas you know nothing about."

"Ms. Adler. I've been in the unforgiving battleground of business for a long time. On the other hand, you're a trust fund baby, a neophyte, playing a game you're ill-equipped to win. You've spent your time leaning on your companies, being managed by others, while you have become a very respected charity princess, admirable work, to be sure. Contrasting that, I've acquired a set of proven, very effective tools to bring people like you to their knees. Don'tconsider us in the same league."

Kate picked up on something. She saw the unsteady grip on his water glass as he took a drink. He noticed it too and set it down. "Does it bother you that a woman claims to be your equal, perhaps your superior?"

"That's awfully confrontational, don't you think? Of course not," Petrovic said too quickly. "I fear no one."

"Who you fear or deny is irrelevant as I'm here to inform you your aggressive efforts towards my company will be met equally and forcefully. You might say, my feminine gloves are off. Given what I perceive to be a slight, because I'm a woman, makes what's going to happen even more enjoyable."

"Whatever you have in mind, Ms. Adler will not be enough to stop the proven business formula generating profits while you were still in university. Just what do you *think* is going to happen, Ms. Adler? I would be most interested."

Kate looked at Penn, who was tapping on the tablet's screen. He got up and handed it to her.

"What's this?" Petrovic asked.

"Trouble. Not trouble for me but trouble for you."

She put the tablet on the table, turned it around for Petrovic to see, and said, "These are the online summary pages for three of your bank accounts in Panama."

"How could you know...." He started to say. He pressed one of the buttons under the window next to the chair. "Get me, Holland," he said.

A man quickly stepped into the area with a laptop he'd been working on under his arm. Petrovic handed him the tablet. "She says these are our bank accounts."

Standing next to them, Holland put his laptop down and studied the tablet's screen. In seconds he said to Kate. "How did you get these?"

Kate put her hand up, wanting the tablet back. "Do you see that button in the corner?" Kate showed him.

Holland didn't say anything.

"Well, I do," she said. "When I press it, you will see the balance in those accounts disappear. It's meant to be a small demonstration of what could lie in front of you if you persist in attacking Morton Roth. We could've gone after your investment accounts."

Before Petrovic realized what was happening, she pressed the button and handed it back to Holland.

He looked at the screen and said, "What the hell. You can't do that." He looked at Petrovic and said, "It's a setup. You need access codes and passwords; one can't just walk into someone else's bank account."

"I'm sorry, Mr. Holland, was it? When you check from your laptop, you will see I've done that." She stood up and handed the envelope to Petrovic. "I think you will find this interesting. I'll show myself out." She said.

Kate, seemingly unconcerned, gathered her things. With Penn, she headed for the plane's exit.

Petrovic, still seated, looked up at Holland and said, "What happened?"

Holland looked at the screen and said, "The money is gone. She did it remotely right in front of us."

"How did she do that?"

"I've no idea," Holland said.

Vanek started for the door.

Petrovic said, "Where are you going?"

"I'm going to stop them."

Petrovic waved a somewhat defeated hand. "No, let them go. They know we can't do anything here. It would cause a scene. Something I'm sure she factored into this meeting. Everyone, prepare for takeoff; let's get out of here. I have some thinking to do."

Holland was opening the envelope as Petrovic was talking.

"What's that," he said.

Holland didn't even go to the second page. He looked down at the seated Petrovic and said. "It's a low ball offer to buy the company."

Looking at Holland, Petrovic says, "Whose company.?"

Holland said, "Your company."

"I'm not putting up with this. It's now personal. How can she even think about such a ridiculous proposal.?"

Holland looked at his boss, knowing what occurred in his therapy sessions. It didn't take a genius to figure his boss out. "I think she was trying to get to you by telling you your business isn't as valuable as you think it is. However, balance sheets, revenue, and profitability are facts. They say the company is worth what we believe it is. The fact she's saying something different doesn't affect anything."

Petrovic heard the words, but inside it wasn't a balance sheet that bothered him. He couldn't tolerate the audacity of a woman questioning his success.

"Vanek?" He said.

"Yes, boss."

"Did you come up with that list of Adler's charity offices?"

"Yes, there're five spread around the world."

"Pick one."

"How's, Brussels?"

"Sounds perfect."

CHAPTER 54

Rotterdam
Netherlands

Kate's plane sat on the tarmac as Captain Silanos went through his pre-flight checklist.

Penn opened his laptop and waited for the Zoom connection from the plane back to the operations room. He sat across from Kate; after the connection, he directed it to the larger screen on the bulkhead. Brad's face came up first on the screen, followed by tiles with Elena and Loren. They were sitting in the conference room observing Penn and Kate on the room's main screen.

How's everything, Brad asked?"

Kate looked across the table at Penn and said, "I think he got the message."

Penn said, "Let's tell it like it is. Kate kicked his butt from here to Tanzania."

"Well," Kate said. "I'm sticking with he knows the free ride is over."

"What did he say about the offer?" Brad asked.

"Well, surprised will not cover it," Kate said. Their CFO was on the plane and understood right away."

Brad said, "I didn't know about any offer. Not that I should, I don't' have anything to do with the Adler industries side."

"Avery put it together at the last minute. It has a clause that says we can back out any time, but they won't get that far. They'll trash it. Anyway, Avery hasn't worked out all the details we need to make a serious offer. But the look on his face was worth it. How are Mr. Okoro and his family?

"They've been moved to a safe place with security. Mr. Okoro is coming around nicely. His diabetes is stable."

"And the Bremerhaven office?"

"No one was hurt; that's the first thing. Second, all the files in all the offices have backup routines. The office manager is in the process of getting new office space. Lang Gerlach estimates they'll be fully functional in two days."

"It pays to have great people," Kate said.

Brad said, "There's good news on our end. I'll let Elena cover it."

Elena started with, "Mom has penetrated at least part of TerraDyne's network. We have access to their email server, voice messaging system, and traffic over the network to their central drive. We aren't into the drive yet, and now Mom is brute-forcing the password system. They're using a VeraCrypt hidden volume with a seven-word Diceware passphrase. They have some serious security in place, so it has taken a while."

Kate said, "That's great news." She followed with a giggle, "I used to be able to understand all that. Being a security analyst in Munich seems such a long time ago."

Elena said, "It means we'll have at least a partial window into their operations."

"Great," Kate said. "I read through the summary of options in the Brimstone report. What do you think we should do next?"

Brad said, "We're working on a couple of options. One is having Mom issue a fake sanction notice to a country's coast guard where one of TerraDyne's ships will make port. That would result in the ship going through a full inspection which takes a lot of time. Even if they find nothing, taking a ship off the clock is serious, given the lost revenue for even an hour. They lose the docking and loading fees they paid and the dock access space given to another ship. They'll have to reschedule the initial docking slot. It will definitely get their attention. I'll let Loren cover the other option."

"TerraDyne," Loren said, "Has an open pit mine operation in Northern Norway. They use these gigantic trucks that cost millions to move the ore from the bucket shovel to the crushing operation. These trucks are state of the art and self-driving as the path they travel, to and from all day long, is very specific. They're all connected via a high-powered private radio to the dispatch computer. If Mom can gain access, we can shut down the trucks and maybe the shovel for as long as we want. Again, those trucks cost seven million apiece, but the loss of production is what will get their attention."

Kate said, "Let's go with the open-pit mine. He'll understand a significant hit to his bottom line, and no one gets hurt. Put together the details, and I'll make the final decision tomorrow morning." She looked at Elena, "I'm pretty sure about moving forward, so make sure we can move quickly."

"That won't be a problem."

Loren had a smile on her face. Kate said, "Loren, do you have something to say?"

Elena interrupted, "She always gets excited when she can reach out into the world and touch something with her keyboard."

"Well," Loren said. "That's one of the reasons I'm here."

Kate said, "Is that all for right now?"

"Yes," Brad said. "We can pick this up tomorrow morning."

Kate said, "Does anyone know where Konner is?"

Brad said, "He's at the residense."

"OK, I'll be going directly to the residence. It's been a great Zoom meeting. Call if you need me."

CHAPTER 55

Vianden Castle

Kate took a chance and called Konner on her way back from Rotterdam. "This was a long shot. Can you talk?"

Konner said, "Great timing. I just got off a video meeting with the prime minister of an important country. There has been a major development. Due to the subject matter of the calls, I decided the office in the residence was the most secure place."

"I think it's nice you feel comfortable there. However, I'm surprised Ms. Myrla didn't shoot you at the door."

"You could've told me that was a possibility."

Kate said, "How much can you tell me?"

"Not much. I don't feel comfortable talking even over the G9t phone."

"Don't tell Elena; she might not let you back into the building."

"Where are you?" Konner asked.

"On my way back from Rotterdam. I just got off of a video meeting with the group. I should be there in an hour or so. Stay put. I'll meet you there."

***

Myrla took Kate's shoulder bag containing her computer and said, "Welcome home, Ms. Kate. I trust you had a nice flight. Are you hungry? What have you eaten today."

Kate smiled at the ritual. "No, Myrla, I'm fine."

"Is Mr. Houston here?"

"Yes," she said. "I have Mr. Houston in the dungeon downstairs." She said with a straight face.

Kate looked at her and wasn't sure how to respond.

Then Myrla smiled, and Kate said, "Myrla is that you? You're making jokes about Mr. Houston?"

"I believe it will not be again as it was not so good. I let Mr. Houston into your office. I believed that would meet with your approval."

"Well, I don't know yet, Myrla. Let's keep those keys to the dungeon handy."

She pretended to pull out something from her dress pocket and held it up. "Of course Madame." She said.

Kate walked to the office and found Konner typing away on his laptop. When he saw her enter the room, he stood up and came over. He held out his arms and moved to envelop Kate in a hug. "Now, this is a good feeling." He said.

Kate looked up, "What have you done to my head of household. You have turned my praetorian guard into a puppy. Somehow she has taken a liking to you."

"Why should that be a surprise?"

"Because there are at least three previous suitors buried in the back yard."

"Suitor?" Konner said. "I'd hoped to have gotten farther along the trail than that."

"Your's is still a temporary position until HR says you're full time."

"I love it when you talk corporate. How was your day?"

"We decided to confront Petrovic and let him know his quest to own Morton Roth was no longer going to unfold per his previous plan."

"Nice, how did that go. How did you get Petrovic to agree to a meeting?"

"Technically, he didn't agree. We ambushed him as he was boarding his plane. Have you seen the size of a Boeing Business Jet? It's huge."

"No, that's not my world. What was his reaction?"

"Informing him was pretty straightforward; it was the offer to buy his company that surprised him."

Konner looked surprised. "I didn't see that coming. When did you decide to do that?"

"After talking to Avery and the financial people. It's a stretch, but he thinks we can pull it off after we get the value of his company down like he tried to do to us. Even if we can't, we can withdraw the offer. It will have made its point."

"Very impressive. I never expected under that Jane Doe persona was a dynamic Titan of industry with a left hook."

"Let's not go that far. I'm still trying to save my company. Actually, my father's company."

"No," Konner said.

"What?"

"Kate, it's time you accepted that it's your company. It's your responsibility and thus your company."

"OK," She said. "Thanks for the suggested change in my thinking. That means you don't have to sleep in the dungeon tonight."

"Dungeon? What's that mean? You have one here?"

Kate looked at him with a satisfied smile.

"Oh," Konner said. "That was a joke, wasn't it."

"Maybe," she said.

I need to set up another video call with Devroe. It's on the current problem, and some of it is quite."

Kate finished his sentence, "Classified."

Konner had a sheepish smile trying not to dwell on the issue. Nonetheless, he wasn't comfortable with how much to reveal about his efforts for Devroe.

Kate said, "You go ahead, and I'm going to take a long bath. Perhaps we can have a glass of wine after."

"It's a date," Konner said.

"You're so romantic," she said, walking away.

CHAPTER 56

Vianden Castle

Devroe came up on the screen, and Konner said, "You look better today. How do you feel?"

Devroe rubbed his face. "Do you ever feel you're the most powerful force in the world, and you can't get anything done?"

Konner laughed. "No, can't say that's ever happened to me. I have some Koffman news that might qualify as getting something done."

"Please don't hold it back."

"Nuri Koffman initially agreed to hold off on any further response to Iran's announcement."

"That's certainly good news. I don't know how you did it, but you may have avoided a catastrophe. Wait, you said initially."

"He was willing until he found out Iran is shopping for or already has purchased u235. Then he went ballistic. He's convinced he must strike first and at the heart of the danger confronting them. I convinced him it was in his best interest to let us find the shipment and eliminate the problem rather than start shooting at Iran. I said the president was committed to eliminating the problem."

Devroe rubbed his face again. "So, where does it stand?"

"We have twenty-four hours to find the shipment, or he'll, and I quote, "defend his country.""

"Did Koffman have anything else that would help?"

"They feel the deal was in the works before Iran's press conference yesterday but don't know for how long."

"How would they know that?"

"I don't know."

Clearly frustrated, Devroe said, "I need to get this to the president. Koffman's finding out about the u235 gives him a bigger reason to strike at Iran. That would be a huge escalation."

Konner waited for a response. "Are you still here?"

"Yes, I was looking something up using online maps. Interesting."

"What's interesting?"

"I can't find an airport anywhere near Natanz. They built it in the middle of nowhere, on purpose, and the only way in is via roads."

"Helicopter?" Konner said.

"Perhaps, but that would take a two-step operation unloading from the airplane and reloading onto the chopper. That increases the number of people involved and exponentially raises the risk of exposure. Plus, it would take a heavy lift chopper which is very visible. When you add up the lead container needed to transport the material and the weight of the u235, you're looking at thousands of pounds. It can be done but wouldn't be the first choice given it's not very low profile or low risk."

Konner said, "Given what's at stake for the Iranians, it seems a little squishy around the edges."

"I agree. Still, I will have the NSA scrub the air for anything that smells of a strange flight path, no AIS transponder, anything. I'm meeting the president in the White House situation room. That ought to tell you how quickly he thinks this could get out of hand."

"I'm here. Let me know what I can do."

"You can call your Syrian friend and drain him for what he knows. We need to find that shipment, take it out of circulation, and not have anyone know we did it. It's a long shot, but hey, I'm desperate at the moment. Call him, and I'll be back."

***

Konner thought for a moment, wondering if he could get the call in before Kate returned. In the little time he'd been with her, he knew she could spend a week soaking in a bath. He decided to try to call the Syrian before she returned.

Konner was amazed that the Syrian answered.

"Catalina, it's Konner. I'm surprised you answered."

"Some of us don't have cushy stateside jobs. Some of us have to work odd and long hours for a living."

"Cushy is not a word I would have used. I have a question."

"Of course you do. However, the last exchange we had was for the visa. For new information, it should cost you again. However, my wife is out of Iran and on her way here. For that, I must thank you. I owe you this for keeping your word. A rare find these days."

Konner said, "I need to get to it. We suspect the Iranians are trying to purchase 90% u235 from an outside source. They plan to get it to their facility at Natanz. If they are, it's a huge development. I'm checking my sources for verification. Do you have anything on this?"

"You do understand the irony here, my friend. You're the United States of America, and I'm a little mouse, a Syrian mouse at that, and you're asking me for help."

"Look, this is important. Do you know anything?"

The Syrian said, "The man who replaced me in Tehran is a fool, so they ordered me to determine the impact of Iran's announcement. Now I'm doing my Paris job and my old job simultaneously. I contacted every source I had, and I'm sitting here writing my report to the devils in Damascus."

Konner was getting frustrated. "Look, we found out the shipment is coming in by air."

"Who said it was coming by air?" The Syrian asked.

"Wait, you know about this? It's from a tip left at our embassy in Belgrade."

"My research entailed more pillow talk. It's my understanding it's coming in by ship."

Konner became focused. His voice went up an octave. "When? What ship?"

"I'm not sure. Not an obvious ship, that's for sure. My source said it was a known smuggling ship called the Doha Sea. But being a smuggling ship, it could be named anything on the stern or its papers. Right now, I know it's running along the coast of Ethiopia, getting close to Iranian waters."

"Do you have any location information?"

"No, but I would hurry if I were you. I also know the Iranians have sent a warship to meet and transfer the u235 at sea. Is the US going after it because Syria doesn't have the reach, and they also don't want Iranians to get anywhere near that stuff?"

Konner said, "I don't see we have a choice.

"Then I'll include it to Assad and his gang in my report. They'll be delighted. I might even get a bonus."

"No, you're not."

"What?"

"You're not telling anyone. Our interest in this shipment is a national secret, and if you let anyone know, I can guarantee your life is over. Not literally, but it might as well be. If you breathe a word of this, it could cost lives, and I mean thousands. Will you keep this conversation a secret? I want your promise."

The Syrian smiled. "To honor that you kept your word, I'll keep your promise, but Paris is expensive, and now that my wife will soon be here, she will want to buy everything. The CIA stipend and my meager salary will disappear rapidly in the Parisian atmosphere.

"I'll see what I can do. But breathe a word of this, and money will be the least of your problems. So, the shipment is real, and it's coming via tanker, and your people think it might be called the Doha Sea."

"I didn't say the ship was a tanker. I don't know that, but the rest is accurate. At least that's what I know right now."

Konner's voice made a desperate note when he said, "Listen, Catalina, you contact me at this number if you hear anything else, can you do that?"

The Syrian said, "Konner?"

Konner said, "What?"

" Are you married?"

"What? Ah, no. Where did that come from?"

"We aren't close friends, but I know what you do for a living can steal your life. Find someone your compliment, and you will get that life back. Because of you, I'll soon be with my wife. If I find anything else, I'll contact you immediately even if you can't get the CIA to increase my payments."

"That's good to know. Look, thanks for your help."

CHAPTER 57

Residence
Vianden Castle

After her bath, Kate knocked on the door to her office."
"It's fine," Konner said. "I'm off the call. I have to say you always look stunning with wet hair and a robe."
She came over and sat on his lap. "You always think of the nicest things to say to a lady. Tough day?"
"Certainly a busy one. How did yours go?"
"How about we retire to my room for the rest of the evening. Talking about business there isn't the same as discussing it in this room. I always get a better perspective without the trappings of the daily grind."
Kate's bedroom itself was not large, but it had several rooms. A walk-in closet large enough to serve dinner for twelve, a bath area with enough square feet it could be listed on the market separately, and a sitting area just inside the double door entrance. Konner walked in and retreated into one of the oversized swivel

chairs. Kate walked over to a table that contained a serving set with an open bottle of wine. "Can I interest you in a glass?"

Konner kicked off his shoes, "Oh, OK, since you're twisting my arm. Again, how did you do today? I'm sure it wasn't just a normal day saving the world."

"As I said before, we met Petrovic on his plane. It was pretty straightforward, telling him it would no longer be business as usual. We were prepared to push back and not only on the financial front. He definitely didn't like that. I not only saw his demeanor change but something else as well."

"What do you mean?"

"I don't know. I expected agitated, given how strong I was talking to him because I'm sure that doesn't happen every day. But then he started to get nervous or something. It was strange."

She walked over and sat on the couch. "Come sit here," she said, patting a spot on the cushion. You're too far away over there."

Konner looked at her and playfully said, "Absolutely."

Shaking her head, she said, "At the end of the day, you're all just horny boys. It's just more comfortable than talking to you over there, don't get your hopes up."

"Hope? I don't know what I could be hoping for, so I don't understand the comment."

Kate rolled her eyes at the comment.

"Kate, I don't think you know what a great job you're doing with your company.

Kate looked at him seriously. "Konner, I want you to know I appreciate your support. It's comforting to always have someone in your corner."

"I'm just stating the obvious. You're an amazing woman Kate."

Kate leaned towards him and kissed him. "You can get your hopes up now."

Konner chuckled. "You said there were other options."

"The team discussed various options Mom presented in her report now that I've decided to go on the offensive. To make TerraDyne feel the heat."

"That's interesting; any favorites?"

"I'm intrigued by one that takes over these huge self-driving trucks at a mine he has in Norway. It would stop production, which would be harmful, but the world is very interested in that capability, and something going wrong with self-driving anything, for no apparent reason, would be big news. You know," she said, waving her hands in the air, "visions of these big giants overtaking the world."

"Not sure about that one," he said. "Surely, there were a few others to consider."

"I was thinking in the bath, and there was an intriguing one that makes more sense." She picked up her glass and savored an end-of-the-day favorite. "It's boarding one of his ships and pointing it at a safe spot on the shore and running it aground."

"You would do that? That would mean pictures of a beached tanker will be on every major news organization along with the name TerraDyne."

"Anyway, what happened with you today? I know it wasn't a casual walk in the park."

Konner was thinking, "here we are again." He didn't like not answering an innocent question couples everywhere shared. It placed an obvious and uncomfortable wall in their relationship; given what he did for a living, it wasn't going away.

Kate sensed the pause in the response. "It's OK," she said, putting her glass down and moving closer.

"No, it's not OK. I want to tell you. I want to share what we do in our lives, and I can't. Discussing what happens when we're not together is a vital part of a relationship."

Kate was clearly tired as she placed her head on his shoulder. He lifted his arm and drew her to his side. She said, "I think you're making a big deal out of it, and it's not."

They both sat there quietly. The silence was a welcome change from the fast-paced day, but Konner was still thinking and said, "Don't you think a one-way exchange of information could be a problem in the long run?"

He waited and then realized Kate, a Titan of industry, had fallen asleep.

CHAPTER 58

Brussels
Belgium

The middle of the night gives those who are awake a quieter and subdued version of the day. Electronic signals are low, traffic has almost disappeared, and activities not suited for the day emerge.

In the darkness, Captain Derik Laven, of the Belgian security service, expected anything but a quiet evening. From a distance he saw the SUV drive up and park a block away.

Vanek looked at the front of the charity office that sat at street level in the city center of Brussels. There would be no subtle entry this time. The front of the office was glass, as was the door. Vanek intended to create as much chaos as possible. It would be a clear message to Kate Adler.

Vanek sat inside the SUV and felt something wasn't right. "You guys know what to do right. Just like the rundown."

One of his men asked. "Are you coming?"

Vanek looked out onto the street. He'd listened to his internal voice throughout his life, and it had served him well. "No," he replied slowly as if still trying to read the feeling. "You know what to do and do it quickly."

Captain Laven counted three men exiting the vehicle and walking up the street towards the Adler Children's Charity offices. He brought his radio up and said, "three men walking towards you."

A voice on the other end said, "I have them in sight."

The first guy walked up and, hiding his face, blinded the security camera covering the front door with a spray can. But it was too late. Mom had already captured what she needed; the facial recognition and the internal travel schedules she could now access confirmed Vanek was in town. The internal memo from Petrovic authorizing the attack included the target's address. However, Vanek was not standing at the front door.

Mom sent a tip to the local police. It contained enough information the authorities took the warning of a break-in seriously.

"Go," the Captain said. The engines started, and lights started flashing as the officers converged on the three men who had no choice but to surrender.

Vanek moved to the contingency escape plan he had for every operation but never needed. Seeing the commotion, he started the SUV and, with a quick u-turn, headed away from the area.

Laven saw the vehicle start-up and move into the street. He called into his radio, "There's a fourth person in the SUV. We need him also." One of the patrol cars went after the SUV. Vanek hung a hard right and then hard left into an alley and stopped the vehicle turning off the lights. He walked to the other end of the dark passage with it's ripe smells and dampness. Exiting the alley, he quickly walked to an unlocked Toyota sedan. If things got tight, he never wanted the delay caused by unlocking the door. He pulled out from the curb and into the night.

Captain Laven asked his men. "Do you have the one who escaped?"

"No came the reply, but we have found the SUV, and he must be on foot."

The captain heard a loud explosion both over the radio and through the night. He motioned the second patrol car to him while shouting into the radio. "What's going on. What happened? He switched frequencies and called the station, "Get an ambulance to my location immediately. Possible officers down."

When he arrived, the SUV was a burning wreck, and two of his men were on the ground about 10 feet away. Kneeling, he could see cut marks on their faces and rips in their clothing due to the tempered glass blowing outward.

"What happened," he asked the man on the ground.

"Don't know. It just blew as we approached."

The captain looked up at the other end of the alley. The fourth man was in the wind.

***

"Boss, it's Vanek."

"So, how did it go?"

"Not well. In fact, nothing happened because the police were waiting for us. I was able to escape, but the police captured three local guys we hired for the job."

"Do they know not to talk?"

"They are completely in the dark and don't know anything that can come back to us."

"What about the vehicle."

"M35. I heard the explosion."

"OK, so do you think they were waiting? Did someone tip them off?"

"I know they were waiting. After all these years, I've got a nose for this. We did everything per the usual precautions. Only a few people knew the operation was even going to occur. I don't like close calls. We need to find out who leaked it."

"Well, I don't see how that could happen."

"It did happen, and I almost got thrown in jail."

Again, it can't happen, so I'll put it off as a one-time. Let's move on.

Vanek was thinking. "Sure, let's move on. You weren't there. It wasn't your freedom on the line."

Vanek asked his boss, "What will we do next."

CHAPTER 59

Oval Office
White House

Devroe's phone let off a loud jazz number, and it buzzed on the table. He looked at the president and said, "It's Konner. I think I should take this."

"Konner, this is early for you; I'm in with the president. Can it wait?"

"No, it can't."

"You're on speaker," Devroe said.

Konner said, "Last night, the Syrian said he's been on the trail of the same information. His contacts indicate the shipment was not coming by plane. He says it's on a ship off the coast of Ethiopia heading for Iranian waters. The Iranians have sent a military ship out to meet and transfer the u235 to the Iranian vessel in open water. They don't want the material coming into port on a civilian ship."

Perez said, "Konner, it's the president. Do you have anything specific?"

"No, the only other information he had was the ship could be sailing under the name Doha Sea. However, the naming of vessels is a fluid issue in the smuggling business.

Devroe had walked over to the other side of the oval office, talking to someone on one of the desk phones.

Perez asked Konner, "How reliable is your source.?"

"His agenda is the same as ours. His government wants to know what Iran is doing, and they don't like the idea of them getting the bomb."

Perez said, "We will have to comb the area for something that stands out. It's certainly a needle."

Devroe returned, "I've Defense Secretary Kyle McKinny, on the phone. He says the closest ship we have would be the USS Nashville, a destroyer on patrol in the area. We'll ask them to check all traffic for transponders and challenge and identify anything suspicious. As long as they state they're looking for illegal cargo or weapons, they can board and inspect any vessel we believe is suspect."

The president's voice went up a notch, "If we're lucky enough to find it, we will not be visibly boarding it unless we're out of options. Mr. Secretary, is that clear?"

"Yes, sir," McKinny replied.

Perez continued, "The Iranians will see that as a blatant effort against them, and we blow our honest broker status. It's not perfect, but it's the only thing keeping this from blowing up right now."

Devroe said, "Previously, we were looking for something in the air. I can re-task NSA to focus on the gulf area for anything useful. It's a pretty broad net. If we're lucky and they find anything, they can feed that data directly to the Nashville. It's all we've got as we can't stop everything."

Perez said, "And then what? Like I said, boarding her is the last resort."

"We have an option." Devroe said, "Tell him, Kyle."

"Sir, the HMAS Adelaide is an Australian frigate in the area. If the Nashville can come up with something, we might get the Aussies to stop it for inspection. It would be within the sanction's rules. However, you would need to call Ackerman the Australian prime minister."

"That's a great idea," Perez said. I'll get on it."

"General," Perez said, "tell the Nashville this is important but under no circumstances are they to board whatever ship we find without my order."

Devroe said, "Mr. Secretary if we get to the point of using the Adelaide, I'll talk to the captain directly. We don't want any misunderstandings."

"Yes, sir."

Devroe picked up his phone and said, "Konner, are you still there?"

"Yes," came the reply. "I heard everything."

"Sit tight. You may have to call the Israelis."

"Right. Let me know."

CHAPTER 60

Residence
Vianden Castle

Kate woke up and found Konner missing. He was in her office on the phone to the states. She remembered falling asleep on the couch. It was a restless night as she had put off until morning reviewing some numbers from Avery on the company's status. She knew it wouldn't be good news. It bothered her through the night and kept her from a deep sleep. She wanted to address the issue early. She peeked around the office door, and Konner was still on the phone. A quick wave let him know she was leaving.

When Kate finally reviewed Avery's report, the news, as she expected, was disturbing. Shipping orders were falling as their empty ships sat in port. Kate thought, "TerraDyne wasn't a business; it was a criminal enterprise."

They didn't know it yet, but they picked the wrong person thinking it was business as usual, that she'd give in to their strong-arm tactics. She'd prove they'd met their match. Handing Petrovic the offer to buy his company was a great feeling, but it wasn't a move that would solve the problem. Avery was still working out the details.

Brad knocked, and without a response, he opened the door and said, "I think you need to come to the operations room."

Walking in front of Brad, Kate entered the room. The rest of the team was standing looking at her with blank faces.

"This isn't good." She said. "Brad?"

"There was an attempted attack on the Brussels charity office that only could've been Petrovic."

"Attempted attack?" She said.

"Yes, the local police received a tip they thought was credible and were waiting. The police captured everyone in the team but one that got away. Mom obtained a copy of the police report."

"Our people?"

"It was early morning, so the office is empty."

"What do you mean a tip?"

"Yes," Elena said. "It was a tip as in anonymous."

It took a second to register that the man simply had no morals. Everyone waited. Kate said, "If it wasn't for that tip, anything could've happened to that charity office."

Brad said, "Police say inspections at the scene led them to believe plans were to set fire to the office. It might have been the same team that attacked the Bremerhaven office, but we don't know."

What followed was an almost tangible silence that permeated the room. Everyone was waiting for Kate to respond.

Then Penn said, "In WWII, a failed Allied operation against the German army became known as "a bridge too far." I think Petrovic just went too far."

Kate's face reflected the anger that was building inside. With a force that never entered her previous conversations, she said, "Options. I want options, and whatever restraints we were working with before are gone."

Penn said, "We talked about the mining operations and or having the coast guard detain a tanker for inspection. However, we didn't present one because we considered it too aggressive. I was going to press for it if things got any worse."

"Consider things have gotten worse. What was it?"

"Hijack a TerraDyne tanker and," he paused. "run it aground. I learned quickly when I was in the field; that some people only respond to force."

Elena said, "Failing a coast guard inspection happens every day and isn't news. However, a huge merchant ship running aground is a photo op and worldwide news."

Loren said, "We would make sure all the right news organizations pick it up

Kate turned to Penn and asked, "Did we do any planning?"

Penn nodded towards Elena.

Elena said, "Yes. We had Mom start searching for TerraDyne ships passing through the Persian Gulf. The candidate list is always changing because the ship's position is important."

Penn said, "The ship's distance from shore is important due to the range of the chopper. We're lucky that Ethiopia has miles of empty shoreline to beach the vessel safely."

After an encounter with her keyboard, Loren said, "Mom's latest qualified candidate is a small dry freighter." She leaned forward, reading from the screen. "Mom has run all the background checks, and even with the attempts to hide its identity, her estimate is 97% it's a TerraDyne ship."

Elena said, "Given the required distance from the coast, the window to board this particular freighter is three hours starting now. After that, it will be out of range, and we'll need to choose another ship which we can do, but it might take days."

"So, what's the next step? What do we do now?" Kate said.

Penn shifted nervously in his chair. "I have a confession to make."

"Confession?" Kate said.

"Yes, after our meeting on the plane, I was sure Petrovic would go after a charity office. At least I wanted to be prepared if he did."

"How would you know that?"

"In my previous life, I was trained to think how your opponent would think. Get into their shoes, and feel what they feel. What would they do? To me, going after a charity office is what he'd do. It was the obvious answer to his increasing the pressure. It would have the maximum effect. It would hit you where you were most vulnerable, resulting in your being more likely to make concessions."

Kate said, "He couldn't have been more wrong. But what are you confessing?"

Penn continued, "I didn't send the rescue team back to base. Instead, I sent them to the UAE, and the Black Hawk followed in another run. They unloaded the chopper from the C130 and finished the checklist. They can move almost immediately."

Kate was grateful for the great team she had inherited with the Cartel. Without hesitation, she said, "Send them."

"There's one more thing we should consider," Penn said. "Sometimes other hijacking gangs try to steal what's valuable cargo and sell it on the black market. Because of this, sometimes TerraDyne puts security teams on their smuggling ships. If this is one of them, our team might meet some resistance. However, we have learned our people are very successful in such encounters."

Without hesitation, Kate said, "Beach the tanker."

CHAPTER 61

Vianden Castle

Warde Hockin was captain of the HMAS Adelaide, a Hobart class destroyer of the Royal Australian Navy. He was part of the United States coalition protecting the busy shipping lanes due to Iran attacking several ships in the area.

Captain Hockin said, "I understand, Mr. Prime Minister." He put down the radio telephone and looked at the handset for an extended second. Getting a direct call from Ackerman, his country's prime minister, was not an everyday occurrence, and the request was truly unusual.

His executive officer knew who was on the line and said, "So, what warranted a call from our esteemed prime minister himself?"

Hockin hung up and said, "We're to assist any US Navy ship in the area in any manner requested."

His first officer asked, "What does that mean?"

"I think we're very close to finding out."

***

Captain Lynzei Ann Fowler of the USS Nashville skippered an Arleigh Burke-class destroyer on patrol in the same area.

The signals officer came up to the bridge and saluted. He handed her a note and said, "Captain, I have an urgent NSA message that came over the secure comm line. There's also a message from someone called Stephen Devroe. He's not on the authorized contacts database. Ma'am, who is he? Can he message us directly? Should I report it?"

"Keep current, son; he's head of national security," Fowler said. "He can do whatever he wants." She took the message and, after reading it, turned and contacted CIC (Combat Information Center). "Graves, what do you have bearing two six zero at twelve thousand yards."

"Give me a sec; I've three ships in that general vicinity. Can you be more specific? Do you have a direct heading?"

"No, that's the best I have. Identify the three and report."

Graves said, "What am I looking for?"

"Anything usual."

In seconds he came back with, "How about no AIS transponder signal? That's more than suspicious."

"Stand-by." She contacted her air commander. "Lieutenant, get the chopper ready for immediate deployment. I need an ID pass on a freighter; CIC will provide coordinates."

"Graves," Fowler said, "relay coordinates to the air commander. Are you still tracking that Iranian frigate?"

"Yes, Ma'am, it looks like it's traveling an area search pattern biding its time at less than six knots. Other than that, nothing new to report."

"Good, keep me advised."

Eighteen minutes later, the chopper was pacing the ship from the stern. The pilot reported, "I have a freighter with a transom ID of Nord Biscay."

She asked her executive officer, "Is it on the suspect list?"

"No, it's not on the list."

Fowler thought about the instructions on the note from Devroe.

Fowler said. "Get me the Adelaide on a secure line."

"Yes, Ma'am."

Seconds later, Fowler was talking to Captain Hockin. "Captain Hockin, this is Captain Fowler of the USS Nashville. My orders are to inform you of a possible sanctions issue with the Nord Biscay located eleven thousand yards from my position traveling on course one two zero. We're requesting you board and inspect."

"Roger that," Hockin said. "Anything specific we're looking for?"

"You will be receiving a message with further instructions but proceed with the boarding as soon as possible."

"Roger that. Adelaide out."

Hockin said, "Find that ship and get exact coordinates."

"Yes, sir," came the reply.

Hockin spoke to his air boss, "I need you to transport a boarding party right now. Coordinates in route."

"Yes, Sir," was the reply."

Hockin connected to Lieutenant Peerson, his security officer, "Peerson, I need a VBSS (visit, board, search, and seizure) crew in the air immediately. Chopper is standing by."

Hockin turned to the communications officer on the bridge. "Son, hail the Nord Biscay to board."

The young seaman switched to open channel communication and said. "Hailing Nord Biscay, Nord Biscay, this is a Royal Australian warship HMAS Adelaide requesting you slow to five knots and facilitate boarding."

There was no response.

"Graves, is there any change in course or speed?"

"Negative Captain."

"Lieutenant Peerson, this is the captain. Upon arrival, proceed with caution. Situation uncertain. Have you deployed a RIB (Rigid Inflatable Boat) for your return?"

"Affirmative."

At least twenty minutes later, Adelaide's chopper was tracking the Nord Biscay just above the bow. The boarding team roped down without incident. They proceeded cautiously towards the superstructure and up the stairs from the main deck.

Standing on the navigation deck, Peerson addressed the captain of the Nord Biscay. He was a large, gruff man wearing well-worn civilian clothes looking anything but professional. Peerson thought he looked like a gangster or a bouncer and not the ship's captain.

"Sir, my name is Lieutenant Peerson, Royal Australian Navy. May I ask why your transponder was not on?"

The captain crossed his arms, making it known he was not pleased with being boarded. When he responded, he didn't look at Peerson, "The transponder is faulty. I'll not stop to get it repaired due to the time it will take. I've got a schedule to keep. That's how I make my living. I'll get it fixed when it doesn't interfere with making port calls on time. Now is that all you want?"

Peerson said, "When hailed, you didn't slow to five knots."

"No, I didn't slow down, lieutenant, for the same reason. Every other time I go past this point, I get boarded, and it costs me time for which I get deductions from my pay. So if you don't like the way things are, and you have concluded your useless inspections, I invite you to get off my ship?"

Peerson said, "Captain, I'll need to see your Certificate of Registry and your declaration sheet. Also, proof of ownership."

The captain all but rolled his eyes. "Again?" He said. "They're almost worn out."

"Please, sir."

"No, I don't think so."

"Why object? If you don't have anything to hide, we can do this in minutes and be on our way."

The large man moved close to Peerson in an obvious confrontational manner. "And if I don't, what are you going to do, shoot me? You have no authority to arrest me. Besides, if you want in that safe, you need me to open it."

Three threatening-looking crew members in similar dress, drifted into the room from port side access to the bridge. Their posture made it evident they weren't happy with the intrusion.

Peerson was getting annoyed. He said into his squad intercom, "Everyone to the navigation deck now."

The Aussie, by no means a small man himself, moved into the captain and, inches away, said, "As I said, sir, we can have this done in minutes with your cooperation, or I'm going to go over there and stop this ship dead in the water myself."

The captain said, "You do that, and you're going to end up in the water. I think you and your *mates* should get off my ship."

Three of Peerson's men came in from the opposite side by the bridge wing, followed by two more. The armed group was an impressive sight in the confines of the bridge.

CHAPTER 62

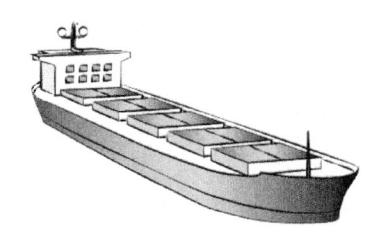

Legacy5 firefight
Nord Biscay

Lange looked at his men sitting on the floor of the chopper. Swirling air flew about the cabin from the open slider as he looked out over a vast expanse of ocean. He switched his radio channel and reported to base using the brevity code, passing templeton." It indicated they were on route. It was a twenty-five minute ride as the Black Hawk was making four hundred knots. Lange could see the ship come into view out the open door as Rondo, the pilot, made a stern pass to check the ship's name. Against the rusty and battered stern of the vessel, Lange could see the name Legacy 5.

"Control, this is Lange confirming the ship's stern ID as Legacy 5. I repeat Legacy 5."

Penn said, "Good copy here."

"Tracking target," Rondo, said. "Hover in four mics."

Back on the squad channel, Lange said. "Trips over, boys, gear check." They started to stir.

First, Rondo brought the chopper alongside, matching the bulk carrier's speed as they moved in unison. Then, he slowly moved sideways over a clear area on the ship's bow.

"Stable hover," Rondo said over the radio.

Lange said, "Cooper take us out."

"Yes, cap." He replied as he slid over to the edge of the choppers opening. He grabbed a rope and was the first going down, followed every ten feet by another man from above. Soon all six men were down.

Lange said to Rondo, "Lange here, all clear."

Rondo gave the chopper lift and banked to the left on his way back to refuel to return later and pick up the team.

Lange reported, "Passing jackpot."

As the team expected a merchant crew, the first shots surprised them. Pings were everywhere as the men dropped for cover behind the large flat cargo doors over each compartment. Each compartment opening rose about two feet from the deck, offering cover for the men.

Lange reported back to control. "Hostel contact repeat hostile contact. Automatic fire."

***

Peerson from the Adelaide was still standing face to face with the ship's captain of the Nord Biscay. Annoyed at the captain's resistance said, "In a minute stopping this ship will be the least of your worries as I can impound your ship for a very long-drawn-out inspection. The captain shook his head, finally relenting, and opened the safe. Peerson, trained to know what he was looking for, reviewed the documents. After taking his time, he handed them back to the captain.

"Thank you; these seem to be in order. You already know it's against maritime law not to have your transponder in working order. There's also the issue of a collision resulting from not reporting your position. That would most dramatically certainly affect your schedule."

"Write me up a moving violation for the transponder, and I'll take my chances with the latter. The company will not blink an eye at paying the fine, which is minuscule compared to being late to port."

Peerson went outside and radioed the Adelaide. "Captain Hocking, I looked at the Nord Biscay documents, and they're up to date and in order. I can confirm the transponder is off, but I don't think it's suspicious. While annoyed, the Captain has been cooperative. The only suspicious thing I see is that the owner is TerryDyne, which means it could be transporting anything under the sun, mostly illegal. Do we check cargo against the manifest?"

Hocking's executive officer interrupted. "Captain?"

"Hold on," Hockin said to Peerson.

"Yes?"

"It's the White House. We put it on four." The officer said.

Hockin said, "As in DC?"

"Yes, sir."

Hockin returned to his boarding party, "Peerson, stay on this line."

A cautionary frown proceeded Hockin picking up the handset. He was not sure this had ever occurred; however, his orders were specific. Cooperate with the Americans. "Captain Hockin here."

"Captain Hockin, my name is Stephen Devroe. I'm President Perez's Director of National Security."

"Yes, Doctor, I'm aware. How can I help you?"

"Actually, you already are, Nashville has you looking for a needle in a haystack, and that can't be easy. We sincerely appreciate your cooperation in this serious matter. I understand you're aware of the vessel vectored by the Nashville?"

"Yes, we have identified the ship as the Nord Biscay. I have an inspection party on board right now."

Devroe said, "Have you inspected the ownership papers?"

"Yes, the boarding officer said the papers appeared to be up to date. The ownership papers indicate it's a TerraDyne freighter."

Devroe took a deep breath, "I want to brief you on what we're trying to accomplish. We aren't trying to find military equipment or smuggled goods in this case. Captain? Are we on speaker?"

"No," Hockin said.

"Good, because what I'm about to tell you is classified top secret. We're interested in locating anything that looks heavy enough to be a lead-lined box or container. Start with storage compartments in the superstructure with direct outside access to the main deck. The boxes will be cumbersome, heavy and hard to transport. Captain?"

"Yes, sir."

"This is important. The box may contain radioactive material, so don't open it under any circumstance. Do you understand?"

"Yes, sir. Understood."

"Have your communications officer keep this line open and have someone monitor it so you know when I come back. Please get back to me immediately with whatever you find. Again, thank you for your help. Any questions?"

"Not right now, no. I'll get back on this line as soon as we know anything."

He punched in the other line and said. "Peerson, you still there?"

Hockin relayed the instructions. There was silence at the other end until Hockin finally heard a "Roger that."

CHAPTER 63

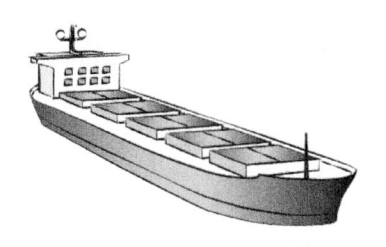

Legacy 5

Brad asked why Lange and his men would receive, "Automatic weapons fire? Why protect a cargo ship with an armed force? Usually, the crew retreats to the citadel or gives up. The fact they arrived via chopper makes it pretty evident this wasn't a typical Somali hijacking."

Penn said, "Remember, TerraDyne often puts security on their smuggling ships to protect their valuable illegal cargo. That means it's precious in the black market and a target for hijacking. That would cause a delay on arrival. They don't want any problems delivering the cargo as the people on the receiving end are, I guess you could say, thugs themselves."

***

Back on the deck of the Legacy 5, Lange said, "Count?"

Pete said, "I counted three before they disappeared back into the bridge deck." Lange said to his men. "OK, looks like they're not going to cooperate, so go to standard ammo. They pulled off the clips that contained non-lethal ammunition and, reaching into the front pouch, replaced it with a thirty-round clip with standard NATO 7.62 rounds. Each provided cover fire for the next as they worked towards the wheelhouse. From the upper level of the superstructure, two armed men quickly appeared around a bulkhead. One never got off a shot and dropped to the deck. The other lowered himself behind the railing to reduce the target area and pinned Lange and his men in position with excellent accurate fire. The shooter moved to a new position and again fired at the group.

The gunfire stopped, and in the silence that followed came the bouncing sound of metal against metal.

Lange yelled, "*Grenade.*" They all went flat on the deck. Hurriedly thrown, the grenade landed well away from the team. It blew the corner of a compartment cover forcing the corner up at an angle. Return fire caught the shooter sprinting to hide in a nearby outside hatch, but he didn't make it. With the above threat eliminated, they rapidly advanced to the base of the superstructure.

Lange sent Jerry to the farthest side on over-watch. His job was to protect the worst part of close-quarter fighting, ascending stairs in an active engagement. Lange and Thomson started up the stairs towards the bridge; weapons raised level to their sights, covering all angles.

Suddenly, another gunman with an AK47 burst out of the bridge area, rapidly approaching the stairs. He was out of Lange's line of sight. In three steps, the man would make the corner with Lange unaware. Jerry said into the network, "Lange cover now." Lange dropped to a knee with his men following the motion just as Jerry squeezed the trigger twice. Lange looked over at Jerry behind a free-standing storage locker and nodded his thanks.

Still on the stairs, Lange motioned to Pete and Thomson to go towards the other corner of the bulkhead. He wanted to approach the bridge from both sides.

Jerry saw another gunman emerge through a hatch with his rifle aimed directly at him. Jerry was ready, and two taps later, the man fell. Yet, another man appeared, and Jerry said into the network, "Someone is coming out with his hands up. He doesn't look armed. Not sure if it's a crew member or a security type. Wait, now there are two."

Lange rounded the corner of the bridge with his weapon up and encountered the two men who had their hands behind their heads. He motioned with his hand and yelled, "Down."

Rob strapped both men's hands as they lay face down on the deck. Rob and Lange burst into the wheelhouse, and it was empty. Then someone out of sight said something he couldn't understand, and an AK47 came sliding into view from a passageway that accessed the bridge from the back wall. The man slowly emerged, dropping to his knees.

Lange's first reaction was to see how thick he was around the waist, indicating a bomb vest. Satisfied, he motioned the man flat to the ground. Lange said into the squad network, "Bridge, all clear."

Rob kneeled, fitting plastic straps on the man, now at Lange's feet.

Lange pointed to Rob and then up the passageway from where the man on the deck appeared. "Find out where the crew is. I want the captain."

Lange reported back to base, "Passed capstone. No casualties."

Everyone in the ops center expressed relief differently.

Kate said, "Those guys don't get paid enough."

Penn said, "They might agree. So far, so good."

The captain and the first mate emerged from the passageway, followed by Rob.

Lange pointed at one of them and said, "Captain?"

The man nodded.

Lange handed him a piece of paper with a new ship heading. Not knowing if the man spoke English, he pointed at the paper and then out the window towards the front of the vessel, indicating the direction.

The captain looked at the note and said in English, "This heading is wrong. It sends us directly towards the coast. There's no port there."

"That's right," Lange said.

The captain shrugged his shoulders like he didn't care. The tanker was old, so instead of entering the information into the ship's control system, he approached the wheel and manually turned to the coordinates.

"Lock it," Lange said.

Lange then pointed at the engine controls and said, "Increase your speed."

Again, cooperating, the captain moved the lever up to 80% and, looking up, said, "If you want to get there, that's all she can take. Your option is to break down and not make it at all."

Lange reported, "We have redirected to the given heading. Estimate landfall in less than an hour."

Roger that. Penn said.

Lange asked the captain, "Where is your crew?"

The captain said, "You have killed most of them; the rest you tied up. They were also the security that was on board."

Lange wondered why the captain's vessel responded with gunfire, yet he willingly followed orders.

Kate listened to the boarding and gunfight and also thought there was something not right. "Colonel Lange, isn't the crew doubling as security unusual?"

"Yes, Ma'am. Very unusual as they're opposite skill sets. Also, we encountered a shooter on the bridge that was not a rent-a-cop. I think the whole crew had advanced weapons training."

"Colonel Lange, can you search the ship? We might find something incriminating to pin on TerraDyne, like smuggled military equipment. A beached smuggling ship owned by TerraDyne transporting illegal weapons would make a great story headline. It has a certain ring to it."

"Yes, Ma'am." Lange switched to the squad network. "Jerry, Thomson, Cooper, and Rob search the ship for contraband. Start at the deck level of the superstructure and work your way up, then go down into the hold. If it's a smuggling ship, it should be smuggling something."

CHAPTER 64

Vianden Castle

Konner was in the operations room listening to the Cartel's team board the Legacy5. He marveled at how professionally they handled these situations. First the rescue of Okoro, and then this. He stayed out of the way and didn't want to distract anyone. He and Kate visually connected a few times, but she was busy, and he was impressed with her decisiveness. He marveled how she could be several people at once—a mother to the charity's children and field marshal at the same time.

Konner's phone went off, and everyone in the ops room heard it. Embarrassed, he smiled and turned the volume down as he left the room.

"It's Koffman, the Israeli prime minister, he thought. This can't be good." On his way to the office he was using, Konner said, "Yes, Mr. Prime Minister."

"Mr. Houston, I understand why, but going through you to the president is an interesting way to conduct foreign policy."

"Sir, in this situation, any interesting method would be worth it to keep things under control. That's also your goal, am I correct?

"Of course. Nonetheless, through you, I must be clear to the president, if there's the slightest chance the Iranians can get that material inside Iran, we'll strike the Natanz facility. The only way that doesn't happen is to guarantee you have the u235 in your possession. I can't allow any situation to lead to our country's elimination. I'm no fan of mutual destruction, but I'm also no fan of unilateral destruction, so I must make my position clear to President Perez. I have a ready alert of three f35B stealth jets sitting on the tarmac with the pilots strapped in and ready to go. They could be in the air in seconds, and I'll not hesitate to use them. You will know immediately when they take off, so notification will not be necessary."

"Yes, I understand," Konner said. "I can assure you all possible assets are engaged in locating the uranium shipment. The president has guaranteed the Iranians will not obtain the material. If it's required, he'll authorize overt action."

"Mr. Houston, with all due respect, you're bluffing. You're buying time in a desperate attempt to find the material without a clue to its location."

"That's not true. We have a boarding party that landed on a suspected ship. It's too early to hear back."

"I'm sorry, that's another half-truth. The United States can't board a ship and tip your hand. We need honest dialog here if we're to solve this problem."

Konner was getting a little agitated and said, "Mr. Prime Minister, you're correct; transparency is critical in this situation. I must point out, however, just because you doubt our updates doesn't affect our efforts. It only affects what you think of our efforts. Please remember, you're not the only party affected if they get the material—the dynamics of the world change. Your job is to protect Israel. My job has a little wider net."

Konner said, "As far as tipping our hand, the boarding party is from the HMAS Adelaide, an Australian ship participating in the coalition's protection fleet. The Prime Minister of Australia has agreed to keep the effort highly classified. The USS Nashville is close by for support but not participating directly. It will engage only as a last resort. I'll relay your position and your concerns to the president immediately."

Koffman said, "Thank you, Mr. Houston. Please remember there are very determined dynamics at play on this side."

Konner had this feeling in the pit of his stomach, and it wasn't hunger. He dialed Devroe and recounted the call as accurately as he could.

"What did he sound like?" Devroe asked.

"What do you mean?"

"The soft information. Was Koffman in control or angry? Was anyone making a commotion in the background?"

"No, just his voice, and it was calm but stressed as we all are. He said we would know when the Israeli planes took off. Is that true?"

"Ah, that's above my pay grade," Devroe said.

Konner said, "Are you kidding? There's only one above you, but I get it. God, I hope we get out of this. Have we found anything on the ship?"

Devroe said, "They're still searching the ship – it's huge. Wait, the Adelaide ship is calling in, and I've got to answer it. Can you hold on as I may have news?"

"Of course."

CHAPTER 65

USS Nashville
HMAS Adelaide

Devroe took a deep breath and said, "Captain Hockin, Devroe here. Do you have anything?"

"We might. The team has located several locked lead-lined containers. They have radiation symbols on the outside."

Devroe sat back in his chair and put his hand on his forehead in relief. "That's great news, captain; any documentation with the shipment?"

"Yes, I've sent scans to the Nashville. I have to say it all looks in order."

Devroe's admin came in and put the scans on his desk.

"I have them here. We'll research the validity and get back. It shouldn't take but thirty minutes. Can your men stay in position?"

Hocking said, "You let us know what we can do. We also occupy part of this planet and know what's at stake."

Devroe looked at the material on his desk. He called Dan Tilde, head of CIA.

"Dan, I have a manifest, invoice, and packing slip here for a uranium shipment. Could you check them out right away? I want to know if it's a legitimate shipment or is someone trying to hide something."

Tilde said, "Send it over. We're on it now."

"Konner, are you there? OK, I'm back."

"Any good news?" Konner asked Devroe.

"Possibly, they found heavy lead containers with radiation symbols on them. We're checking to see if it's a legitimate shipment. I'll be back to you as soon as I know anything so you can get to the Israelis."

"Great," Konner said, "Hope to hear from you soon."

***

Konner walked back into the ops center after the Israeli phone call.

Kate says, "You look worried."

He shows Kate the phone in his hand like it's the issue and says, "I am; it's a big problem. On the other hand, your operation is important, and I want to be here, but I may have to step out." Kate sensed something big was wrong in Konner's world.

"Should I be worried?"

Konner gave a non-committal shrug of his shoulders.

Kate said, "We boarded the ship we want to run aground."

Konner said, "Ignore me, do what you need to do. They need you."

Kate smiled and put a hand on Konner's shoulder as she turned to those in the operations center. She listened to the men on the Legacy 5 talking back and forth over the speakers, and something hit her. Kate said into the intercom, "Colonel, this is Kate; before we go any further can you determine if this is a TerraDyne ship? I want to be absolutely sure? I don't want any stupid errors."

Konner leaned over to Loren and said, "Did they board OK? Is everyone alright?"

"Yes, they're fine, but not until after a firefight with TerraDyne security people or armed guards or whatever you want to call them. Anyway, they've redirected the ship to the new heading that will impact an open beach on the coast of Ethiopia. Then the fun begins."

"What's that.?"

"The team will leave the ship at the last minute and make a pass taking photos. They'll be in the press releases we send out."

"You're good at this, aren't you?"

"Yes, I enjoy the press side, but I prefer physically changing the world from my keyboard. Haven't you ever wanted to remotely blow up someone's computer because that person deserved it? Because of Mom, I'm able to do that and more."

Konner laughed. "I'll be sure to remember that."

* * *

The Nashville recovered the chopper and resumed its previous monitoring pattern. They were at a slower speed to stay in the area of the Adelaide.

Fowler heard the speaker come to life. "Captain, Graves here, that Iranian destroyer just changed its heading now bearing one eight five degrees headed south in our direction at flank speed."

To captain Fowler, this was significant as Iranian ships rarely did anything over standard speed. The slower pace dramatically lowered their fuel and maintenance costs, with sanctions making replacement parts hard to get. "Tag it." She said. "Keep me informed."

She turned to her executive officer and said, "XO, sound general quarters."

The executive officer selected the ship's intercom and said, "This is the XO, General quarters general quarters; this is not a drill."

It meant the ship was on alert, and each crew member was on station and ready to perform their duties. It was a level down from battle stations.

CHAPTER 66

White House Situation Room

Devroe was in the White House situation room with the president having just brought him up to speed on all the moving parts. Neither was in high spirits.

Perez said, "I feel like I'm in the middle of a room full of dynamite, and someone is getting ready to strike a match."

"We're not there yet. With a little luck, Dan at the CIA will tell us the shipment the Adelaide found is the u235 going to Iran. If that's the case, the Aussies can take possession and say they discovered it on a routine inspection of a suspicious vessel. We can deny any operational involvement."

The president said, "Did Koffman actually say he has planes on ready alert?"

"That's what Konner said. He also indicated he was stressed but in control."

"Is there any way for me to know for sure about the planes?"

"I've ordered a re-task of our NRO L-32 satellite overhead soon." Devroe looked at his watch. "The National Reconnaissance Office should have verification in 10 or 15 minutes."

Perez said, "I've no reason to doubt Koffman. I just wish he was a little more flexible."

"I don't think it's him. On this subject, I don't think anyone in their government knows what flexible means."

Devroe's phone went off. He looked at the screen and said to Perez, "It's Dan."

"Dan, good news, I hope."

"Fraid not. We checked all angles. That shipment is legit. Qatar's medical institute ordered it. According to the papers, it's useless for anything other than radiation treatments for cancer patients. We checked several sources at the hospital, and it all checks out. Sorry, it's a legitimate transaction."

Everyone in the room felt it at the same time.

Perez could see his friend sink into this chair without any visible movement. It was a physiological reaction to the news.

In a subdued voice, Devroe said, "Thanks, Dan, for the quick turnaround."

Perez said, "You don't have to say anything; your body language is shouting right now. So what's the next step?"

"Honestly, Mr. President. I don't know.

CHAPTER 67

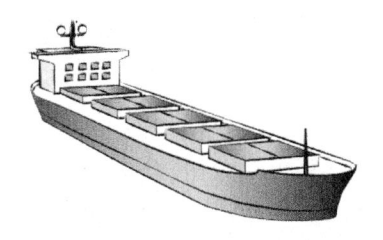

Legacy 5
USS Nashville

Lange walked over to the ship's safe and kicked it with his foot. "Open." He said to the captain. The captain hesitated, then started nodding no.

"Look, you understand me just fine. I'm not asking you to open the safe; I'm telling you."

The captain said, "Either way, I open that safe, and all hell breaks loose."

"Let me worry about that. I'll need to see your manifest, ownership, and registration documentation."

The captain said, "Well, turning over that information will be easier since you killed the one who could report me.

"Report you to whom?"

"To those who would come after me."

Lange said, "What's that mean?"

On his knees, turning the dial, the captain didn't respond to the question. Instead, he said, "Do you know the meaning of an international incident?"

Curious, Lange said yes, "Why?"

The captain stood up and handed Lange the papers. He pointed at the documents and said, "Because I'm not sure why, but you're now holding one. Mysterious things have occurred on this voyage from loading my cargo to your boarding."

Lange looked through the small stack of pages. "Control, Lange here; I have got the ship's documents."

Kate said. "First, is there any ownership information?"

The sound of shuffling papers was followed by Lange saying. "This is a mess. I've docs going back ten years. The latest ownership information I have is Santiago S.A., and back then, the flag was Panamanian."

Kate looked over at Loren.

Konner was still sitting next to her as she went through the TerraDyne database provided by Mom. She entered the search string and was not satisfied.

Penn said, "Colonel, hold for a sec."

Loren entered another set of search parameters while the room waited. Again, nothing. She said to herself, "Let's try this."

After a few seconds, she said, "Gotcha. Santiago S.A. is a leasing company that's a subdivision three levels down from Aray S.R.L." She looked up with a grim and said. "And Aray S.R.L. is a subsidiary of TerraDyne marine."

"Yes," Penn shouted.

Kate said, "I just wanted to make sure it was a TerraDyne tanker. If we had made a mistake, it would have been twice as bad for us than for them." Kate looked at Konner and smiled.

"She was happy." Konner thought. "That was nice."

"Control, Lange here; the ship's log is a mess, but it seems the ship made recent port calls in North Korea and Hai Phong in Vietnam. The ship's registration has changed using several names over the last few years. Probably not important for what we're doing."

Kate said, "Colonel, can you read them anyway?"

Lange read off, "The Atenor, Macoma Bay, Doha Sea, and Sea Clipper, to name a few. Want me to keep going?"

"No," That's fine, Kate said.

Lange looked at his watch, "It seems we're now less than an hour out. We want to be off the ship when it hits. I'm going to tell Rondo to start on his way back."

Konner listened to the discussion over the speakers and then tried to figure out why his brain was uncomfortable with something. He looked at his phone like it contained the answer. When the dots connected, it was a shock.

He stood up and interrupted everyone; he said, "I'm sorry, could you have the colonel reread the names of the ships.?"

Given his previously intentional low profile, Penn and the rest of the room were surprised by Konner's outburst. He'd made a point of not wanting to be a distraction. Konner looked at Kate, and she saw him intensely focused and, she thought, agitated. Kate cocked her head and said. "Konner?"

Penn said, "Colonel, what were those previous registration names again?"

"You want them all or just the ones I read."

Penn looked at Konner and said, "Lange can hear you. Go ahead."

Konner said to Lange, "Just the last three, I think."

Lange read them off, "The Atenor, Macoma Bay, Doha Sea."

Konner said, "How's Doha spelled?

"D O H A," Lange said.

Konner was shaking his head. What appeared to be happening was beyond coincidence. Konner ignored everyone else in the room, "Kate, something is going on you should know. It's dangerous, and I'm sorry, but you're right in the middle."

"What is it?"

Konner thought about where he was and, with few options, started towards Kate's office while saying, "I need to talk to you in private."

A confused Kate followed him. In her office, she said, "Konner, you have me worried; no, you have me scared." She pointed back towards the ops center. "You were a little strange back there."

Konner was thinking at lightning speed. "I'm dealing with something that's highly classified. The US is desperately looking for a ship carrying a shipment of military-grade u235 uranium headed for Iran. If we don't find it, the Israeli air force is sitting on the ground with engines running, waiting to bomb the Iranian facility taking delivery. It could start a war."

"Konner, that's all very serious, but what does it have to do with me or us?"

"That shipment is on the Legacy 5, also known as the Doha Sea."

Konner's phone rang. He looked up and said. "Its' Devroe."

"Yes," Konner said.

Devroe said, "We have detected the ready alert has moved from the tarmac to taxi positions. That means they're hot and burning fuel."

Konner could hear the president in the background say, "We need more time" Devroe said, "You need to call Israel and get more time."

Konner said, "You're on speaker with Kate."

"Why? She's not cleared."

Ignoring his comment, Konner said, "I'm pretty sure I've located the shipment."

"What?

Konner looked up at Kate and said. "Kate and her tier one team just boarded the ship that I think has the u235."

CHAPTER 68

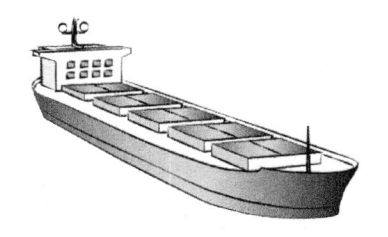

Legacy 5
White House Situation Room
HMAS Adelaide

Konner's said to Devroe, "Look, it's a complete surprise and a bigger coincidence. And that was surpassed only by finding out Kate and her team are involved." The president and Devroe looked at each other with empty stares.

Finally, Devroe said, "Did you just say you've found the shipment? Wait—you *think* you found the shipment? You can't be serious."

"I'm very serious."

"Why? What's the position? Where is it?"

Konner looked at Kate and said, "Can you get the coordinates?"

She picked up the phone as Konner continued.

"It's in the Arabian Gulf," Konner replied. "But where isn't as crucial as we found the ship."

Kate handed him a slip of paper. "OK, I've got the coordinates here."

Konner read the coordinates while an analyst in the situation room entered the information into the system. The position came up on the screen in seconds.

The president said, "Konner, do I understand you're not positive it's the ship?"

Konner said, "Yes, that's correct. I need to verify the material is onboard. However, all information points to this ship, including the boarding party fighting their way on board. They killed three of the security guards."

Perez said, "Let's assume, for a moment, it's there, and then what? That Iranian frigate will not play nice. If it's there, can Kate's people get that material off the ship and move it somewhere? I have no idea where yet?"

After getting the coordinates, Kate was still on the phone and heard the president's question. She said, "Penn, I need you in my office right now."

Konner said to Devroe, "We're checking to see if Kate's team can move the material."

Penn hurriedly walked in with a curious look on his face. In the background, Konner could hear the president talking to those gathered in the situation room.

Konner asked Penn, "Can your guys lift a shipment and get it off that ship?"

"That's rather vague," Penn said. "What shipment? We have a chopper on the way to exfil the team now. We might be able to use that to lift something."

Devroe said, "Penn can you hear me?"

"Yes, sir," Penn said, "I can hear you, but you can't hear the team on the ship."

"Got it; you'll need to relay to me what's going on there. As far as the shipment, it's a lead box or cabinet that probably weighs a thousand pounds. We think it's on the ship you boarded. If we find it, we need to move the box to another location. I don't know where yet."

Penn listened and, assimilating a few disconnected facts, said. "Wait."

He walked over to Kate's wall monitor, changed to the ops room feed, and said, "You need to see this. Earlier, Kate thought something wasn't right and had Lange start a search of the ship. As a result, Lange has the captain opening the hatch to a suspicious compartment. He looked at Kate and Konner and said, "Lange turned on the video feed when the two of you left the ops room."

Those in Kates's office looked at the screen and heard Lange say to the captain. "What's in there? Open this hatch."

Konner said to Devroe. "We're looking at video from the ship. After searching the ship, the team found a suspicious compartment they are trying to open."

The captain said, "My orders are specific. I give the combination to the SSD officer on the Iranian ship when we make the transfer at sea."

Lange said, "What Iranian ship?"

"We were to meet an Iranian IRGC military ship and make the transfer at sea. They're waiting for us, but then you changed my course."

Konner said, "Devroe, the captain says he was meeting an Iranian ship to transfer the shipment at sea."

Devroe said, "Konner, we have been monitoring an Iranian frigate that in the last hour has changed course, and it's heading directly towards your position at battle speed."

"Got that," Konner said, "with or without that shipment, we need to get Lange and his men off the boat and fast.

Kate said, "Colonel, can you hear me?"

"Yes, ma'am."

"Time is getting short. We need to get your team off that boat; you need to get that hatch open quickly, so we know what we're dealing with.".

"Copy that," Lange said. He turned to the captain and said, "What's your name?"

"Anton Kikorov."

Well, Captain Kikorov, it's been a lovely chat now, let us into this compartment and now."

The captain looked at Lange with a pained look. "I'm going to pay dearly for this."

"Look," Lange said, "I don't have time for this. No one is going to know if you open it. We tied up the rest of the crew, leaving them in the citadel. For that matter, go with us and say you were a hostage. Open the compartment now."

"You'll take me? How?"

Lange said, "We have a chopper on the way; now open the damn hatch."

Looking relieved, the captain entered the code unlocking the hatch.

Stepping in, Lange saw a box eighteen inches square sitting on a rolling dolly. Lange walked around it so ops could see the package on video.

Everyone, including those in the situation room, heard Penn say, "Good God, there it is."

Kate said, "How do you know?"

"Let's just say another life."

"After trying to move it, Lange said, "It's an incredibly heavy box."

Konner said, "Devroe, I think we have it. We're looking at a video of a very heavy lead container without any markings. It was behind a newly installed hatch with a special combination lock. The captain says the package secretly came aboard just before departing North Korea.

Devroe said, "That pretty much nails it down. We need to get that box off the ship."

The president said, "Even if we can, what will we do with it?"

The defense secretary said, "Take it to the Adelaide."

Konner looked at Penn and said, "Can you do that?"

Penn looked at Kate for direction.

She said, "Whatever we can do without putting my people in danger."

Penn said, "We can try."

All three of them could hear Devroe say to the president, "We have serious security issues here."

The president said, "We don't have a choice. Get the shipment. We can sort out clearances later."

Devroe said, "Konner, are you still there?"

"Yes,"

"Penn," Devroe said, "can you hear me?"

"Yes, I'm here."

"Your people need to know the box contains 90% grade u235 uranium, so instruct everyone not to open the box. We're desperate to keep it from going into Iranian hands. It's dangerous, and we need to do this as quickly as possible for several reasons. Ten thousand innocent reasons, to be exact. You need to do this while an Iranian frigate is fast-tracking to your location with swords drawn."

Kate said, Mr. President, this changes things substantially."

Penn was concerned, "If there's an Iranian frigate on its way, I need to get my people off that boat. The Iranians are equipped with surface to surface missiles that can turn that ship into wet dust."

Devroe said, "You're correct, but they won't use them because that will sink the ship and the uranium along with it. They need the shipment and the boat intact."

Penn said, "Copy that. But it doesn't mean they won't try to rope down and board her. The team is not armed for that kind of firefight."

Loren said, "The Iranian ship is an Alvand class and doesn't have an air arm. It doesn't have a chopper, so they can only get on that ship with a ship-board RIB (Ridged Inflatable Boat).

Kate said, "Dr. Devroe, That doesn't mean if they get close enough, they can't fire upon the ship putting everyone in danger."

Devroe said, "This is going to come down to timing. We'll give you all the support we can, but we can't have any Americans associated with that shipment."

Kate said, "Mr. President, We'll do whatever we can up to the point of putting my men in an impossible position."

Devroe said, "Konner, you need to get to Koffman and get us an hour if you can."

"On it. If Koffman has those planes running, it's not going to be easy."

Perez said, "Get back to me with what he says. Be sure to remind him we never talked to him and will deny it if it comes out."

"I'll be back." Konner turned to Kate and said, "I'm so sorry. I had no idea this involved you in any way."

Kate said, "Let's get this fixed. You call whomever you need to, and I'll return to the ops room. You're aware the team will learn about this secret operation?"

Konner said, "From what I heard from the president, it's the least of our problems right now." He started dialing.

***

Captain Fowler was in CIC looking at the radar screen. She picked up the radiophone and said, "Yes, Dr. Devroe, Fowler here."

Devroe said, "Captain, I want to update you. We have found the package. It's on the dry freighter, the Legacy 5. I've sent the coordinates."

The Nashville's radar operator pointed out the position on the screen to Fowler.

Devroe continued, "An independent team is aboard and is transporting the package to the Adelaide. Monitor the situation and be available, but under no circumstance are you to board that ship without the president's approval."

"Copy that," she said.

Devroe said, "Are you aware of an Iranian frigate in the area?"

"Yes, I'm in CIC and see it's changed course and increased speed. Its current heading is to intercept the Legacy 5."

Devroe said, "How long does the team have?"

Fowler looked at her radar operator, and he said, "Thirty maybe forty minutes."

"Doctor, we estimate forty minutes give or take," Fowler said.

"I've clearance for you to monitor the boarding team's efforts. The frequency is also in my message. Await further orders."

"Roger that."

***

Penn said, "Colonel, we have a problem. That box you just found contains weapons-grade uranium. A fact so classified it would make your head spin."

"Penn, I wasn't born yesterday. Lead-lined boxes don't usually transport popcorn."

"I just wanted you to understand the seriousness of the situation. We need to get that box off that ship using the Black Hawk. Then we need to take it to another ship in the area."

"OK, I mean, I guess we can do that. We could have a problem. The Black Hawk, when it arrives, will have just enough fuel to make it back. With an extra thousand pounds, it might not make it that far."

Penn said, "Yes, I thought of that and haven't had time to develop a solution. You work on how to get it off the ship with the Black Hawk, and I'll work on the fuel issue. Ah, there's one more thing."

Lange almost laughed, "Penn," he said, "just how much can you fit into a single can?"

"There's a very angry Iranian warship headed your way that knows what's going on. They want that box and will be willing to fight for possession."

"Well, I say we get our butts out of here ASAP. How much time do we have?"

"Right now, about thirty minutes or so.

Lange said, "Get back to me on the fuel problem. There aren't a lotta gas stations out here."

"Colonel," Penn said.

"More?" Lange replied.

"If you pull this off, I'll buy the beer."

"Ha, If I pull this off, you're going to buy me a whole damn brewery. Gotta go."

CHAPTER 69

Vianden Castle
Legacy 5
USS Nashville

Konner said, "Mr. Koffman, thank you for taking my call. I can now inform you we have located the shipment, and we're in the process of transferring the material to a secure location. We just need another hour to complete the operation."

"Mr. Houston, believe me when I say I want to believe you but without proof that shipment could be anywhere. Including in Iranian hands."

Konner said, a little taken aback, "I'm sorry, sir, but I'm saying it representing the president, and that should count for something. We talked about transparency; it's not in our interest to mislead you at this point."

"Mr. Houston?"

Konner felt an important sentence coming and was surprised when he said, "Please hold for a second."

Konner waited no more than thirty seconds before Koffman came back on the line.

"Thank you for holding. I needed to get to my office as I want you to understand my position. I'm the youngest prime minister to ever hold this office. Most of the people I deal with, especially the military, were around when we were fighting for our lives and almost lost the country. I'm a politician, but most people in that room can still smell the smoke of Arabs trying to destroy our nation. I must go forward unless I have solid proof to present to some very restless members of my government. That's the reality of things right now."

Konner said, "I think I'm right when I say you're monitoring Iranian communications."

"Perhaps," was the response.

"The Iranians have a frigate on its way to intercept the ship that has their u235. Hopefully, we'll be gone, along with the shipment, when they get there. When the Iranian boarding party reports it's gone, it will ripple through the Ayatollah's circle. Your monitoring will detect this. That will be your proof. Mr. Prime Minister, we're close to solving this problem without bloodshed. We need another hour."

"There's a certain unreal element to this conversation," Koffman said. "I've no idea who you are except Devroe saying you speak directly for him and the president."

Konner said, "I'm sure you have gone over my file with a microscope, so you know who I am. Let's not dwell on secondary issues. You know why we need to handle our communication in this manner."

"Regardless," Koffman said. "I'm inclined to release the operation against the Natanz facility. Mr. Houston, you cannot imagine the heated exchanges in this room, the atmosphere heavy with history. I'm sure you've made a valiant effort, but my hardliners want solid proof, and, your word aside, or a message we might or might not intercept, you have none. I'm afraid my hands are tied."

Konner's knuckles went white as he squeezed the phone in frustration. "What if I could get you proof?" They were desperate words that came out before Konner thought it through.

"You have two minutes."

"Can you hold for one minute?

"That leaves you with one."

"Can you give me another cell number for a video feed if we stay on this line?"

Konner wrote it down and ran back to the ops room.

Kate saw him urgently burst into the room. His movements were quick and, in his urgency, restricted to the bare minimum.

He addressed no one, saying, "Can we send the team's video feed showing the package to this number?" He held up a piece of paper.

Loren took it and said, "Are they ready on the other end?"

Konner nodded.

"Then yes," she said.

Penn got on the line and said, "Colonel Lange, Penn here, be aware we're taking your video feed and sending it somewhere important. Try to provide as much video as possible of you preparing the shipment.

"Roger that," Lange said.

The room could see the feed from the colonel's helmet camera on the monitors.

Back on the phone, Konner said, "Mr. prime minister, as soon as we can make the connection, I'll send a video feed of the team getting the package ready to transport off the ship."

The video in the ops center presented a clear picture of the box right in front of Lange.

Back on the phone, Konner said to Koffman, "Mr. Prime Minister, you should be receiving a video feed showing the u235's lead container. Can you see it?"

"Yes, I can see it. What am I looking at?"

"A team moving the shipment from its current location onto the boat deck. A helicopter will then transport it to another location."

"How do I know that's the shipment?"

"The box you see is lead-lined and weighs over a thousand pounds. Unfortunately, no markings indicate it's stolen u235 or headed to Iran. However, it's a TerraDyne ship, and we know they participate in all manner of illegal shipments and will do anything for money. Also, the ship made a port call in North Korea five days ago, one of the few sources that could provide the u2355 material. The ship in question also had its transponder turned off and an armed security team waiting for my boarding party. The NSA had a source that said the ship carrying the shipment was named the Doha Sea. This ship, named Legacy 5, had documents onboard indicating one of the ship's previous registrations was the Doha Sea. That's a lot of coincidences."

"I'll have to agree with that," Koffman said.

"There's one more thing. The Iranians have a military ship heading towards the team at flank speed. It looks like the Iranians are making sure they get what they paid for."

Konner said, "You can stay on the line up to the point we make the drop at the third-party location. Can we have the time to complete our operation?"

"Wait," Koffman said, "you need to hold on." Konner could hear voices in the background, and one, in particular, was definitely shouting."

Because Koffman was close to the phone, Konner could hear him clearly say, "General, when you're prime minister, you can make that call. Right now, it's my call, and I suggest you fall in line."

"Mr. Houston? Is an hour enough?"

Konner's body went limp with gratitude."Yes, and thank you. One more thing, can you pull back the ready alert on the runway so my friends in Washington can see we're making progress?"

"I'll take them off the runway but only back to their line position in full view from above. We'll shut the planes down to refuel in case this goes south."

"Thank you," Konner said. "You can get me on this line. Call me before doing anything else. Again, I'll let the video run until it leaves the ship, then we go black."

Konner put the phone down. He bent at the waist; his head went forward into his hands as he took a deep breath. Kate came over and, putting a hand on his back, said. "It's been quite the day. Our team has it under control. They've been in worse situations than this."

Then she added, "Perhaps without the uranium."

Konner nodded, but Kate saw the effect the pressure had on him.

The video was still up on the screen, and they heard Lange say, "Boys, we need to get this out on the deck so we can hook it to the chopper, and we can't drop it."

Lange pointed at Pete and said, "Go find something we can use to secure it to the Black Hawk. OK, let's roll this thing away from the superstructure and out to a clear space so Rondo won't hit anything."

"I heard that," Rondo, the pilot, said from the Black Hawk over the intercom.

They started pushing the dolly and its cargo down the ship's side next to the guardrail. OK," Lange said, straining. "Now over between the loading hatches towards the ship's center."

Pete came up from behind with a bundle of nylon straps with a metal hook on the end. He also had four large new rolls of the same material.

The control room could see Pete standing there with the straps.

Kate said, "Everyone is that going to hold it? Penn said it was a thousand pounds. We need a weight check of everything before lifting all this. We don't want it in the water."

Konner and Kate exchanged concerned looks.

Rondo came over the intercom, "I've already completed the calculations on the weight. The chopper can lift the package and load all of you with 300 lbs. to spare. Oh, I forgot. That's leaving Pete behind."

Kate said, "Mr. Rondo, we need you on task here."

Over the radio, everyone heard, "Rondo here, sorry ma'am."

Lange said, "Three hundred pounds is cutting it pretty close since I've added the captain." As far as the straps holding, I don't have a clue. We don't want this thing in the water."

Kate looked at Loren and said, "Lange, hold on, we're checking on the straps."

"Already there," Loren said. "How wide are the straps?" She asked.

"Lange?" Penn said, "Did you hear that?"

"It looks like two inches," Lange said.

Loren said, "Good news. It says here the straps are good for seven thousand pounds per inch of width. That's amazing."

Pete was shading his eyes, looking into the sky. "We've got company," he said.

Lange looked at Pete, then looked up and saw a drone. "Well, nothing is a secret now." He said.

Lange said, "Control reporting a drone over our position."

Kate said, "What does that mean? Is it armed?"

Lange said, "No, it doesn't look armed."

Penn said, "That has to be Iranian. Nothing you can do but get out of there as quickly as possible."

"Roger that," Lange said.

Instructing his men, "We don't have the time or equipment to leverage the containers up to put straps underneath. So let's run the straps under the dolly and take them both."

The people in ops looked as the video feed showed the men running the straps under the dolly and bringing them together at a loading ring and then the single length to the hook.

Jerry said, "How are we attaching it to the Black Hawk?"

Rondo said, "Someone needs to count me down to a point someone can attach the hook underneath. We can't use the wench. It's too heavy and will rip it right off the side. Standing underneath could be dangerous, so don't use Pete he owes me money."

Lange said forcefully, "*Rondo.*"

"Oh, sorry again."

***

Captain Fowler was down in CIC following the Iranian ship closing in on the Liberty 5. Fowler asked, "How much time before the Iranians get there?" In front of the screen, the technician said, "Eighteen to twenty minutes tops. That's assuming they don't start shooting at the Liberty 5 before then."

Fowler said, "That's unlikely, as it will draw attention to something they want kept secret." She turned to the navigator and said, "I want an exact location of the Iranian ship, and stand by; I'll be on the bridge."

"Yes, Ma'am."

CHAPTER 70

USS Nashville
IRIS Sabalan
Legacy 5

Konner called Devroe. "I need some good news." Devroe said.

Konner brought Devroe up to speed on the additional hour Den-David granted and the tight timing getting the team off the ship before the frigate arrived.

Konner said, "This is going to come down to minutes. Where is the Nashville?"

"Close enough, but we can't be shooting at an Iranian warship."

"Have you gotten anything from the NSA on the status of the Israeli planes?"

"Yes, the Israelis are backing off. We have a live feed-up and can see them pulling the ready alert off the flight line. Nice work, Konner. Really—I mean it, nice work."

"Thanks, but it's temporary and not over yet. I'll get back with anything from here."

***

Captain Fowler, monitoring Lange's communication, concluded the Sabalan was close enough that the team, whoever they are, would not make it off the ship in time. She picked up the phone to the navigator and said, "Listen very carefully. Plot a course intersecting with the Iranian ship at thirty degrees, moving it off course. When we get close, I'll decide how close."

"Yes, Ma'am," Came the reply.

"Radar, as we approach, I want to know the second that ship changes course or speed regardless of the degree."

"Roger that."

A short time later on the Sabalan, the Iranian captain saw the Nashville coming directly at him on a collision course. The captain shouted, "Hail that ship and insist we're the stand-on vessel and demand a change of course."

Captain fowler heard the hail and didn't respond. They listened to the demand again with more urgency. "Steady," she said to the helmsman, "Be prepared for hard a port."

The demand again came over the radio, but this time with a loss of professional decorum. The voice yelled, "Collision imminent, change your course."

Fowler waited, and her radar operator said, "Iranian ship changing course now heading two five zero."

Fowler said to the helmsman, "Hard-a-port."

"Hard-a-port aye." The helmsman responded"

Fowler said, "Come to two four zero

"Right to two four zero, aye."

Fowler was standing and grabbed the chair arm as the keel shifted, and the destroyer performed a battle turn."

Swearing came over the radio from the Iranian ship, accompanied by shouting.

Fowler said to her XO, "It will take them another 16 to 20 minutes to go around us and return to course. It might just be enough time to allow the team to lift off."

The XO said, "But we still might have a problem."

"You're right." Into the phone, Fowler said, "Weapons officer stand by to lock onto that Iranian ship."

"Yes, ma'am,"

* * *

Konner and the ops room watched the video as Rondo carefully lowered the chopper to Lange's hand signals. In the background, the Ethiopian coastline loomed large as the freighter headed towards a disgraceful fate.

The downward air thrust made it challenging to work underneath as Pete struggled to maintain balance. Lange sent everyone but Pete to the side. Lange was thirty feet towards the bow, so Rondo could see him waving instructions.

As Rondo slowly brought the aircraft down, Pete sat underneath, wearing a pair of goggles. Finally, with a slight jump, he secured the hook. One by one, the men threw their gear up and into the opening of the chopper. Then using the rope ladder, all of them, including the captain, made it into the opening, now ten feet off the deck.

Kate said, "Colonel make sure that package is secured properly; we don't want it in the water."

"Yes, Ma'am. I'm waiting to see it fully suspended in the air before we take off."

All the while, Rondo was keeping the aircraft steady as he slowly started lifting and the straps drew tight. The last one still on the deck, Lange saw the package lift and hold the heavy cargo.

Satisfied, he said, "Everything looks secure." He ran and grabbed the hoist line from the winch hanging down about thirty feet. Lange held onto the winch line as a heavily accented voice came over the radio.

"This is the IRIS Sabalan calling Black Hawk helicopter. We're monitoring your activities. Don't remove the cargo from the ship, or you will be fired upon. I repeat, or you will be fired upon."

At the same time, Rondo saw the Black Hawks air defense panel light up as the craft's sensors detected a fire control radar locking for a firing solution. Rondo shouted, "We're lit up. Someone has a lock on us. We're seconds from being dead."

Simultaneously on the IRIS Sabalan, the operations officer informed the captain, "Sir, imminent threat, we're being targeted by missile direction radar. It shows the missile has been armed but not launched."

"Who's doing it? Where is it coming from?"

"I can't tell, sir; the signal's power has the sensors saturated and unable to lock on a source. The computer is trying to sort everything out now, but it has to be the American ship."

The captain heard a siren start over the intercom.

"Sir, we now have a level one system failure. Systems are down, sir; if a missile is launched, it won't take long to arrive in these close waters, and right now, we're blind."

"Get it up and running now." The captain shouted.

"Sir, at best, we can re-sequence everything, but that's going to take some time we don't have."

The captains' reactions were conflicted. He had specific orders to offload that shipment at all costs. He also remembered what happened to the captain that lost a ship to the US navy in 1988. Failure on either front would result in the end of his Naval career or worse. After what seemed like an eternity, the operations officer's voice brought him back."

"Sir?"

The captain said, "Stand down, fire control. XO, prepare to board on my order."

"Rondo says, oh man, oh man, it's gone. Let's get this over with."

***

On the USS Nashville, Captain Fowler, monitoring the conversations on the open line, just smiled. She picked up the ship's phone to her weapons officer and said, "This is the captain, nice job."

"Ma'am, that was about three times the normal energy we need to paint a target that close for a solid lock. It's the first time we have used the Agus system for EW (Electromagnetic Warfare). It worked."

Fowler said, "I wanted to make sure they got the point.

***

Konner said to Koffman, "Mr. Prime Minister, does the video provide enough proof we have the material and it will not fall into Iranian hands?"

"Yes, our thanks for the video. It was key in convincing us your efforts were successful. However, you still have the problem of an American team performing the operation. Something that visible is going to be hard to keep secret. I, for one, hope you're able to pull it off, but I used to be head of Mossad and know a thing or two."

Konner looked at Kate and Penn and said, "It wasn't our team. There's nothing to hide."

Konner could hear Koffman smile when he said. "Indeed, Mr. Houston, the world is an interesting place. My concerns are only with the uranium. For that, I'm grateful; whatever you did on your side to make it happen is not my concern."

***

Having gone through channels and with the Australians in agreement, Penn said. "Control to Rondo, proceed immediately to the HMAS Adelaide. Hover to release the cargo, then land and refuel when they clear the deck."

Rondo says, "Did someone say land on an Australian warship?"

Lange said, "Just follow orders. What's wrong with landing on another military ship?"

Rondo said, "Did everyone forget we're civilians? You normally need some sort of engraved invitation."

"You landed on a nuclear carrier once without permission. I think you will be alright, and you'll still go to heaven."

"Yes, but that time it was that or die."

"Rondo," Lange said sharply. "On task."

"On my way," was the response.

CHAPTER 71

Oval office

Devroe, in the oval office, sat on the couch. His feet were on the table directly in front of him. He took a deep breath while looking out the opposite window onto the rose garden.

"We have a problem." The president said.

"I thought we just solved one, actually more like twenty?"

"It created another. What do we do with the u235 on board the Adelaide?"

Devroe's shoulders slumped. "Got any ideas?" he said.

Perez said, "Uranium has a signature. An expert can detect the origins of that uranium down to the originating mine. There's no way to eliminate that, so someone can prove it's that specific Iranian shipment any time in the next ten thousand years. If someone finds and identifies that exact shipment in our possession, all of this goes out the window."

Devroe, on overload, raised his arm and pointed out the window. "Have you ever sat here and just enjoyed the green outside the window?"

Perez said, "Do you remember what President Obama did with Osama bin Laden after raiding his compound?"

"Where did that come from?"

"Pay attention; it's the solution to the problem. Obama didn't want bin Laden's body to become a shrine to rally terrorists, so they made sure no one in a hundred years could find him."

Devroe's eyes got wider when he understood. "They dumped him into the sea so he'd disappear."

"During the time you orchestrated this miracle, I called the Australian prime minister again."

"Did you give him our sincere thanks for his deft handling of a touchy situation?"

"No, I asked him for another favor."

Devroe looked over at Perez in his chair. "You didn't."

"Yes, I did. I asked him to dump the u235 overboard in the deepest part of the Gulf of Aden, where it's unrecoverable. I looked it up. It's almost nine thousand feet deep. I asked him not to enter the location or the disposal in the ship's log."

"And?"

"He agreed."

Devroe smiled. "Brilliant solution to an impossible problem. If you ever decide to run for president someday, I would be happy to run your campaign."

Perez laughed. "You did that already, remember?"

"Oh," Devroe said, "I'm too tired to remember."

CHAPTER 72

Belgrade
Serbia

A concerned Vanek came into Petrovic's office reading several messages. The first message was sent to TerraDyne's shipping company by the captain of the Legacy5.

"Not good," Vanek said out loud.

"What's not good?"

Vanek understood the significance of the Legacy 5 shipment and knew the players involved. He'd warned Petrovic not to take this deal. Vanek thought Petrovic's ego made him reach too far and feared he was in over his head for the first time. Usually in total control and a master of his business, this was a bigger venue with unforgiving players and less room for error. Vanek insisted they weren't ready to deal with competing sovereign states battling on a world stage, and the stakes were high enough to threaten the business. He tried, to no avail, to point out the exposure brokering a deal of that magnitude. But Petrovic, driven by hubris and a constant search for fast profits, wouldn't listen. Noting his displeasure, Petrovic isolated Vanek and ran the operation himself. It was just another incident that made Vanek rethink his position.

"What, let's hear it," Petrovic said. "You look worried."

"We have a serious problem here. We have several messages, and none of them are good. First, someone just hijacked the Legacy5 and removed the u235 shipment—it's gone."

The familiar and unwanted wave approached and went over Petrovic. The tightness started, and he knew it was just the beginning. At first, Petrovic didn't fully realize the meaning of Vanek's statement. It didn't fit into his self-image of not failing. He expected what worked in the past would also work in the future. He came back with, "That's impossible.

"Yeah, that's what *I* thought. The captain sent the message to us just before armed operatives boarded the vessel and removed the u235. First, he sent one to our contact reporting directly to the Ayatollah, asking for help. So the Iranians know the shipment was removed and is now in the wind."

Petrovic's face changed the instant he realized the impact it would have on his business.

"Second, the Iranians demand you return the money they paid for the material or deliver it per the agreement."

Vanek looked down on the seated Petrovic and could feel the momentum in Petrovic's life re-route itself into unknown territory. Petrovic was shaking his head, "We were only holding the money. We were only brokering the deal. I need that money to pay the North Koreans."

"You're right on that count, as the third message is from the North Koreans, who have completed their part of the deal and are asking for payment. They don't know the shipment is missing yet."

As the realization became clear, he almost shouted, "Where did they take the shipment?"

"At the time of this message, I guess the captain didn't know."

Petrovic was pacing the room and said, "The only way out of this is to get that shipment back. You need to find it quickly. I need something to say to the North Koreans."

Vanek, no stranger to power plays but on a smaller scale, thought, "The man's ego, now energetically in motion, kept him from realizing he was a dead man. Other than drug lords, North Koreans and the Iranians top the list of the people you can't cross, and Petrovic had managed to infuriate them both."

Someone knocked and came into the office. They handed Vanek another message before leaving as fast as they entered.

Vanek said, "We have a new message, and it's from the Iranians. According to the Iranian ship that was going to meet the Legacy 5, if the freighter stays on course, it will run right into an empty beach on the coast of Ethiopia. That will not be a pretty sight in the news."

Vanek looked at Petrovic, expecting him to draw his imaginary samurai sword, explode, and vow to kill somebody. Instead, he saw the parts of his personality that governed his world withdraw into an uncontrolled dark space. The feeling deep inside that he could handle adversity transformed into an awareness of impending doom and a loss of control. Vanek saw the first signs of an anxiety attack when Petrovic started having trouble breathing.

"Deep breaths," Vanek said. "Take deep breaths." Petrovic's doctor warned his problem could become intense unless he changed his lifestyle.

Petrovic put both hands on his chest as his eyes started glazing over. Returning to his chair, he leaned forward onto the desk.

Vanek said, "It's not a heart attack; it just feels like one. Where are the pills?" Vanek asked. There was no response.

He opened the right-hand drawer, then went around behind Petrovic and opened the left-hand drawer with no success. He grabbed him by the shoulders and leaned him back against the chair. Vanek pulled open the center drawer, located the bottle, and hurriedly poured the tablets into his hand. With most falling to the floor, he selected one pill and reached for a water bottle.

"Open your mouth." He ordered and inserted the tablet. "Here, drink this."

Petrovic managed both without a word. Vanek looked down. This tower of power right now looked helpless.

"It's OK," he thought. "It wasn't his problem anymore. After a relatively short search, he had found a more legit company that needed a director of security. He was going to own part of the company. It was a drop in salary, but it came with equity in the company that could pay off big later.

Most importantly, he turned down better offers to be with a company located in Frankfurt. After a life of living on the edge, taking chances, and performing acts others wouldn't, he wondered if he could work himself into the mainstream. He would call her, first just to hear her voice, then who knows, but he would try. It was his chance to go legit before being thrown in jail and the opportunity disappearing. The failed attempt to torch the charity office was a night of reckoning. Thankful, he'd followed his gut feelings; he managed to escape capture. Then there was the evening over a few drinks when Holland said, "You're young enough to start over. Do it before it's too late." It was a strange comment coming from the firm's most trusted employee.

CHAPTER 73

Vianden Castle

Kate had intensely listened to the operation unfold and was exhausted. The package was on its way to the Australian frigate. Barely an hour ago, they were trying to run a ship aground to fight the war Petrovic insisted on having. The day then turned into something else entirely, but she knew there was still the problem with the shipment.

Kate said to Konner. "What happens now."

"The Nashville will shadow the Aussie ship as they exit the area. I don't know what Devroe will do with the u235. I don't know what his options are."

Standing, Kate looked down at a clearly exhausted Konner, who had almost fallen into the chair after his last call with Koffman. She brought over a water bottle. "I think you need this." She said.

He grabbed the bottle and produced a smile for her. Kate saw behind his attempt to hide what he felt. She knew he was still recovering from an intense encounter with uncertainty and the need to perform perfectly.

His glazed eyes returned to normal when his phone cried out. It was Devroe's number. Konner listened to him for a few seconds, then looked up at Kate, and handed her the phone. "It's the White House." He said.

Kate, with a bewildered look, said, "White House?"

Konner didn't respond as he held the phone out, waiting for her to reach for it.

"Kate?" Konner said, still holding the phone outstretched.

"Yes?" She said.

"I would take it."

"Of course," she said, " back to the moment, grabbing the phone. "Kate Adler here."

"Kate, this is Martin Perez."

"Yes, Mr. President. How can we help you?"

Perez laughed heartily. Recovering from a light moment in a day of panic, he said with a broad smile. "Kate, you and your team just helped us avoid people dying. I can't think of anything more important, so you have helped enough. This call is to thank you."

"Oh," Kate said. "In that case, your welcome, Sir." She chuckled. "It's not like we planned to be in the middle of an international crisis. We tend to avoid those on a daily basis."

"Normally, I would say I can't get into details because it's classified. However, despite the classification, I think that firewall disappeared a long time ago when we needed the help of you and your people. You rescued us from a delicate situation."

"I don't know how we could've said no under the circumstances. It would be bad form to say something like we don't work weekends."

The president laughed again. "It goes without saying; I owe you one big time."

"Oh, I think clearing our civilian chopper to land on your nuclear aircraft carrier was a pretty big favor. That act also saved lives. Those same lives were part of the team that performed this afternoon. Ironic, don't you think?"

"Ironic and fortunate. Kate, do you play golf?"

"No, Mr. President. Why."

"I'm giving you a presidential mulligan. You can use it at any time just call me. Ah, you will probably have to go through Devroe, but I'm here."

"Mulligan. Is that a drink?"

Kate heard the president try to talk and laugh at the same time. When he came back on the phone, he was almost breathless. "Ms. Adler, it's anything you want it to be. Thanks again."

Kate looked at Konner and said, "What's a mulligan?"

"A what?" He said?

Kate looked at him impatiently. "Come on, what's a mulligan? The president said he gave me a mulligan."

Konner couldn't help himself and, standing up, hugged Kate in front of everyone. Elena and Loren were both pleased but surprised at the gesture. Kate pushed him back and said. "I asked you a question."

Penn said. "I'm sure you'll never need it. I'm very sure."

Konner said, "It's a do-over. A kind of gift. The president is an avid golfer, and he was saying, in his own way, he owes you one big time."

"Well," Kate said, looking very pleased with herself. "I would say that's kind of nice to have in your back pocket."

Brad said. "From the most powerful man in the world. I would say so."

Kate said, "Unfortunately, being heroes doesn't remove our existing problem. We wanted to create a problem for TerraDyne; what about the ship?"

Penn said. "Oh," rather loudly. "It's still heading for the coast. We left that ship on a course at three knots to hit a deserted beach where it wouldn't harm anyone. Authorities can pull it off at high tide. The captain left with the team, and they tied the gunman or crew up in the citadel."

Loren said, "There's zero chance of it sinking, and someone will find the crew as soon as it hits the beach. I've notified the local press that it's coming, so coverage is not a problem."

Everyone looked at Kate. "No one gets hurt, and for trying to smuggle uranium, I say we let it go. Loren, get the best photos from the locals and send out the press releases."

"Brad, can you make sure that anyone in our office who could've heard anything knows it's top secret. I'm OK with the security team, but given the confusion, we probably weren't as careful as we should have been."

Konner said. "That's a great idea," he motioned her towards her office.

When they were inside, he said, "Kate Adler, this is a day your father would have been proud. It's definitely why he created the Cartel in the first place. I'm very proud of you."

Kate looked at him and said, "I'm starving. How about dinner? Your place or mine?"

Konner said, "Let me think. Since I've no place, why don't we make it yours."

Kate said, "Excellent choice."

CHAPTER 74

Residence

Nona had cleared the remains of a wonderful dinner and left the room."

Konner said, "Do you eat like this every night?"

"Good heavens no. How could I keep this gorgeous figure."

Konner's smile was mischievous at best.

"Don't change the subject, Mr. Houston."

Konner put his wine glass down and said, "What's next for you?"

"I need to follow up on some final details with Avery on a business matter. Then tomorrow, I will confront Mr. Petrovic about his continued attacks on my company. Now that he's suffered a few attacks on his own company, perhaps we can get this straightened out."

"You just call and get an appointment?"

"We got the last meeting because we sort of ambushed him. This time the call left the impression I was now willing to negotiate due to the falling value of my company. He'll jump at the meeting."

Over coffee, Kate says, "You know one way to make the relationship work is to work on the same problems, like this time, don't you think?"

Konner said, "What are the odds of me being right in the middle of a super-secret operation that, somehow, is connected back to you?"

"I don't know, probably not very often. I now know why you looked so preoccupied when you returned to the ops room that first time. I knew something was up."

"I had many moving pieces on the chessboard, and not many were working at the time. Plus, all of it was beyond top secret."

Kate said, "Despite it being highly classified, many of my people might have ended up knowing things they shouldn't."

"A small price to pay for the eventual outcome." He said.

Chapter 75

Vianden Castel

"Alright," Kate said as everyone grabbed morning coffee and sat around the conference table. "That whole operation with Konner was more than enough drama and a diversion. We need to get back to our original plan."

Brad said, "The picture is in all the papers. Loren, nice job."

Penn said, "I wonder what Petrovic is thinking this morning?"

"I don't know for sure," Elena said, "but I know we have his attention."

Kate waved her hand, "No, we have more than his attention. I can assure you of that."

An assistant came in and said, "Kate, I have Avery on the line. You want it in your office?"

"Yes, thank you. Brad, time to get the plane ready."

"When are you leaving?"

"*We* are leaving right after Avery's call. You will need a suit."

In her office, Kate said, "Avery, where are you?"

"I'm en route to Belgrade. I left early, and I'll stay on the plane until you get there."

"Did you see the headlines?"

"Yes, the timing is great."

Kate said, "I saw TerraDyne stock dropped like a rock after the pictures of the ship stranded hit the newswires. I wanted it that way just before this meeting, and it almost didn't happen for reasons you would never believe, but I can't tell you."

Avery said, "I guess I have to leave it at that. Have you contacted Petrovic?"

"Yes, he's expecting a meek Kate Adler ready to give in to the big bad wolf."

Avery said, "It was a great idea making sure we were ready with the materials on our side."

"It won't be long before we find out."

CHAPTER 76

Belgrade
Serbia

Kate sat outside Petrovic's office with Avery and a neatly dressed Brad. She didn't feel safe walking into the lion's den and remembering Brad's skills in saving her life in Munich; she brought him along. Penn and Avery insisted on the vehicle sitting outside with Colonel Lange and two men. The three of them dressed in expensive suits with weapons under a tarp in the rear of the SUV.

The assistant right outside Petrovic's door said to Kate. "I'm sorry. If you're important, he makes you wait."

Kate said, "Is he on the phone?"

"No, and there's no one with him." She said, nodding her head to the door.

Kate stood up and, in a few steps, turned the door handle and walked into Petrovic's office unannounced.

Petrovic almost shouted. "What do you think you're doing?"

"We had an appointment," Kate said, sitting in front of his desk. And I don't like to be kept waiting. It's rude."

"I was about to call you in, so there was no need for the theatrics."

Kate didn't respond.

"So, Petrovic says, "you admit you have lost this battle, and it's over. It was inevitable. I'm in a position to offer you a fair price for Morton Roth and its offices, although substantially less than the last offer. I gave you multiple opportunities to accept, and you should have accepted the first and highest. One could chalk it up to a lack of business sense."

"Do you mean the offer right after you started attacking my business to lower the price? First, you murdered Nymagu to retain the lost contracts. Then you attacked my company directly by ransacking an office, then setting another one on fire. Kidnapping one of my employees, set you and me on a path of confrontation. However, changing your tactics from my business to my charity touched me in a place that sealed your fate."

His palms were up as he shrugged his shoulders, "I've no idea what you're talking about." He said. It was a passing attempt to deny his past actions. "You would be wise to accept it as I'm quite done with these games."

"The games you just denied knowing anything about?"

He said, "Sometimes people can be too clever and outsmart themselves. I think that's the case here." If we go to round two, it will be a very different fight."

"That I can guarantee you," Kate said, "I've learned a lot about my company and even more about myself. I have to admit it's over." Kate let that comment hang in the air.

A confident Milosh Luka Petrovic puffed himself up in his chair. Used to winning, he never got over the thrill of a victory as he laid it directly at his father's feet. The hell with the doctor; this is the way to run a life. Win at all costs. Let the rest lie in the gutter with Darwin's castoffs.

"Good," he said. He moved a folder across his desk towards Kate. "I've prepared the paperwork for the final offer."

Kate didn't move towards the folder as he had expected. It was the first thing Petrovic noticed that something was not right.

Kate said, "Mr. Petrovic, your biggest mistake was going after anything related to my charity. That changed everything."

That was the second thing he noticed. Kate's voice was defiant. "Something is not right," he thought. There was no contrition in her voice or her movements. She sat up straight, contrary to the defeated profile of the many others after losing the battle.

Petrovic pointed a finger at the folder. "You're not accepting my offer?"

Kate didn't respond. She wanted the realization to work into his mind slowly.

"If you aren't here to capitulate to my wishes, why *are* you here?"

Kate finally said, "No, it was just a way to get you to a meeting we knew otherwise you wouldn't grant. I'm here to lay out what your new world looks like."

Petrovic stood and said, "This is ridiculous, and I."

"Sit down, Mr. Petrovic," Kate shouted.

The words were overshadowed by how they were delivered. Petrovic thought, "No one ever talks to me in such a manner, and if they did, regretted it quickly and sometimes permanently."

"There's something you should know." he said, "You don't come to my office and insult me. You asked for this meeting under false pretenses." Petrovic was starting to breathe heavily. "I suggest you leave right now before you can't."

He hit the intercom on his desk and said, "Get Vanek in here."

Kate said, "Mr. Vanek left your employ and has joined another company. Tetra Marine Security, to be exact."

Kate looked at Brad, "Ask Mr. Holland to come in."

Brad sent a text to Holland, who was in his office steps away.

Petrovic's dominating countenance and posture changed as he sat down.

He said, "What do we want with Holland? If we're to resolve this situation, TerraDyne's decisions start and stop with me."

Holland came in the door and stood until Kate motioned him towards a chair. An act that didn't go unnoticed by Petrovic. "What's going on?" He thought.

Petrovic, now clearly agitated, said. "What in the living hell do we want with him?." Petrovic looked at Holland and almost shouted. "You aren't needed. Return to your office now."

Holland didn't make eye contact but unbuttoned his coat, indicating he wasn't leaving.

Petrovic stood up again behind his desk. "OK, I've had enough of this. I want everyone out of my office. I don't have to accept any of this." Looking at Kate, he said, "Especially from you."

Kate matched Petrovic's eyes for an uncomfortably long silence as she also stood. She moved forward and put both hands on the front edge of Petrovic's desk; she leaned in towards the man before saying, "Mr. Petrovic, what you think no longer matters. I suggest you sit down."

"I beg your pardon?" he said in a threatening manner. He started around his desk threateningly and bumped chests with Brad, who was a few inches his senior. "This is my company, and you will all leave at once." He reached over to hit a red button on his desk intercom to summon his heavy security.

Kate returned his stare and shook her head side to side. Petrovic didn't understand the gesture. Then he realized no one answered, and the line was dead. He then hit the button for his secretary and didn't get the usual instant response.

Kate says, "Again, I think you should sit down for this. In fact, I insist."

Petrovic started to feel the familiar but rancid feelings of weakness and panic. He'd conquer them this time as there was no option. Something was in play that needed his full attention. Suppressing any outward sign, he tried to breathe deeply, determined to fight the demon that penetrated his cloak of invincibility.

Kate said, "Listen carefully, Mr. Petrovic; your phone doesn't work because you're no longer with the company."

Again Kate let the words sink in. It was all part of what she had rehearsed in her mind. She was enjoying it.

Petrovic's mind didn't understand what she said. He couldn't comprehend anything close to what she said. They were just words with no meaning.

With an aura of power only a Petrovic would understand, Kate slowly said, "I'll deal first with your company and then deal with you."

"You're aren't going to deal with anything. I'm still the CEO of this company, and nothing you say will change that. I'm not sure you have grasped the hidden attributes and the far reach of my management style."

Kate said, "I'm very aware of your history. I'm also very aware you can't make payroll. I know this because I'm the reason you're short of funds. We have a unique ability to infiltrate the strongest of security networks. I've taken the liberty to temporarily transfer all of TerraDyne's monetary assets into holding accounts I control."

Petrovic sat there speechless.

"Mr. Petrovic, you incorporated in Switzerland and claimed it as your residence because they've no extradition treaty based on corruption. My lawyers inform me the laws of Switzerland also require an appointed fiduciary in the event the Chairperson is incapacitated. That fiduciary can, upon proof, assume direct control to protect shareholders. You entered Mr. Holland's name as a formality for the required co-chairman because you knew you controlled him, and he was but a pawn. Holland has held a board meeting because you're no longer fit to run the company. He removed your cronies that you were paying for their rubber stamp approvals.

"Mr. Holland now works for me, and his charter is to remove the company from any marginal activities and turn it into a clean company making a profit.

"Your company Mr. Petrovic is bankrupt, and I'm here to save and reinvent the organization."

Avery leaned forward and, symbolically moving Petrovic's offer aside, placed another folder on his desk containing the details.

Kate said, "What you have built using the worst tactics now belongs to me."

Avery said, "This morning, Mr. Holland and I completed a major stock transaction, and Morton Roth, a division of Adler Industries, has taken control of TerraDyne."

Petrovic said, "You control nothing. Holland did what?"

"That's going to come as a surprise," Kate said. "He was quite helpful. It turns out he was the source who left anonymous tips giving us a heads up of your intentions. We eventually obtained full access to your network. The security was well designed but couldn't hold up to our capabilities. We uncovered a memo Holland submitted where he said; I'm paraphrasing, 'The company has substantial legitimate income and can transform into a legitimate company at a reduced revenue posture over time.' You put him on leave after presenting his study. You also threatened him in writing, saying he could never leave the company because of what he knew. That's when we knew we had inside help. He's been indispensable in making this a smooth transaction."

Petrovic said, "What transaction?"

Kate said. "Mr. Milosh Luka Petrovic, I now own your company."

Petrovic was sweating and could feel it run onto his forehead. Proudly he couldn't bring himself to wipe them away.

"You can't own my company; you don't have the assets."

She nodded towards Avery and said, "Mr. Stanton and I've put together a plan where he secured the funding to buy the company. We'll add the marine fleet to Morton Roth, and by selling off the mining and other operations, we'll pay off the original loan. It's called a leveraged buyout."

"Holland has no authority except if I'm incapacitated. As clearly I'm not."

"What I see is a man thinking he could do what he pleased, in the pursuit of profits, without regard to anyone or anything around him. I see a man who once was very wealthy and could command great droves of people for purposes great and small as long as they generated wealth. A man of your intellect must surely know nothing ever is; it's either been or becoming, and you sir are now history."

Petrovic stood up again and angrily started for the door. Kate said to Brad, "Now."

Brad opened the door, and four men from the Cartel's tactical team in the SUV entered the room.

"You will never get away with this."

"Quite the contrary, I already have."

Petrovic, a man at the end of ordinary thought, looked at her without response.

"Now to deal with you. In addition to your legal troubles, Iran and North Korea didn't trust each other, and you volunteered to broker the deal. We have provided considerable evidence to Iran that the Iranian funds you were holding until delivery have mysteriously disappeared. We also informed North Korea that the u235 shipment is in your possession and that you intend to find another buyer. These aren't people you double-cross and walk away."

"Lies" he yelled. "Lies, I've done none of those things."

Kate looked at him with a particular contempt and said, "Interesting thing about the truth. It's not so much the reality of the thing but the understanding of the thing. If you think someone is following you, it's because they probably are. I would say you need to disappear permanently or find yourself, in the case of the North Koreans, in the custody of some of the worst examples of humanity who answer to no one."

Petrovic was stunned. His heart was pounding, and he was burning up on the inside. Beyond rational thought and reduced to simplicity, he illogically said, "What do you think you're doing.?"

"I would think that's obvious, Mr. Petrovic. I'm bringing you to your knees and leaving the option of your continued existence to others. Never underestimate the power of your enemy."

CHAPTER 77

Belgrade

    Petrovic's apartment on Cara Dusana, was across the Danube river and near the Mihajlo Pupin bridge. Petrovic packed a few things and planned to leave the country quickly and go into hiding until he could straighten this mess out. Fully aware of the danger the North Koreans and Iranians posed, he hired a local security company. They symbolized his new life. They fanned out along the street in front of his building. The security supervisor stood out front and motioned Petrovic to stay in the glass lobby. The supervisor listened to his men reporting back on the radio and got the all-clear. Only then did he turn to Petrovic and signaled him it was time.
    Fortunately, his limo and plane were under his name and were not part of the theft of his company. The limo sat right outside the building's entrance. He called his driver from inside the lobby, in another sign of his new life; he had the car started before rushing from the lobby of the building to the limo's open door. The supervisor and his men boarded the two SUVs to trail the limo to the airport.
    The shame of letting a woman outsmart him was already wearing off. It didn't matter. He'd start again. In business, contacts are everything, and he had them worldwide. Re-establishing an empire would be easy, and he'd never forget one Kate Adler. She'd be forever in his sights. Sitting inside the confined space of the vehicle made him feel more comfortable. He told the driver, "Get me to the airport. I've got a lot of things I need to put in place. I've no time to lose."

The Danube at that point was more than seven hundred meters wide, yet the people across the river vividly saw the explosion and wondered at the cause. The impact stayed within the armor plating surrounding the vehicle's rear passenger area, eliminating any innocent casualties.

The men from the security team pulled the driver out alive, saved by the armor behind him, and placed him on the ground away from the destroyed vehicle. The intense heat from the flames prevented any further rescue efforts. One man called the emergency number for an ambulance. Simultaneously, halfway across the bridge, a pedestrian pulled down a set of binoculars and placed them in his pocket. He removed the battery from the burn phone used to trigger the blast and put both in a small cloth bag with a weight inside. He dropped the bag into the water.

Jourdan Duma pulled a picture out from the inside pocket of his suit. While looking at the image of the handsome Nymagu family, a thousand memories vividly flashed in his mind. Skiing vacations, being his best man and godfather to his children. Looking up at the smoke rising, he had taken the revenge Adi's family couldn't. He cupped the picture in his hand and said out loud, "He was your husband and my best friend."

CHAPTER 78

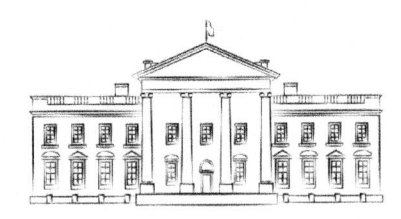

White House

Devroe said, "So I brought the president up to speed on all the details and the layers of events you handled." Through an approving smile, he said, "I have to say even I was impressed."

Konner said, "Well, that's definitely a milestone. However, I have a feeling this is not an "atta boy" phone call. So before you start in on the real reason for calling, I have a proposal."

"Fire away. I've got an open-door policy here, haven't you noticed?"

Konner ignored the comment that would have customarily elicited a witty response. "Most of what I've been doing the last two years is centered in Europe."

"Ah, OK, and your point?"

"Would you consider my being stationed here rather than in Washington? Before you answer, consider the world has very successfully turned to remote communication. I can be on a secure video feed from any of our embassies here. Besides, there's the wear and tear factor of being a DC to Europe yoyo."

He quickly responded, "The United States doesn't execute foreign policy in a zoom meeting."

"Come on, Devroe, don't be a dinosaur."

That seemed to catch Devroe off guard. He didn't have an immediate response.

Konner said, "I don't think that came out correctly."

Still quiet, Devroe finally said, "I think I just learned something about myself."

Cautiously Konner said, "Like what?"

"Things are changing faster than in the past. Still, I've to ask, is this purely a plan to stay closer to Ms. Adler?"

"If you can't justify my request at face value, then say no. Don't make it into something it isn't. I'm a big boy and will go with your decision."

Devroe said, "I need to run it by the president, but your stock is trading very high right now, so I don't anticipate a rejection." Then he said, "There's a catch. It's temporary; let's see how it goes. I can pull you back at any time."

"Thanks, Stephen; I appreciate it."

Devroe said, "Oh, and there's another detail."

"As you say, the other shoe."

"A nice shoe. I've put you in for a nice raise. It won't put you in Gulfstreams, but it's a good bump."

"Nice, it's sincerely appreciated. I'll spend it wisely."

"Since you will be spending more time in Europe, I'll also be more generous with your expenses. Not a lot, but I'm upping you to a full three meals a day."

Konner laughed. "That's beyond generous, Doctor; I don't know what to say."

Devroe said, "So that's all the good news for today and back to your day job. We need you to look into a man living in Helsinki, who appears to be running terrorist operations from there."

"What? They have terrorists in Helsinki?"

"That's precisely the reason he's in Helsinki. In this case, it's someone who's young and starting to manage operatives worldwide. We can't find any affiliation with traditional funding sources, so he's a bit of an enigma. I need you to get as much on this guy as you can as we think he is planning something big. The CIA had him under electronic and physical surveillance, but the agent ruffled plenty of feathers, and the Finnish Security Intelligence Service wanted him out. Going through channels will take time we don't have, so you're going in as non-official cover. If you get in trouble, you're on your own. We can't claim you as ours, so don't get into trouble. We need you to keep a low profile while following him around and observing his contacts. We need a positive ID and at least a photo we can put into the database."

"It sounds simple, which means it isn't. When do I leave?"

"Tomorrow morning out of Luxembourg International. See, I, at least, made concessions based on where you are right now. You have a meeting with the Helsinki station chief at our Embassy there. He'll bring you up to speed."

"Why not just have him do it."

"He's been burned. We're bringing him back and replacing him, but we can't wait on this. So there you have it. It's all in an email, including all the background information. Have a nice flight."

CHAPTER 79

Kate's residence

Konner said to Kate, "That was quite the wild ride. The magnitude of what you did is hard to describe. Perhaps thousands of people were affected."

Kate said, "We look for areas where we can be of help. Opportunities where we can apply our set of skills. It's not often we have one thrust upon us."

"In this case, everyone is glad you were there. I've got a question. When you took over TerraDyne, Petrovic didn't have the money to pay both the Iranians and North Korea. It's actually what brought him down."

"I think Avery and his finance team would have another opinion."

"Still, how did you resolve having to pay both?"

"We didn't. We sent the money Petrovic had from the Iranians to North Korea. The Iranians will suffer the loss but can't make a case because it would make public their efforts to purchase the material. Making it public would require Israel to respond. They're stuck with bad options on every front."

Konner said, "Well done." He looked at Kate in a way that moved the conversation in another direction.

Kate sensed the change and said, "So, where do we go from here?"

"I talked to Devroe. The good news is he's agreed to relocate me to Europe, but I would still require a lot of traveling. It sure cuts down on the long flights back to DC."

"The bad news?"

"I leave tomorrow."

"Where.?"

Konner looked at her, and she said. "OK, I won't ask. How long will you be gone? I guess I won't ask that either."

"I leave from Luxembourg International. He said it was a concession to where I am now."

"How romantic of him."

"Do you think you can get me to the airport? Otherwise, I have to leave tonight."

"You mean like you will owe me a favor?"

"One could say that if one was inclined." He chuckled.

"I'll have Captain Silanos get you there on the helicopter. But I'm not sure I want to participate in making it easy for you to go away."

"It's only temporary."

"Really, how can you know?"

"I don't. It's my job, and I like it. My boss is Devroe, and he must react to events. He's not the bad guy. Still, asking for more time off after the time in Tanzania is probably not a good idea."

Kate was in thought, playing with her water glass.

Konner said, "It seems one of us is always in some kind of emergency. I don't see us able to spend a lot of time together without a bunch of distractions at best and emergencies at the worst."

Kate thought that was a telling statement. Thinking back, she could almost feel the kiss that sent her off to a place that needed sincere self-evaluation. At that point, she was very cautious but was very interested in where this was going. Now it seemed things had moved back a little.

Konner moved his napkin and looked under the table. That's your foot on my leg, Ma'am. Are you trying to change the subject?"

"*What?*" She said in mock horror. "I'm a proper lady. I would never be so bold or forward to suggest anything of the sort. I would, however, be very open to *your* changing the subject."

***

The next morning a distracted Kate was standing with Konner at the open door of her home. The morning air was cold, and she wondered why she hadn't grabbed a jacket. "Your car is waiting." She said. It was a hollow statement as she dealt with swirling emotions trying to keep them behind the wall she needed in times like this.

Konner said thoughtfully, looking at Kate. "I think I'm tired of wondering if this will work out. Before I leave, I want you to know I'm committed to this relationship. From now on, I consider us a," and he struggled for words, "a thing." He winced at the choice of words.

He said, moving forward with outstretched arms, "What I meant to say was…"

Kate cut him off. "Thing? I'm no."

Before she could object further, Konner wrapped his arms around her, pushed the hair from her face, and kissed her. Not just any kiss. It was another one of those long warm, lingering kisses that curled her toes.

She thought, "Damn, he's good at that."

He pulled back a little and said in a smooth, sensual tone, "I need to know if we are together."

Kate was still trying to keep it together, "Actually, I've been there for some time now." She said.

Konner had a broad smile at the revelation. "Well, that couldn't be better news." He said. "And thanks for last night."

"You're referring to dinner, right?"

"I don't think so." He said with a grin. He looked back at her as he turned towards the open car door.

Kate said, "Let me know where you'll be, so I don't worry." She realized she had crossed an invisible line as soon as it came out. "I mean." She started to say.

He looked back at her knowing she had accidentally let slip a guarded emotion from behind the protective armor—or maybe not.

Her arms were crossed and held tight as the car pulled away. Myrla came up from behind and placed a sweater over her shoulders. Kate followed the vehicle down the long driveway until it was well out of sight.

Standing next to her, Myrla put an arm around Kate's waist and said, "The Mr. Konner is a nice man. You think so yes?"

"Yes, Marla, a very nice man."

She took a deep breath, and her phone rang. She pulled it out and saw Brad's name. "It's a little early, isn't it?"

He said, "We have a problem."

The End

ADDITIONAL BOOKS BY RICHARD D TAYLOR

GENEVA INTRUSION

A Kate Adler Book # 1

IRAN WANTS TO START A WAR HIJACKING TANKERS. KATE ADLER ESCAPES AN ASSASSINATION ATTEMPT AND IS RUNNING FOR HER LIFE TOWARDS A BIG SURPRISE.

A Cartel thriller delivering constant surprises.

Enjoy a sample of Geneva Intrusion

CHAPTER—1

BOARDING THE *MONTCLAIR STAR* — THURSDAY PM

Panama-flagged oil tanker *Montclair Star*
Location: The Persian Gulf, 25 miles off the coast of Iran.
US Fifth Fleet in the area

"Pirates, pirates on port side," Juarez, a deck hand, breathlessly shouted as he careened up the stairs to the bridge.

Captain Carlino Bertucci, standing on the tanker *Montclair Star*'s bridge wing, was aware of the situation. A man with twenty-four years' experience, he was tracking the pirates on radar and concentrating on the small boat through his binoculars.

He lowered the glasses, walked into the wheelhouse, and quickly radioed the US Maritime Administration emergency group.

"Mayday. Mayday. Mayday. This is the *Montclair Star*. Hijacking in progress. Request any aid. Coordinates 26 degrees 30 minutes by 53 degrees 15 minutes, course 135, speed 19 knots."

"*Montclair Star*, this is the warship *USS Connolly*. We copy your transmission," said the young ensign on the Arleigh Burke-class destroyer. "Relaying your information to coalition channels now."

"They're on approach, situation is critical, *Montclair* out," Bertucci said, leaving the channel open.

Five men in a small, sea-worn skiff violently attacked the choppy waves fighting their way towards the massive oil tanker in the Strait of Hormuz. The leader, a large man, stood at the front with knees bent, absorbing the powerful surges of the bow as it dove deep into the water then thrust upward. He studied the distance as they approached the plodding behemoth. It required his total concentration to maintain his balance atop the erratically battered boat. Drawing his forearm across his face once again failed to wipe away the saltwater stinging his eyes. A fatigued AK-47, whose violent history would never be known, lay at his feet covered in the spray that filled the air.

"Faster," the leader shouted, "faster." The skiff suddenly shifted starboard under his feet, causing him to slam his foot against the outboard rail to stay aboard. He looked disdainfully at the frail young man soaked to the core, trying to control the screaming outboard motor. "Keep her steady, or we lose speed," he yelled with a wave of his arm. Eyes fixed on the tanker, he waited until the last moment to pick up the semi-automatic rifle.

Bertucci walked over to the wall speaker and pushed the ship's PA button. "This is the captain, pirates alongside, this is not a drill, repeat this is not a drill." With the ship's phone in his hand, he selected the engine room and said, "Banoy, you heard the announcement, pirates will attempt to board. Give me all the speed you have."

Banoy said, "Do you authorize full ahead?"

"Yes," the captain yelled to his chief engineer, "do it *now*."

The radio speaker came alive. "This is the warship *USS Connolly* to the *Montclair Star*; what is your status, over?"

Bertucci looked over the port side wing and saw a man on the skiff below with a gun pointed directly at the bridge. "Everyone down," he shouted, taking an awkward dive for the floor as bullets pinged off the outside of the bridge.

On the *Connolly*, the ensign turned to his captain. "No response, sir, but I heard automatic gunfire."

The *Connolly*'s captain turned to the executive officer and said, "Get a helo in the air, and you," he pointed at another ensign, "turns for flank speed and, navigator, get me to their position."

"Yes, sir," was the reply from each of the crewmen.

The craft was still trying to gain on the tanker as it fought against the dangerous waves generated off the enormous ship's bow. The leader put down the AK-47 and picked up a Soviet-made grenade launcher. Holding it up to his eye, he observed the larger ship move in and out of the weapon's sight and fired.

The unstable platform on which he stood caused the grenade to errantly head for the upper corner of the superstructure, where it entered the side window of the bridge and went out the front without an explosion. Glass rained down on the *Montclair*'s bridge crew.

Captain Bertucci commanded the helmsman, "Hard-a-port," attempting to run into the smaller craft, making it more difficult to board.

Bertucci's voice was tense as he turned to his first mate. "Let's get those jets on." The man moved swiftly to the control panel and threw the master switch. "Jets on," he shouted as the four-inch water jets around the ship created a non-lethal means of making it more difficult for the pirates to make it to the ladder from their small craft.

Just then, automatic gunfire came in the open door. The captain watched as the overhead exploded in a sequential pattern of bullets above him. He looked at his crew face down on the deck.

"Change that order," he said to the first mate. "Get your men to the citadel. Leave the jets on."

The first mate rushed everyone off the bridge and into the companionway.

"All hands to the citadel — *now*," Bertucci said over the PA. He then picked up the telephone. "Banoy," he said. "Shut down the engines and electrical power and get your guys to the safe room."

"Aye, sir," Banoy responded.

Another cartridge-full of ammunition came up from below, pinging off the outside hull and taking out more glass. Bertucci, on his knees, could feel his heart pounding as he turned the dial on the ship's safe. He pulled at the door and grabbed the ship's log. Bent over, he exited the bridge descending five flights of stairs into a room designed to deny the pirates the leverage of hostages. They knew untrained pirates could not start the engines, and short of an explosive charge applied to the hatch, they were reasonably safe. They expected the pirates to leave once they realized time was short, help was on the way, and that they could not navigate the ship to a friendly port.

Bathed in the water from the jets, the leader motioned for a crewmember to throw up the ladder. The third try caught the tanker's bulwark. He and his four men ascended the ladder, all barefoot and dressed in the typical Somali pirates' threadbare clothing. Clearing the bulwark, the men took cover behind a raised oil tank access hatch and, from the duffel bag, unwrapped four KL-7.62 semi-automatic assault rifles from their waterproof covers, several flash/smoke grenades, extra ammunition, and a medical backpack. The lead man felt the engine's muted vibration under his feet come to a stop, and the noise generated by the defensive water jets fade as they shut down. The five men moved quickly towards the main superstructure in practiced precision. The trailing two men concentrated on the superstructure's gangways, with the rest looking for any threat at deck level. Silently and methodically making their way to their destination.

Seconds later, the five men stood on the port bridge wing just outside the pilot house. The group leader, gun at his shoulder, nodded as one of his men pulled open the hatch to the wheelhouse. A second man rolled a flash/smoke grenade into the room. Their backs were against the outside bulkhead as it went off. The leader entered, quickly swinging his gun's barrel into the space, ready to open fire. Two men who covered the right and left sides of the area immediately followed him. It was unoccupied. Not surprised, the leader knew the crew would be locked away but was trained not to take any chances. The smoke that hung in the air streamed towards the broken windows and outside as if needed elsewhere.

Silently he pointed at one of the men who went over to the helmsman's console. Looking at the dark gauges, which showed no sign of damage, the man nodded his head, indicating everything seemed okay. The leader turned to another man also at the console, looking at a sheet with the new coordinates. He motioned for them to stay. Both men pulled on latex gloves before they touched anything. He nodded for the other two men to follow him.

Having previously studied the ship's layout, they proceeded directly down to the engine room, guns raised around every corner, expecting the unexpected. As they approached the engine room, one of the men had another flash-bang grenade ready. The group leader looked through the round window in the hatch and found the room empty. He waved his hand at the grenade, and the man put it away. As the door opened, they all entered the dimly lit, pale green engine control room. There was a shadowy quiet and the thick and stale air smelled of diesel. Large windows overlooked the massive silent engines in the dark room two decks below as the start team technician stood at the engineering console. With an assistant, his job was to start the engines. He surveyed the panel and nodded to the group leader with thumbs-up.

Finally, alone, the group leader turned to the start team and spoke aloud in a Persian dialect. "Time for you to do your job. Let me know when you're ready." The start team put their guns down, and the still-armed leader moved to the entrance door to protect their position.

The assistant pulled on his latex medical gloves as he approached the thirty-foot-long gray control panel that resembled a lineup of ten tall refrigerators, each with a withering array of gauges and dials. He came to a stop in front of the electrical generator module. He pulled open his vest and extracted two plastic-covered sheets of instructions. As he looked at the papers, he flipped the breaker switches in the proper sequence and watched the red status lights turn green. He pulled down on the master handle and heard the generators restart. Their eyes adjusted as the regular lights took over from the dim battery-powered lights.

"Electrical on," the assistant said.

"Check," said the tech as he stared at the control console indicator lights.

More switches set by the assistant started to bring up the hydraulic and lube oil pressure.

"Check again," the tech said, monitoring the pressure gauges.

Moving down the control panel, throwing another multi-breaker switch sequence started the air compressor. The tech watched the indicator on the control panel rise to 128 PSI. He checked the fuel flow indicator and several other gauges and said, "Check, starting main engine one." He held down the large red button labeled "M/E One Start" until the green light above it came on. The deck vibrated beneath their feet as the room filled with the groans and deep moans of a powerful giant awakened. The same sequence was employed to the "M/E Two Start" button and so on until all three engines were idling.

"Normal idle in three minutes," he said to the group leader at the door.

"Good," the group leader said. "Full ahead when you're ready. Lock the door behind me. I will be on the bridge. Don't forget, nothing is to be left behind when you leave. Wipe down any questionable areas."

"Yes, Captain," both men said. The tech looked at his assistant and then put his hand on the maneuvering handle that engaged the propeller shafts and looked at the maneuvering chart that said "Max 105, Full 95, half 65." After four minutes and with full green indicators, he moved the handle slowly, first to 65 RPM. The tech felt the additional vibration on the console and in the room, as the noise level rose significantly. The immense vessel was now ready for its new heading.

Look for Geneva Intrusion available on Amazon now.

[Link to GENEVA INTRUSION On Amazon]

Sign up for my newsletter and receive release dates and book information.

[Link to subscribe to my newsletter]

Enjoy a sample of Primary Protocol.

PRIMARY PROTOCOL
A Kate Adler Book # 2

WITH 70,000 LIVES AT STAKE, KATE ADLER AND THE CARTEL RUSH TO STOP AN ATTACK ON THE FRENCH NATIONAL STADIUM

A page-turning suspense terrorist thriller that delivers constant surprises.

CHAPTER—1

Vianden Castle Luxembourg

The confidential referral was from *Tangent Day,* the code name for Martin Alejandro Perez, President of the United States. Brad Danner sat at his desk in Vianden Castle in Luxembourg, headquarters of the secretive Cartel, waiting for a call from the French ambassador to Mali. A unique referral was required before anyone could directly contact the Cartel, and *Tangent Day* was about as unique as it got.

The ambassador's call would almost certainly involve a problematic issue needing a somewhat unconventional solution. The kind of solution where a national power would find their options limited due to the restrictions of law or convention. For the past two years, Brad managed the outside world's contacts for the organization and contributed as a special advisor to Kate Adler, the acting chair. Out of college, he joined the military for action, but his computer skills landed him in an intelligence tent at Bagram Air Base. The experience qualified him later to be a bodyguard to Kate in what was supposed to be an NSA intelligence center in Munich. The problem was Kate didn't know about the arrangement, which resulted in a rocky start to their relationship. Kate was his boss, having taken over the Cartel two years ago, fulfilling her late father's wish to further the group's agenda into the future. She was flying in today from New York. She would undoubtedly want an update on the ambassador's call.

The phone vibrated on the hard surface spinning on its axis as its bright screen lit the dark lampshade above it. He picked it up and entered the "one-time" code into the touchscreen.

"Hello, this is agent 2810. Can I help you?" Brad said in a balanced voice.

"This is Renee Magnant, French Ambassador to the Mali Republic."

"Madam Ambassador, I want to thank you for your call, and I must tell you this conversation will be recorded and available only to those in the Cartel."

"I would hope so because if it gets out, I'm dead. Who is this I'm calling? Who is the Cartel?"

"We are someone your referral thought could help in some way."

"Well, that was evasive enough," she said, "I will get right to it. I have information regarding a probable terrorist attack and have not been able to convince anyone it's real. I guess you are my last chance at avoiding a disaster."

"We will certainly do what we can to help."

"I don't need help. I need a miracle. As you know, at the request of the Mali government, the French military came in, confronted, and defeated a terrorist group named Ansar Dine. They killed all the leaders except a man named Mokhtar Belmokhtar. I have it on good authority that Mokhtar's group, and several other offshoots located in Southern Libya, Tunisia, and the northern parts of Niger, have formed an alliance."

"What sort of an alliance?"

"An alliance to finance a vindictive response to Ansar Dine's humiliating defeat and a warning to the French to stay out of their area of operation."

"Did they say what form this response would take?"

"That I don't have. I just know, as a group, they have raised over thirty million euros, and revenge is their goal. I can guarantee it's going to be big, and many French people are going to die somewhere."

"Why do you want us involved? Shouldn't you go to the French government?"

"Really, Mr. 2810? I have been in this business for a long time; don't you think that was my first thought? I called DGSI (French for General Directorate for Internal Security), and they could not find any chatter or Intel to support my alarm. All I got was they would investigate it, which means they didn't believe me. I called French President Maurice Jossart, who agreed to make some calls and also found DGSI didn't have anything to substantiate the claim. I know my sources here on the ground, and this is real. Mokhtar and his band of lowlifes are being very quiet about it. I insisted to Jossart that someone needed to do something, or the prospect of dying Frenchmen would land in his lap. In confidence, he provided the information to contact US President Perez, who I have known for some time.

"Perez was very gracious but came to the same conclusion after checking with his people. I'm not exactly shy and probably pursued this a little aggressively with the President. I also hung on him the prospect of thousands of lives on his shoulders. He finally gave in, providing me with the method of contacting you people. By the way, who are you, and what's with the writing letters and this funny phone I have?"

Brad, who had been taking notes, replied, "I can assure you we have the same goals regarding your concerns. Innocent people should not have to suffer at the hands of a few who are radical in their beliefs. To my knowledge, we have not picked up any information regarding an attack on French soil. Who were your sources?"

"That's another problem I had with the DGSI. It's from previously used anonymous informants that I trust, having used them for years. Their information once saved my life during an assassination attempt. However, it's not the kind of information that the formalized institutions of my wonderful country consider the last word."

"Who did you talk to at DGSI?"

"I was given to a man named Durand. I was told he was high up, had access to all the information that would be available, and could make decisions. He was polite but didn't believe a word I said."

"Madam Ambassador, I want to thank you for providing this information. We have certain capabilities that we will incorporate to see if we can discover more information concerning your suspicions of an attack. I can assure you we will follow up on this. Please keep this phone in a safe place and tell no one of our conversations. I will get back to you with whatever we find. I will send you a meaningless text with a new code and a time on your mobile when we need to have an encrypted conversation. You will then repeat the procedures you used to make this call. Meanwhile, keep listening to your sources. If they have any updates, use the text feature of the G9 phone to get back."

"Well, Mr. 2810, this has been an interesting conversation. First, how do you know my mobile number? Second, I'm not used to sharing this kind of information with someone I don't trust or, in fact, know yet. Even if you find out what they're going to do, what can *you* do about it but wave another unnoticed flag?"

"As to your mobile number, well, as I said, we have our capabilities. Second, we don't publicly wave flags. If we find something vital that's not addressed by the traditional authorities, we are capable of handling it."

With a challenge in her voice, she added, "A well-funded group bent on killing as many as possible somewhere in France?"

"Anywhere."

"As I said, this has been an interesting conversation. I will wait for your text."

Brad put the phone down and started filling out the call log on the screen. He could understand the ambassador's skepticism due to the unusual secrecy involved in her eventually making contact. He didn't take the time to explain that the Cartel determines where to apply its resources in two ways. One is from a POC (Pattern of Concern) generated by Geneva9, also known as Mom, the Cartel's massive intelligence and surveillance asset. The other is information received from a secure phone conversation after receiving a written request for contact. All requests came in through letters re-posted several times to new addresses before arriving at the Cartel's headquarters and onto Brad's desk. In the age of computers, it turns out regular mail is the safest way to transfer information anonymously around the world without any digital trail. Each country's mail privacy laws and the sheer volume of mail within any country inhibited regular scrutiny. A letter is old fashioned and uncomplicated, but it is foolproof.

Look for Primary Protocol on Amazon.

Link to Primary Protocol On Amazon

Sign up for my newsletter and receive release dates and book information.

Link to subscribe to my newsletter

Enjoy a sample of Islands of Peace

ISLANDS OF PEACE
A Kate Adler Book # 3

WILL ONE MAN, AVENGING HIS BROTHER'S DEATH, USE RISING TENSIONS BETWEEN THE USA AND RUSSIA TO START A WAR? CAN KATE ADLER AND THE CARTEL STOP HIS DEADLY PLAN IN TIME?

A mystery/thriller series full of unexpected twists and turns delivers nonstop action.

Enjoy a sample of Islands of Peace

CHAPTER 1

MOSCOW

Kate Adler entered her penthouse suite in Moscow's Ararat hotel and surveyed the utter chaos. Someone had ransacked her room while she attended a state dinner. Moving farther into the suite revealed a man ripping cushions apart. He looked back at her.

"What the hell are you doing here?" she asked, frozen.

Turning to escape, someone grabbed her from behind. She instinctively resisted but felt the grip tighten. Hearing heavy breathing and becoming overpowered, her body tensed. Angry at being accosted, she felt her high heel give way upon stabbing the man's foot.

"Bitch!" he yelled, reacting to the pain and violently throwing her to the floor.

Kate glanced off a couch and fell hard against the coffee table. An upward glare revealed a 9mm Glock held by a furious bald man with hollow eyes. Pumped on adrenalin from the struggle, he shouted in a thick Russian accent. "Where is the information from Tonkov?"

Kate frowned. "I can't help you and probably wouldn't even if I could. I'm sure you know by now whatever you want isn't here."

The other man pulled the purse from Kate's hands and dumped the contents onto the carpet. Looking down, he sifted the items with his shoe. The bald man put a finger to his earpiece; receiving instructions, he said, "We can't stay any longer; we need to leave now." Still holding the gun, he looked intensely at Kate on the floor, the stare threatening and unmistakable. Both men turned and left.

In her thirty-five years, she had been shot at several times and survived a bombing but never experienced a physical assault. She thought briefly about calling hotel security but then mused; This is Moscow. Instead, she reached for a specially designed secure phone lying on the carpet, along with the remains of her purse. Seconds after she hit the button, she heard Brad Danner's voice, a friend and associate.

"Hi, Kate," Brad said, "how was the dinner? Boring? I have you on speaker in the operations center. The team says hi."

"Hi, Brad, hi everyone; I have bigger concerns than the dinner at the moment. I came back to my room and look at what I found." She held the phone up to show a video of the disarray the men had left behind. Everyone in the center could see the images on one of the many large display screens on the walls.

"As I walked into the room, someone grabbed me and threw me to the floor, but I'm fine. I don't know what the men wanted, but I think it has something to do with Russian President Kozloff and my friend Aleksis. Tonight, after the dinner, Aleksis received a troubling phone call, and he told me to leave the country right away. I need the team to safely get me out of the hotel before someone else arrives."

Brad didn't need any more information, as this was as important as it got. His voice tightened, "Are you safe right now?"

"Yes, I have both entrances to the suite locked, and I have closed the curtains."

"Good, we will work on it and be right back." Three years ago, Kate had inherited her father's industrial empire, placing her high on the world's multi-billionaires list. High society knew Kate as the very public face of the Helmut Adler Children's Fund, named in memory of her father. Only a handful knew she had also inherited her father's powerful covert organization called the Cartel.

Everyone in the Cartel's operations center heard her request, and in practiced precision, each addressed their specific assignments.

Elena and Lauren, the two with direct access to the Cartel's supercomputer affectionately known as Mom, queried for any Moscow police or security notifications out of the ordinary. In charge of field operations, Penn Hauer sent an alert to the Cartel's special operations group. He then brought up his contact list, looking for someone from his past. Another agent in the room placed the status of the Cartel's small fleet of private planes on a second screen.

Penn looked up. "We can't use her plane sitting at Moscow International airport. Whoever did this will already have it under surveillance. Someone call Captain Silanos on the plane and tell him to take off ASAP before they impound him and the plane, or worse. We will give him coordinates in the air."

A voice in the room answered, "I'm on that."

Penn found the name and reached for a secure phone. He heard a voice asking, "Hello, who is this?"

"Freddy, it's Penn Hauer. Where are you right now?"

"On my way to meet a few friends for a beer. Oh, by the way, it's nice to hear from you, too," the man said, outright laughing.

Freddy Faraday was more than just an old-time friend; he was a man of many talents, not all reputable. These talents made him extremely resourceful, depending on the need.

"Hold on a sec," Penn said to Freddy

"Lauren," he began, "I need a small airport well outside of Moscow that can take Captain Silanos and the Gulf Stream 650."

"Yes, I'm ahead of you. Kaluga is two hours or so outside of Moscow by car via the E101." Lauren queried the keyboard. "It has a 7,000-foot runway. The Gulf stream only needs 5,600 fully loaded."

"Great, get those coordinates to the Captain. Freddy, are you still there?"

"I'm here; where else would I be?"

"My principal could be in danger, and I need to quietly get her out of Moscow. Can I count on you?"

"You always have; why stop believing now, brother?" Did you know I had dinner with Ms. Adler tonight?"

"No, I didn't, and don't know why you would. Hold on."

"Brad," Penn said. "Can you get to Kate and tell her a Freddy Faraday will call to escort her out of the hotel?"

"On it," Brad said.

"Freddy, I need you to pick up Ms. Adler at the Ararat Park hotel. I need you to go to her room and stay with her through the lobby and outside. Then I need you to drive her south toward an airport in Kaluga. Do you know where it is?"

"Hell no, I only live here—I was born in Cincinnati, remember? Send the directions to my phone. There went my beer and poker game with a few heavy rollers. You're going to owe me big time, my friend."

"Really, Freddy?" Penn had to crack a smile. "This is a hardship? When was the last time you had a beer?"

Freddy chuckled. "At lunch."

"That's what I thought. Freddy, take this seriously."

"You have that tone in your voice again. I know this is serious. I'm a highly respected psychologist in my spare time."

"What do you mean, my tone?"

"Every time you mention her name, you get all wobbly on me. You were going to introduce me to her sometime, but that never happened."

"Not in a million years would I introduce her to the likes of you," he said, laughing. "Besides, being concerned for her is my job, Freddy. She's a high-value target wherever she goes."

"Yeah, thanks for the company line. What's Ms. Adler's status? Is she ready? Do I go now?"

"How far away are you? More importantly, do you have a car more reliable than the one you had on my last trip out?"

"How about an Audi R8, their big guy? It's the baddest vehicle Audi makes. This thing is a rocket and chick magnet."

"How in the world …?"

"Some people just shouldn't play poker," Freddy laughed. "You declined last time here, smart man. I was already downtown, so I'm perhaps eight blocks away. I just hung a U-turn, and I'm on my way. Hey, Penn?"

"Yes."

"Not that it matters, but just how serious? It's a tactical question. What are we facing?"

"She attended a Kozloff state dinner, and when she got back to her room, someone had tossed it. Two thug types attacked her at gunpoint. Do you have a sidearm in the car?"

"In Moscow, it's not good when thugs come out of the woodwork, especially brandishing guns. That means it's serious. To answer your question, I always have one installed in a fake door panel, and the Audi is no different."

Get your copy of Islands of Peace today.

Link to ISLANDS OF PEACE On Amazon

Sign up for my newsletter and receive release dates and book information.

Link to subscribe to my newsletter

A COMPLETE LIST OF

IMPORTANT CHARACTERS AND TERMS

CHARACTERS
Adi Nymagu President of Tanzania
Akanni Okoro—Morton Roth office manager.
Anakin Holland—Works for Petrovic and TerraDyne.
Anton Kikorov—Captain of North Korean ship with u235
Asim Ahmadi—Syrian gives info to Konner has wife in Tehran
Armin Guyer—From the Conklin Maritime Alliance, an insurance consortium.
Avery Stanton— CEO Adler Industries Chairman
Brad Danner— Co-worker of Kate. Cartel communications, Security group, a friend of Kate
Captain Silanos— Head of the Cartel's civilian air operations
Captain Soren Oppegard—Head of the Cartel's navel operations
Colonel Lange—Former SAS commando, Cartel commander of Alpha Team 4. Team, Pete, Jerry, Thompson, Cooper and the pilot Rob.
Danny McBride—Cartel team EMT
Dan Tilde— Assistant Director CIA
Derik Laven—Belgian security service
Dr. Stephen Austin Devroe— Director of National Intelligence   (DNI)
Elena Maleeva— Manager of Geneva9 surveillance system (Mom) and security group.
Havel Vanek—Enforcer for Teradyne
Helmut Adler—Kate's father, founder of Adler Industries and the Cartel

Jaron Gabai—Israeli programmer

Jamil Novak—Vanek's man in the van.

Jonadab Hagen— Manager over Jaron in the Israeli software unit.

Jordan Duma—Agent providing security for Nymagu who is also his close friend.

Jozef Mati—Petrovic's doctor

Kate Adler (Katerina)—Protagonist, Executive Director of Cartel.

Kim Il Sung—leader of North Korea

Kevin Wainwright—General Manager of Helmut Adler Children's Fund.

Konner Houston—Special assistant to U.S. president and Kate's love interest

Lang Gerlach—Managing Director at Morton Roth

Legacy 5/Doha sea—Smuggling ship

Lynzei Ann Fowler—Captain of USS Nashville

Lt. Rondo Kane— Flamboyant Black Hawk chopper pilot

Loren Sorrel— Assistant manager of Geneva 9 asset field operations, Directing the G9 asset in the real world.

Mr. Marcks—Writes article about Morton Roth troubles

Martin Perez—President of the United States (POTUS)

Mansell Brin—Palange's second in command

Milosh Luka Petrovic—CEO of TerraDyne

Mrs. Doris Hayward—Assistant to POTUS

Mrs. Ethel Bannister— Maintains safe house in Paris

Myrla Villar-Noelle—Manages Kate's household.

Nador Morocco—Location of Cartel base.

Noha—Israeli programmer

Nuri Koffman—Prime Minister of Israel.

Patterson—Agent of Duma's security agency.

Penn Hauer—Director Cartel Field operations, security group Security Group – Brad, Penn, Elena, Loren, and Kate.

Tangent Day—Cartel code name for POTUS

Umma Galicki— Head of Mossad

TERMS AND PLACES

Adelaide Australian boat.

Adler Industries—Billion dollar empire Founded by Kate's father and source of her wealth.

<u>Asmara</u>.—Capitol of Eritrea

Cartel—Secret private group promoting its agenda from the shadows.

Conklin Maritime—Alliance, an insurance consortium.

Fordow—Iranian nuclear enrichment facility.

G9t phone—The Cartel's secure cell phone encrypted by Mom

Geneva9 / Mom—Cartel's surveillance computer

Helmut Adler Children's Fund—Charity created by Kate in memory of her father.

Kates residence—Châteauesque style mansion residence just outside Vianden

Morton Roth—Maritime management and shipping company, Division of Adler Industries

M14 incendiary—Thermal granade

NGO—Non Governmental organization

Nord Biscay—Suspect tanker

Nador Morocco—Location of Cartel base.

POC—Pattern of Concern is a warning generated by Geneva9

Security Group—Brad, Penn, Elena, Loren, and Kate

Seastate—Industry magazine and website.

TerraDyne—Large natural materials and shipping company.

Vianden Castle Luxembourg—Cartel headquarters

Seaward—company Terry Dyne was going to purchase.

SSD—State Security Department Similar to secret police

Wonsan   North Korean military base.

Zanzibar Resort—Resort in Tanzinia

Printed in Great Britain
by Amazon